PRAISE FOR AMANDA ROBERTS, ONE OF TODAY'S FAVORITE FEMALE SLEUTHS AND AWARD-WINNING AUTHOR

$3.00

SHERRYL WOODS

❧

"A brilliant job. . . . A tale that showcases a writer whose talent is increasing by leaps and bounds."

—*Affaire de Coeur* on *Wages of Sin*

❧

"Believable, appealing, and immensely entertaining, Amanda Roberts is a woman of today."

—*Mystery News* on *Body and Soul*

❧

"Energetic, outspoken. . . . Amanda goes after her story like a dog who has latched onto a dirty sock for life."

—*Mystery Scene*

❧

"Ms. Woods has really hit upon a winning ticket with the feisty Amanda."

—*Rave Reviews*

❧

"Sherryl Woods continues her patented blend of humor, Southern charm, and convoluted plot twists, featuring the gutsy, fast-talking, fast-thinking Amanda Roberts."

—*Romantic Times* on *Wages of Sin*

❧

"Particularly wonderful is the mix of Southerners invaded by some Northern folks. . . . Realistic characters are captivating while she advances us through a suspenseful, sometimes humorous, whodunit."

—*Mystery News* on *Ties That Bind*

SHERRYL WOODS has published fifty novels since 1982 and has sold over five million books worldwide. She has written seven books in the highly acclaimed Amanda Roberts mystery series. A former news reporter in the South, very much like her highly praised fictional sleuth Amanda Roberts, Sherryl Woods now divides her time between Los Angeles and Key Biscayne, Florida.

OTHER BOOKS BY SHERRYL WOODS

RECKLESS
BODY AND SOUL
STOLEN MOMENTS
TIES THAT BIND
BANK ON IT
HIDE AND SEEK
WAGES OF SIN
DEADLY OBSESSION
WHITE LIGHTNING

Sherryl Woods

White Lightning

A Time Warner Company

If you purchase this book without a cover you should be aware that this book may have been stolen property and reported as "unsold and destroyed" to the publisher. In such case neither the author nor the publisher has received any payment for this "stripped book."

WARNER BOOKS EDITION

Cover design by Jackie Merri Meyer
Cover photograph by Herman Estevez
Hand lettering by Carl Dellacroce

Warner Books, Inc.
1271 Avenue of the Americas
New York, NY 10020

A Time Warner Company

Printed in the United States of America

First Printing: October, 1995

10 9 8 7 6 5 4 3 2 1

CHAPTER

One

There was no one who could turn a simple request into a command quite like Miss Martha Wellington. Even after being awakened by the phone at 5:15 A.M., Amanda recognized Miss Martha's imperious tone. Less familiar was the weak, quavery fragility behind it.

"Miss Martha, are you okay?"

"No, I am not okay," the grande dame of Georgia society snapped impatiently. "Do you think I make it a habit of calling people in the middle of the night because I feel like chatting?"

Amanda flinched. "Of course not," she soothed. "Obviously, you're upset about something. What's wrong?"

"I'm dying, that's what's wrong. And don't go asking a lot of questions, because I don't want to talk about it."

Oddly, Amanda found she was alarmed less by the bluntly spoken news than she was by Miss Martha's flat tone of resignation as she delivered it. Though she was well into her eighties, Miss Martha was a cantankerous, stubborn old woman. She had always struck Amanda as someone who would defy death. Amanda would have expected Miss Martha to put up a fight to the bitter end, unwilling even to concede she was mortal.

Almost as startling as the news itself and Miss Martha's uncharacteristic attitude was the fact that she had chosen to share her present circumstances with Amanda. The last time they'd met, they hadn't parted on the best of terms. Miss Martha had quietly declared herself disappointed with Amanda's reporting on a scandal involving Georgia's senior senator. Though she normally considered herself immune to what others thought of her aggressive journalistic tactics, Amanda had been stung by the unexpected disapproval from a woman whose grit and determination she had come to admire. She had wondered if they would ever see eye to eye on the difficult decisions her job as a reporter sometimes required her to make.

Somehow, though, none of that seemed important now. And since Miss Martha had declared the topic of her health off-limits, all that mattered was doing whatever she could to ease Miss Martha's mind, maybe helping her to get back her fighting spirit.

"What can I do?" Amanda asked at once. "Is your housekeeper away? Do you need someone to take you to the hospital?"

"Della's fussing over me like an old hen. As for the

hospital, I've been. More than once, as a matter of fact. With luck, I'll never set foot inside another one. I'm planning to die right here at home in my own bed, but not before I set a few things straight. That's where you come in."

Something in her tone alerted Amanda that Miss Martha wasn't talking about apologizing to her for their recent set-to. Whatever she intended to set straight, as she put it, she obviously figured she needed Amanda's journalistic assistance to pull it off. She had never quite grasped the concept of an independent media.

"What can I do?" Amanda asked again, though with considerably more caution than she'd displayed a moment earlier.

"I'll tell you when you get here. Della will have a pot of tea ready and one of those coffee cakes you love so much. Bring your tape recorder. I want you to get every word of this down in case I don't live long enough to see it through."

Amanda's first instinct was to balk at being summoned like Miss Martha's personal press secretary. As the older woman had noted, it was practically the middle of the night, especially by Amanda's night-owl standards. Surely this could wait until dawn, at least. Still, her curiosity, always her downfall, was piqued. She'd never get back to sleep anyway. And Donelli was not in his usual spot beside her in bed, which meant she couldn't rely on her husband for diversion. No doubt he was already out tilling fields or whatever the hell farmers did at the first hint of spring weather.

"I'll be there as quickly as I can," she promised,

trying to gauge how long it would take her to shower and dress, then scoot all the way over to Gwinnett County. An hour plus, unless she skipped a few essentials and defied the speed limit. "Give me forty-five minutes."

Miss Martha sighed. "Thank you, dear. I knew I could count on you."

It was not what she'd said about Amanda a few months earlier. As Amanda hung up the phone, she couldn't decide whether she ought to be relieved to be back in Miss Martha's good graces or not. She had a feeling she wouldn't be able to determine that until after she'd heard exactly what it was the elderly woman wanted from her this time.

On her way out the door fifteen minutes later, Amanda paused to scribble a note for Donelli. She considered fixing breakfast for her newly adopted, teenage son, Pete, who ate more ravenously than she'd thought possible for a human being. Though she'd gotten in the habit of preparing Pete's breakfast, suddenly the very thought of frying bacon and scrambling eggs made her stomach turn over in a totally unexpected way. In fact, just thinking about food made her oddly queasy. She plucked a box of cereal out of the cabinet instead, reassuring herself that the eggs and bacon would have been cold and inedible long before Pete woke up anyway.

Still, she felt incredibly noble. She figured both the note and the cereal were evidence of her new domestication. As she shot down the driveway, sending up swirls of red dust, she couldn't help wondering, however, exactly how long it would be before she slipped off that particular wagon and proved that she wasn't cut out for marriage, much less parenthood. Lately she seemed to end each day on a note of surprise, stunned to discover that she'd survived another twenty-four hours without visibly failing in either role.

Fortunately she didn't have much time to ponder how long she could expect that to continue. The roads were practically deserted and, judging from the official lack of interest in her excessive speed, the local police were changing shifts. That particular combination of factors reduced her traveling time to less than forty minutes. Not bad for a drive that generally—and legally—took twice as long.

Miss Martha's housekeeper was watching for her. Della had the front door opened wide before Amanda could cut the car's engine.

"How is she, Della?" Amanda asked as she rushed up the winding brick walkway to the lovely old house. At the moment, with spring flowers a few weeks away from blooming and winter's grip still firmly on, the grounds seemed more desolate than usual. Or maybe Miss Martha's news had finally begun to sink in, filling her with a chilling hint of dread about what she might find inside.

The elderly black woman shook her head. "Agitated." She scowled at Amanda, as if her mistress's mood were Amanda's fault. "She's got no business getting herself all in an uproar this way. If you ask me, she ought to let sleeping dogs lie."

The housekeeper's dire tone carried a warning that Amanda couldn't mistake. "I'll try not to let her get too upset."

" 'Tain't up to you. She's made up her mind about this and nothing you or anybody else is gonna say is gonna stop her. Lord knows I've talked myself hoarse trying to get through to her." She gestured toward the stairs. "You go on up. She's waiting for you. I'll be bringing the tea in a minute."

Amanda would have killed for a cup of strong coffee in place of that weak tea Miss Martha was so fond of. "I don't suppose . . ." she began.

"She ordered tea and tea is what you'll have," Della said, then softened. "But if you want to stop by the kitchen on your way out, I'll have a pot of coffee waiting."

"Thanks." Amanda started up the wide, carpeted stairs, which she'd never before climbed. Somehow that took on a depressing significance. She'd never known Miss Martha not to receive her guests in one of the beautifully decorated downstairs rooms. The sound of her gold-handled cane tapping briskly along on the gleaming wood floors had always heralded her arrival.

Sighing, she glanced at Della. "Which room?"

"Second door on the right." Della hesitated, then added, "Don't be too alarmed by how frail she looks. The doctors say she could last quite a while yet, if she takes it easy and doesn't put too much stress on that tired-out heart of hers. Not that she pays their instructions any mind. She tossed the last bottle of pills they sent over straight out the window."

Amanda found her steps slowing as she reached the upstairs hall. Miss Martha had always seemed so strong, so indomitable. She wasn't sure she wanted to remember her with her energy sapped out of her and her spirits flagging. Unfortunately, before she could turn tail and run, Miss Martha must have heard her footsteps, because she hollered with surprising volume.

"Amanda? Is that you? I heard your car in the driveway. What's taking you so long?"

Amanda followed the sound of her querulous voice and the fit of coughing the shouting had apparently brought on. She entered a room filled with chintz and sheer white curtains. Miss Martha was propped up against a mountain of pillows in a mahogany four-poster bed. An extra touch of blush was the only thing that kept her skin from looking far too translucent and pale. Her blue-veined hands fluttered against the deep rose comforter in a way that hinted of both nerves and a lack of real strength.

Amanda leaned down and kissed her cheek, then took one of those small, cold hands in her own as she sat in the chair that had been drawn up next to the bed. "You look good," she lied, hoping to cover the distress that swept through her at the sight of her old friend.

Miss Martha waved off the compliment. "Nonsense. I look like a sick old lady, which is exactly what I am. Did you bring your recorder?"

"It's in my purse."

"Well, get it out, girl. There's no time to waste."

For once Amanda took the command in stride and fetched her tape recorder. Before she could turn it on, though, Della appeared with the tea and coffee cake. She spent several minutes fussing over Miss Martha, until the older woman lost patience. "Della, that's enough. Bring me that folder I had you get from the vault."

"Should have left it there, if you ask me," Della muttered under her breath.

"I didn't ask you," Miss Martha said, proving that whatever else might be failing, her hearing was as acute as ever. "Just get it and give it to Ms. Roberts. I want to get things started."

With obvious reluctance Della opened the drawer of the nightstand on the opposite side of the bed and pulled out a manila folder bulging with papers and held closed by a rubber band. She handed it to Amanda, muttered something under her breath again about sleeping dogs, and left the room.

Amanda held the folder gingerly. "Why doesn't she want me to see this?"

"Because she figures I might live another day or two, if I don't get myself stirred up over the past." Her hand hovered over the plate of still-warm coffee cake, which filled the room's too-still air with the scents of cinnamon and pecans. "Shall I cut you a piece?"

Faintly surprised that she wasn't the least bit tempted—in fact her stomach churned for the second time that morning—Amanda shook her head. "Maybe later. You know, it's possible that Della is right. Maybe you should leave this alone."

"Why? So I can hang on for a few more days? A week or two, maybe. What would be the point of lingering? I'm eighty-six years old. I'm ready to go," Miss Martha said. "Or I will be once this is taken care of. I've waited too long to do something about it as it is. If I'd gotten into it years ago, maybe my life would have been different."

Her blue eyes, which Amanda had seen alight with humor and snapping with determination, suddenly turned misty. "Very different," she repeated softly.

"Different how?"

"Less lonely," she said at once, then waved off Amanda's expression of sympathy. "Don't look at me like that. As you know perfectly well, I've had a good life. I've been blessed with wonderful friends. I've done just about everything I ever wanted to do, seen every place I wanted to see and a few I could have done without. I've done it on my own and I take pride in the fact that I've never relied on anyone for anything. I've even been able to do for others who were less fortunate." Her expression turned wistful. "That doesn't mean that I didn't have dreams once."

"What sort of dreams?" Amanda asked, unable to keep the slight catch out of her voice despite Miss Martha's determination to shun any display of sympathy. This nostalgic mood of Miss Martha's, these hints at heart-aching regrets were filling Amanda with a terrible sorrow. Pretty soon she'd be shedding the tears Miss Martha was holding resolutely at bay.

The older woman smiled. "You may not be able to believe this, but I was young once. Cut quite a figure in fact."

"Oh, I can believe that," Amanda replied, instinctively smiling back, even though her sad mood hadn't quite been dispelled.

"I'll bet you didn't know that I was engaged, though, did you?"

"I've heard rumors that there was a love affair that went wrong," Amanda admitted. Few people in Atlanta hadn't heard something about a discreet romance that ended badly. Details had been sadly lacking, but Miss Martha's position in society had guaranteed that hints of such a secret wouldn't die. "I never wanted to pry."

"That must have been very trying for you," Miss Martha countered dryly, eyes twinkling.

Amanda couldn't help laughing. "As a matter of fact, it just about killed me," she admitted.

"Then I appreciate all the more the fact that you didn't ask. Let this be a lesson to you. Sometimes patience does have its rewards. I want you to know about William Ashford," she said, her expression turning dreamy. "A lot of it is in those papers you have there, but a lot of it was never reported. No one ever wrote that he was a true Southern gentleman, who suffered greatly when his wife died. No one ever wrote about his tenderness or his charm or his wicked eyes. No one ever talked about the kind of father he was to his boy."

Miss Martha sighed. "And no one ever made the connection that he was the man I loved with all my heart and soul, the man I could never forget. Our engagement lasted only a few days. Almost no one knew of it. When he was in the darkest hour of his life, I kept silent. William's been dead for ten years now and more than half a century has gone by, but I will never forgive myself for abandoning him then. I should have stood by him, no matter what. I should have held my head high and acknowledged him and what we felt for each other."

She turned a steady, determined gaze on Amanda. "I intend to make up for that now, with your help."

As the implications sank in, Amanda's mouth gaped. "You want to make up for something that happened more than fifty years ago?"

"I want to prove that something didn't happen more than fifty years ago," Miss Martha corrected. "Leastways not the way they said it did."

"I don't understand."

"You will when you've read through all the clippings in that file. There are letters there, too. Letters that William wrote me when we were very much in love. I want you to read those as well."

Given the thickness of the folder, that struck Amanda as a daunting task, and she wasn't at all sure how much time Miss Martha had left. That was hardly a question she dared ask.

"Maybe you'd better summarize it for me. We'll get everything you remember on tape first and then I can go from there."

"In case I die," Miss Martha said succinctly.

"No," Amanda said just as firmly. "So I'll understand your version before I start digging into all this research you say is filled with lies."

Amanda wasn't sure what she intended to do with any of it. At the moment, she was merely placating a friend, maybe satisfying her own curiosity. If this was something Miss Martha needed to get off her chest, then Amanda could at least do her the courtesy of listening.

After that, well, quite likely there was no story, not after all this time.

Miss Martha hesitated, then drew in a deep breath. "William was a bootlegger," she said at last. "There was never any question about that. As for the rest of it, it was all wicked lies."

Then before Amanda could snap her mouth shut and hide her astonishment, Miss Martha added, "They said he killed the revenuer who tried to shut him down."

If Miss Martha had declared that she had once been a stripper in a Paris nightclub, Amanda couldn't have been any more stunned. That this genteel Southern lady had been in love with a bootlegger accused of murder certainly was enough to capture Amanda's full attention. It would probably set all of Georgia society on its ear.

Unfortunately, though, the trail was cold. Amanda couldn't imagine how she could gather enough information for even the most cursory story.

"It's been such a long time," she said carefully, hating to dash Miss Martha's hopes. "Witnesses will be dead or their memories will have faded. I really don't see how I can be much help."

"Just because it's not easy? Since when did you walk away from a challenge?" Miss Martha demanded.

"But . . ."

Miss Martha impatiently waved off her protest. "Besides, you're wrong about everything being so far in the past. When you look in that file, you'll see that history seems to be repeating itself. There was a Department of Revenue agent killed less than a week ago during a raid."

Amanda resisted the urge to say *so what*. "And you think there's a connection?" she said skeptically.

"I know there's a connection. It's plain as day. The raid took place on William's property, land that's been in his family for generations." She looked Amanda straight in the eye. "And that's not all. The man they arrested is William's grandson. I don't believe for a minute he's one bit guiltier than his granddaddy was. Making and selling moonshine may be against the law . . ."

"Even now?" Amanda asked. She was astonished. Despite herself she was growing more and more intrigued. "I thought all of that died out with the end of Prohibition."

"Georgia still has local option laws," Miss Martha replied. "Have you ever tried to buy a beer on Sunday around here?"

"So people make white lightning to get around the laws."

"Exactly. The laws and the taxes on liquor. Making and selling moonshine is still a crime all right. But saying a man is guilty of that doesn't mean you can automatically call him a murderer, does it?"

"No," Amanda agreed slowly.

"Well, then, there you have it. We just have to prove that the charges against William and most likely his grandson were trumped up. Somebody had an axe to grind against them, no doubt about it."

"But . . ." Amanda's protest trailed off when she realized that Miss Martha had drifted off.

Apparently, trying to convince Amanda that the man

she'd loved and his grandson were innocent of murder had cost Miss Martha the last of her energy. Amanda would have to wait for the answers to the hundreds of questions suddenly reeling through her mind.

Sighing, Amanda studied the sleeping woman. She looked at peace, as if a great burden had been lifted.

Unfortunately, that burden had been transferred to Amanda's shoulders. Miss Martha didn't expect much, Amanda thought irritably. She just wanted Amanda to link a fifty-year-old crime to a recent murder and solve the two of them. Worse, she expected her to do it with one hell of a deadline staring her in the face.

CHAPTER

Two

While Della fussed under her breath, Amanda sat downstairs in Miss Martha's bright, cheery kitchen, drank the promised cup of caffeine-charged coffee, nibbled unenthusiastically at a chunk of the pecan coffee cake she normally gobbled down, and examined the first clipping in the file she'd been given upstairs. It was a terse summary of the shotgun slaying, which had taken place on September 21, 1942.

In it William Ashford was alleged to have cold-bloodedly gunned down a Georgia Department of Revenue agent—Randy Blaine Alcott—just as the man set foot on his isolated property. No one had witnessed the shooting, but the gun was Ashford's and ballistic tests had proved it to be the murder weapon. The motive seemed clear-cut. The two men had reportedly played a long-running game of cat-and-mouse over the location of Ashford's illegal stills. Alcott was about to win. Ashford didn't like it. *Bam*! He blew him away. As simple as that.

The article was accompanied by a grainy police head shot of the accused. Amanda skimmed over the bare-facts story and concentrated more intently on the photo. William Ashford, despite the fading and yellowing of the newsprint, clearly had been a handsome devil. His black hair was thick, with just a hint of wayward curl to it. Not even the prison garb and unflattering police lighting could mask the burning intensity of his gaze or the hint of a dimple carved in his shadowed cheek. A comparison to Clark Gable seemed inevitable.

What struck Amanda most, however, was the glint of amusement in his eyes, the faint hint that he couldn't believe that anyone could take the accusations against him seriously. She doubted that such arrogant self-confidence had gone over well with either the police or the victim's family. Heaven knew what a jury would make of it.

She glanced up to find Della regarding her with that by-now familiar disapproving expression written all over her round face.

"You really want me to stay out of this, don't you?" Amanda said.

"It's not you I'm worrying 'bout. You like digging in other folks' business, that's your right."

"But you think my investigating this particular story will hurt Miss Martha?"

Della sighed heavily, pulled out a chair across from Amanda, and sank onto it. She too was beginning to show signs of age. Given the years she had worked for the Wellington family, she had to be almost as old as Miss Martha. Her tongue was as tart as ever, but her movements had slowed and hinted of aches she would never admit to.

"The way she is now, this darkness in her, it worries me. I just have this feeling she's tying up loose ends, if you know what I mean."

Amanda's gaze narrowed. "You mean getting ready to die."

"Exactly."

"That seems natural enough to me, if the doctors have given her a poor prognosis."

Della shook her head. " 'Tain't natural at all, not what she's thinking, not what I overheard her saying to that doctor of hers."

Amanda was intrigued. She felt the first faint stirring of anxiety herself, even though Della's comments were pretty oblique. One worrisome option seemed likely for a depressed woman facing a terminal illness: suicide. "What are you trying to say?" she asked, trying to force Della to confirm her suspicion.

Instead, Della fell silent, clearly struggling with her conscience. Finally, looking miserable and uncertain, she said, "It's not my place to talk about it. Could be I'm getting worked up over nothing."

She gazed at Amanda and sighed heavily. "It's just that you don't know what it was like for her back then. How it got her all mixed up in her head. When William was accused of this crime, she took to her bed. She wouldn't tell a soul what was wrong. I knew because I'd seen her sneaking 'round to be with that man, all the while his wife lay at home dying."

Della gave Amanda a look that pleaded for understanding. "Don't mistake what I'm saying. I'm not suggesting they was having an affair. Miss Martha had had a proper Christian upbringing. She had values. I don't think either of them would have done a thing to hurt his wife. That's why they were so discreet about meeting in out-of-the-way places. Always seemed to me that was part of the attraction. Miss Martha'd spent her whole life doing what her parents intended, going to the schools they picked, spending time with the men they approved. Then along comes this man with a hint of danger about him, a man who would have given her folks a fit if they'd known about her taking up with him. It's not surprising that she got all caught up. Must have seemed awful exciting."

Amanda understood all too well that attraction to danger. She'd had a mild flirtation with a French arms dealer during a period when she and Donelli had been at odds. "So Miss Martha had led a pretty sheltered life up until she met William?" she said.

Della hooted. "Sheltered ain't the word for it. Her daddy would have locked his precious baby away if he'd had his way about it. And her brother, Donald's daddy, wasn't one bit better. Her mama fought like a she-devil just to get the two of them to agree to let Miss Martha attend a finishing school for young ladies in Atlanta."

"Then how on earth did she manage to meet William in the first place?"

Della settled back and cradled her cup of tea in her big hands as if the heat were soothing to arthritic joints. "Back during Prohibition and for years afterward, William's daddy supplied her daddy with liquor. William was always underfoot, same as I was, 'cause my mama worked for the family. I'm not sure Miss Martha had any notion of why that boy and his daddy were here, but she befriended him. While the menfolks did their business, she and William would sit out back and talk. Even way back then, that boy could talk your ear off." She smiled at the memory. "Oh, my, he was something. I used to hide nearby and listen to him myself. I always thought he'd wind up a preacher or a politician."

Amanda tried to imagine the lonely little rich girl and the bootlegger's son forming a fast friendship that would later become a tragic love affair. Obviously it hadn't happened overnight. William had, in fact, married someone else.

"If they were in love all those years, how did he happen to marry another woman?" she asked Della.

"I don't know as they recognized what they felt as love, not at first. Miss Martha went off to that fancy school. William, who was three years older, was already involved in his daddy's business. Matter of fact, he pretty much had total responsibility, which must have made him an attractive catch in certain circles. Next thing anybody knew he was married to a woman named Laurabel."

There was no mistaking the distaste in Della's voice when she mentioned the other woman's name. "So he and Miss Martha lost contact?" Amanda guessed.

"I should say so. This Laurabel wasn't the kind of woman he'd be bringing around a lady, if you know what I mean. Before he took up with her, she'd gotten something of a reputation over in Dahlonega, close by to the Ashford property. She and her *girls*, so to speak."

Dear heaven, the man had married a hooker! Amanda found the whole scenario too bizarre to link with the epitome of Southern propriety now resting upstairs. Maybe she'd misunderstood. "Surely, you're not suggesting . . ."

"That she was a madam," Della supplied. "Oh, yes, indeed, at least up until the day she married William. Then she turned so uppity, a person would have thought she'd been born too good for the rest of us."

"If Miss Martha had lost contact, how did you know about all this?"

"Because my cousin went to work for them. William came around one day and asked me—I was working here by then—he asked if I knew of anyone looking for household work. I 'spect he had in mind stealing me away, but I wanted no part of him or his fancy lady. I sent Etta Jane over to them. She needed work and wasn't half so picky. She carried tales home to the family." She shook her head. "I had to feel sorry for poor William. It seemed to me like he made a bad bargain."

"In what way?" Amanda asked.

"First his wife gets this attitude 'bout her, then she turns all poorly after she had his son. She never did recover from that birth. Can't say what it was exactly, but Etta Jane said she took to her bed and that was that. Doctors never put no name to it. My guess is she was trying to tie that man to her by playing on his sympathy."

"Apparently it didn't work, if that was when he started seeing Miss Martha again."

Della shook her head emphatically. "It wasn't as if he came sniffing around trying to take up with her because of the way things were for him at home. They met sorta by accident one day when Miss Martha was out shopping. They had a cup of tea together. Nothing but two old friends catching up. Pretty soon it became a regular thing. He needed someone to pour out his troubles to. She just loved to listen to him talk. He wrote her these sweet-talkin' letters, too. Philosophical-like, she always said. You'll find 'em in that folder, tied up in a pretty ribbon. She saved every one. After he went off to jail, she used to sit up in that bed of hers and read 'em over and over, tears streamin' down her face."

Her expression turned grim. "I could see right off which way the wind was blowin', but I couldn't tell that woman a thing. She didn't want to hear a word against him. Said she was old enough to know her own mind. Worried her mama half to death, when she discovered what was going on. She didn't dare tell Miss Martha's daddy or her brother, 'cause they would have taken a shotgun to William and that would have stirred a scandal, sure enough."

"And all this time they were sneaking around seeing each other, William was still bootlegging whiskey?"

"The finest in all of Georgia, from what I heard,"

Della confirmed. "Had a taste of that peach brandy myself now and again. Went down smooth as silk, not like some of that rot-gut that can kill you."

Amanda tried to think what it must have been like for the two young, star-crossed lovers. She could only imagine how difficult it must have been, especially at a time and place in history when friends and family—especially family as rigid as the Wellingtons—would have been far more judgmental about their illicit feelings. And yet she knew from her own short-lived attraction to that intelligent, sexy, charming French arms dealer how easily emotions could be exaggerated when they were dangerous and deliberately, painstakingly denied.

"How long did they go on seeing each other?" Amanda asked.

"Round about six, seven years, I'd say."

"And you're convinced they weren't having an affair?"

"Absolutely not. Then when his wife died, it finally looked as if things would work out. A month after Laurabel was gone, he gave Miss Martha an engagement ring. They had agreed she would wait a proper length of time to put it on, but they finally had an understanding. I never saw her looking so happy before or since. Then that very day the Revenue agent was shot and William was arrested for murder."

The timing of the engagement startled Amanda almost as much as that of the shooting. "He had never tried before that to get a divorce so that he and Miss Martha could marry?"

"No," Della said. "I doubt Miss Martha would have

had him, if he had. His loyalty to his sickly wife and his love for his son were two of the things she admired most in him."

Amanda couldn't imagine Miss Martha fitting comfortably into the role of the patient, long-suffering other woman. How it must have chafed her pride. And how deeply she must have loved William Ashford to endure it. Amanda's sense of the tragedy of it all deepened.

"You want another piece of coffee cake?" Della inquired as she heaved herself up and crossed over to the stove to check something that smelled a lot like chicken stewing.

Amanda considered the offer, tested the idea on her repeatedly queasy stomach, and declined. "I think I'd better get going. I want to go through this material and make a few calls before lunch."

"You're not going to stick around to talk some more with Miss Martha?"

"Oh, I'm sure I'll be hearing from her the second she's awake, whether I'm here or she has to track me down by phone," she said dryly. "She'll probably feel better knowing I'm already digging into the story."

The creases in Della's forehead deepened. "You'll be careful what you tell her, won't you?"

"Della, you know she'll guess if I'm keeping things from her."

Della sighed. "That she will." She straightened her shoulders. "Then I suppose it's just up to me to see to it that she takes it easy and builds up her strength so she can cope with whatever happens. This chicken and dumplings I'm fixing for her lunch ought to be a start."

"She's always said it's her favorite dish and that nobody in all of Georgia makes lighter, fluffier dumplings than you do," Amanda said.

Della responded at once to the flattery. "I could fix you a batch to take on home with you," she offered, already reaching for a fancy covered dish in the cupboard next to the stove.

Given the odd way she'd been reacting to food all morning, Amanda would have declined, but she thought of how Joe and Pete would react when they discovered an excellent home-cooked meal on the table, albeit—no, preferably—one she hadn't prepared herself. Her skills in the kitchen were less than laudable, as the two males had pointed out on more than one occasion. They would consider the chicken and dumplings a very special treat.

"If you're sure you have plenty," she said.

Della gestured toward the huge pot. "I always make enough for company and Miss Martha's eating like a bird these days. This 'll just go to waste if you don't take it." She ladled up a generous portion and handed it over.

The aroma of the traditional Southern dish made Amanda's stomach churn. Back in her car, the effect was only intensified until she rolled down the windows and allowed the cool March air to blow through.

She blamed her decision to head back home on the need to get the chicken into the refrigerator, but the truth of it was, she flat-out didn't feel like driving all the way into town. She didn't have an article scheduled for the next edition of *Inside Atlanta* anyway. The magazine could get by without her for one day. She called her boss on the car phone and let him know she was taking the day off.

"What's wrong?" Oscar Cates asked in a tone of dread more generally used to inquire about major calamities. Maybe he figured Amanda's first unscheduled day off in all the time she'd worked for him qualified.

"Nothing serious," Amanda assured him. "I may be coming down with the flu or something. There's no point in sharing it with the rest of the staff."

"Sounds to me like you're calling from your car. Where the devil are you?"

"I was over visiting Miss Martha."

"Why?" Oscar asked, his voice filled with suspicion. He'd been targeted for articles on some of Miss Martha's pet projects more times than he cared to remember, too.

"I'll tell you all about it tomorrow," Amanda promised.

"You're not gonna come sneaking in here and try to get space for a story at the last minute, are you? If that's what you're thinking, there's something you ought to know."

"Oscar, I never sneak."

"Amanda, don't you . . ."

"Bye-bye," she said cheerily. "See you tomorrow."

"Amanda!"

As she hung up, she suddenly realized she was so exhausted that even driving the remaining few miles back to the farm seemed overwhelming. Somehow, though, she managed it. On the lane leading up to the house, she paused for a minute to watch her husband, an ex-Brooklyn homicide cop, happily tilling his fields. Donelli was, quite possibly, the only truly contented man she'd ever known. His satisfaction in working the land, after years of battling street action and violence, still astonished her. She tooted her horn and waved, drawing his attention all too briefly before he turned and headed the tractor away from her again.

Amanda drove on to the house. Less than an hour after leaving Miss Martha's, she crept back into her still mussed bed and pulled the covers snugly around her. For half a second she considered looking through the thick folder she'd brought home with her. She even removed the rubber band and took out the little ribbon-bound packet of letters, but she couldn't keep her eyes open long enough to read the first one. Within minutes she was sound asleep, the tantalizing letters scattered around her.

That was where Joe found her when he came in from the fields for lunch. Amanda awoke to find her husband sitting on the edge of the bed, his forehead puckered by a frown, his hair still damp from a shower. His callused fingers brushed across her cheek.

"You okay?"

"Just tired," she said, yawning and stretching.

"At noon?"

"My stomach's been jumpy all morning. I think maybe I'm coming down with the flu."

He caressed her brow, then lingered, his touch light against her cheek. "No temperature."

She grinned at him. She did feel better. "Maybe the nap did the trick."

"In that case, are you sure you wouldn't like to linger here just a little longer?" he inquired hopefully.

An intriguing notion. "Depends on the payoff," she taunted.

"I'll try to make it worth your while."

"Oh, really? How?"

His dark brown eyes sparkled with mischief right before he brushed a quick, tantalizing kiss across her lips.

"Nice," she declared, "but you'll have to do better than that to compete with all this." She gestured toward the scattering of love letters. "I'm told they're filled with passion."

Donelli apparently was willing to accept the challenge. He cupped her face in his hands and slanted his mouth over hers. This time the kiss was long and slow and deep, the kind of moist, breath-stealing kiss that drove out thoughts of anything except the man whose touches were becoming more and more provocative.

Amanda had discovered that one of the very best benefits of marriage was the increasingly certain knowledge her husband had of her body. He could coax a shattering response from her in the time other men took to strip off a shirt. Or, as now, he could tease and torment with a sweet deliberation that kept her just this side of release.

"Busy morning?" he inquired as he lazily stroked her hip. "I saw you take off at the crack of dawn."

"Miss Martha called," she managed to reply between gasps.

"A command performance at six A.M. Isn't that a little extreme even for her?"

"It's a long story."

He gathered up the thick envelopes with the bold handwriting. "And it has to do with these, I suppose?"

Impatient now, Amanda ignored the question and peeled his T-shirt over his head. His back was already bronzed by the first few weeks of work in his beloved fields. She ran her hands over the firm, well-muscled flesh, then tasted the salty tang of his skin. She reached for the snap of his jeans.

"Slow down," he whispered. "It's raining, so there's not a thing I can do in the fields. Pete won't be home for hours yet."

"Hours, hmm?"

He grinned. "I told you I'd make it worth your while."

Not even Miss Martha's intriguing tale of moonshine, murder, and two wrongly accused men could compete with an offer like that.

CHAPTER
Three

Amanda and Joe had barely made it out of bed and into the kitchen, when Pete came in from school. He glanced at the clock over the stove, surveyed their disheveled, hastily donned clothing, then shot them a surprisingly knowing look. Amanda could feel her cheeks turning pink. It was not the first time Pete had taken one glance at the two of them and surmised what they'd been doing. Adopting a streetwise thirteen-year-old definitely had its down side.

Fortunately, before Pete could comment on his suspicions—which Amanda was certain he wouldn't be able to resist doing—the phone rang. She grabbed it gratefully.

"Amanda, what have you found out?" Miss Martha demanded.

Whoops! "Not a thing," she admitted. "I'm afraid I came home and took a nap. I wasn't feeling well."

"I noticed you looked a bit peaked this morning. Wouldn't be a bit surprised if you're pregnant," she said matter-of-factly. "Are you?"

Before Amanda could sputter an indignant denial, Miss Martha rushed right on.

"Doesn't matter," she said dismissively. "I'm sure you won't let that slow you down a bit. Women nowadays don't. I'll expect a report first thing in the morning. I have plans to make that can't wait."

"But . . ." Amanda began, not sure whether to protest Miss Martha's outrageous assessment of her physical condition or her assumption that Amanda would be reporting in.

"Nine o'clock sharp," Miss Martha ordered, then hung up, obviously to emphasize that she would accept no arguments nor tolerate any excuses.

Amanda very slowly and very carefully replaced the receiver, praying that neither Joe nor Pete could see how stunned she was. Pregnant? No, it was impossible. Well, actually, it wasn't *impossible*, but it was unlikely. She and Joe hadn't planned . . . They hadn't actually discussed . . .

Except, of course, for the time Pete had announced that he wanted a baby brother or sister and informed them they weren't getting any younger. That night she and Joe had talked a little about how a baby would fit into their lives. Amanda had been panicked by the very idea. They had postponed further discussions until after they saw how Pete settled in, how their brief marriage adapted to that major adjustment. They had agreed that a pregnancy was something they would plan for carefully.

They hadn't planned. Therefore, she wasn't pregnant. She had the flu. Period.

"Amanda, you're white as a sheet," Joe declared, grasping her by the shoulders and maneuvering her toward a chair. "Sit. Take a deep breath."

"Maybe she ought to put her head between her knees," Pete suggested, peering at Amanda over Joe's shoulder. "I saw that on TV once."

"Certainly the best place I know of to pick up a medical education," Amanda commented dryly.

"Do it," Joe insisted.

Amanda lowered her head. "Can I sit up now?" she asked after a minute. "All the blood's rushed to my brain."

"Exactly," Pete said, obviously pleased.

"Your color is better," Joe observed.

He was studying her as if she were an unfamiliar suspect in one of his homicide cases. Amanda had noticed that a cop could give up his badge, but he could never turn off the way he automatically assessed people, taking in details to which others were oblivious.

He reached into the refrigerator, found the pitcher of orange juice, and poured her a glass. He watched her closely until she'd finished every drop. "So," he said then, "what brought that on?"

Amanda had no intention of getting into Miss Martha's wild conjectures. "Miss Martha was just issuing orders. You know how that irritates me. Plus, I never did have any lunch," she said, giving her husband a pointed look.

This time it was Joe who turned crimson. The color crept up the back of his neck in a way that Pete seemed to find perfectly fascinating. Joe shoved his chair away from the table and headed for the refrigerator. "I'll get dinner started."

"Actually, Della sent over chicken and dumplings."

"All right!" Pete enthused. "Who's this Della? Can she cook?"

"Like an angel," Joe commented, retrieving the covered dish and peering inside. His expression turned almost as rapturous as it had been back in the bedroom.

"I'll get her recipe," Amanda offered.

"Who'll cook it?" Pete demanded. "Joe cooks Italian and you can't even boil water."

Amanda grinned at him. "Then I guess it'll be up to you."

"An interesting idea," Joe agreed. "Perhaps you'd rather cook than work with me in the fields."

Pete looked horrified. "Not a chance, man. I'm not putting on some frilly apron and cooking. I wouldn't be able to run far enough, if the kids at school ever found out."

"Then I guess you'll have to survive on the charity of strangers," Amanda said.

Pete hauled out the chair next to Amanda and sprawled in it. "So who is this Della dame anyway?"

Amanda winced at the description. Pete really was going to have to stop watching old James Cagney and Humphrey Bogart movies. "She is Miss Martha Wellington's housekeeper."

"Am I supposed to know who that is?"

"You are if you expect to get by in this part of Georgia," Joe said.

"Some rich b—"

Joe cut him off. "Pete," he warned.

Pete stared at him blankly, then muttered, "Oh, yeah. I forgot about the cussing." He looked at Amanda. "So she's a real muckety-muck, huh?"

"That about sums it up," Joe agreed. "I don't care if she is in her eighties, she scares the dickens out of me."

"You never liked her because she preferred my ex-husband to you," Amanda taunted.

"Your ex is now in jail. Need I say any more about her judgment when it comes to men?"

Pete's eyes widened. He regarded Amanda accusingly. "I didn't know you were married before Joe."

"An unfortunate mistake," Amanda said succinctly.

"And one she prefers not to be reminded of, because it shatters her impressive record of perfection," Joe chimed in.

Amanda scowled at him. "I have no idea how Mack Roberts got into this conversation, but I'd like to get back to more important topics."

"Such as?" Joe asked.

"How to go about investigating a murder that took place more than fifty years ago. Any ideas?"

"Oh, boy, here we go again," Pete said, his eyes alight with excitement.

Joe seemed less enthused. "Why would you want to start digging around in a murder case that's been closed for decades?" He groaned. "Let me guess. It's Miss Martha's idea."

Amanda nodded. "She seems to think it's linked to a case that's more recent."

"How recent?"

"Last week."

"Involving?"

"Her late fiancé's grandson and a Georgia Department of Revenue agent."

"The guy who was shot when he tried to close down that still over near Dahlonega?"

Amanda beamed. "You know about it? Terrific. Tell me everything you know."

"Forget it. You are not going crawling around in the Georgia backwoods looking for moonshiners," Joe said, gesturing emphatically with a ladle. "The Alcohol–Tobacco Tax guys who get paid to do that are trained in law enforcement. You're not. You have questions, talk to them."

Amanda scowled at him. "Excuse me?"

"Uh-oh," Pete murmured. "I've got homework." He practically bolted from the kitchen.

"Chicken," Amanda called after him.

"Smart move," Joe countered. "Amanda, those people are dangerous. They are operating outside the law. They do not want strangers poking around on their property. They shoot first and ask questions later. Why do you think that state official wound up dead?"

Before she could even draw a breath to reply, he said, "I'll tell you why. Because he was poking his nose into their business."

"With the intention of closing them down," Amanda reminded him. "I just want information."

"Which you intend to publish, am I right?"

"Well, probably," she admitted. At his skeptical look, she amended, "Okay, yes."

"This is not a business that thrives on publicity. Quite the contrary."

She was beginning to see how reporting this particular story could get tricky. As far as she was concerned, though, that just made it a more fascinating challenge. "I'll promise to change names and leave out precise locations."

"I'm sure that will be a comfort to them."

"You don't have to be sarcastic."

"Apparently I do. Common sense doesn't seem to be having any effect."

Amanda sighed. "Joe, I will not do anything foolish."

He rolled his eyes heavenward.

"I won't," she insisted. A brainstorm struck. "You could help, you know. Miss Martha would probably hire you to investigate if it would mean getting to the bottom of this faster."

"No way," he said without giving the idea an instant's thought. "You know perfectly well that I don't take cases this time of the year. I'm plowing my fields. I have crops to plant."

"You could still spend a couple of hours a day on this," Amanda argued. "You could go with me to ask questions. Maybe you'd spot some clues the police overlooked."

"As always, I have considerably more faith in the police than you do."

"I'll refrain from commenting on that for now," she

shot back. "Come on, Donelli, just think about it." She searched for the right cajoling note, the strongest incentive. "Think of all the seeds you could buy with the extra money. Maybe you could even hire an extra hand for harvesting."

She watched his expression closely to see if she was hitting the mark. She caught the quick spark of interest in his eyes, before he deliberately turned his back to her.

So, then, she thought triumphantly, he was tempted despite himself. He'd lost some of his crops the previous year because he'd been short of help to harvest before the first freeze. She also knew that in spite of his expressed disdain for Miss Martha and her fondness for Mack Roberts, he really liked the elderly woman. She reminded him of his grandmother. With that in mind, Amanda pulled out her final piece of ammunition.

"She's dying," she said quietly.

His head snapped around. "Who?"

"Miss Martha."

"Amanda, that's nothing to joke about."

"Who's joking?"

He regarded her as if he still suspected her of making it up. "What's wrong with her?"

"She refused to discuss it and Della was just as tight-lipped. The only thing Della mentioned was her weak heart, but I got the feeling it was more than that. She looks terrible, as if she's wasting away. At any rate, that's why she called. She wanted to get the whole story about what happened with William off her chest. She wanted to set things right before she died. She's determined to see justice done, etcetera."

"Well, hell," he muttered in apparent defeat.

"Can I tell her you'll help?" she asked, pressing her temporary advantage.

He sighed heavily. "I'll help. I'll call her myself, though." He crossed the room, leaned down, and gazed directly into Amanda's eyes. "But from the moment she hires me until this case is solved, I am in charge of the investigation. You will do exactly as I tell you. You will not go anywhere near that property unless I am with you. You will not so much as say *peep* to some moonshiner unless I arrange it. Are we clear?"

Amanda automatically bristled all over again at the barrage of orders. Maybe this hadn't been such a terrific idea after all. Donelli did have a bossy streak that really grated on her nerves. She opened her mouth to form a protest, but he cut her off.

"Are we clear?" he repeated.

She was prevented from having to lie through her teeth by the timely ringing of the phone. "I'll get it," she said and practically knocked her husband back on his heels as she bolted past him.

"You're just buying time," Donelli commented. "I'm not going to forget that you haven't answered me yet."

She made a face at him as she yanked the receiver off the hook. "Hello."

"Ms. Roberts? Amanda Roberts?"

"Yes. Who is this?"

"Willie."

"Willie? I'm afraid I don't know . . ."

"Willie Ashford. This lady—Miss Martha Wellington she said her name was—called me a little while ago and gave me your number. She said you might be able to help me."

Amanda glanced over her shoulder, hoping that her husband was once again absorbed in dinner preparations. He wasn't. His interested gaze was fixed right on her.

"I'm going to try," she said.

"Then I need to see you."

"When?"

"Tonight. Now."

"Where are you?"

"Jail, of course."

"I'll be there as soon as I can," she said and hung up. She reached for her purse and cast a defiant look at her husband. "Well, don't just stand there."

"Where are we going?"

"To see the accused murderer."

"Now?"

"He's apparently in the mood to talk. I intend to be there to listen. Of course, you could always stay here. I should be safe enough with all those nice cops standing guard."

Joe cast a regretful look in the direction of the chicken and dumplings, then turned off the stove. "Let's go." He crossed the kitchen and yelled at Pete, "We have to go out for a while. The food's hot, if you want to come in now and have some."

Pete appeared in the doorway within seconds, drawn either by curiosity or the mention of food. Amanda couldn't be sure which. Probably dinner, since he reached for a bowl first thing.

"What's up?"

"We're going to jail," Joe announced.

Pete paused with a ladleful of chicken halfway to the bowl. "No joke?"

"It's hardly something I would joke about."

Pete's gaze shifted to Amanda. "You in trouble with the law again?"

"Why would you ask a thing like that?" she replied indignantly.

"Because he's already all too familiar with your track record," Joe said. He guided her firmly toward the door. "Come on. If we're going, let's go."

Amanda called back over her shoulder. "Donelli's no angel, you know."

"That is no way to be talking about the boy's new father," her husband informed her. "Besides, next to you, I'm a veritable saint."

CHAPTER
Four

Damn, but the Ashford genes were good! Amanda would have recognized Willie Ashford as being part of the same clan as his grandfather even if they had met on the street, rather than in a county jail interrogation room. She wouldn't have needed to see his name neatly printed by a black marker on his prison jumpsuit.

Of course, there had been some allowances made for contemporary style. Willie's thick, black hair was drawn back in a long ponytail. He had one pierced ear, though whatever he'd worn in it had been confiscated. The intense gaze and the dimples, however, were exactly the same as his grandfather's.

His look of relief when he spied Amanda seemed genuine. "I wasn't sure you'd come," he said, standing and pumping her hand enthusiastically.

"There was never any doubt," Donelli said dryly.

For the first time Willie's gaze turned wary as he studied Joe. "Who are you?"

"A private detective," Joe supplied.

"My husband," Amanda added, since the job description hadn't seemed to reassure the accused.

Willie nodded and turned his gaze back to Amanda. "Oh, yeah, Miss Martha said you were married to an ex-cop." He gestured for the two of them to have a seat in the two chairs facing him across a nondescript metal table. The room's ambience was definitely functional, rather than welcoming. It was doubtful anyone would choose to linger.

"Joe's going to help me with this investigation," Amanda told Willie.

"I wouldn't go bragging about your past then," he told Joe. "Folks in my particular profession get kinda antsy when the cops show up."

"How do they feel about nosy reporters?" Joe countered with a pointed look in Amanda's direction.

"Not much better," Willie conceded. "But a pretty woman always has a way about her that can get around suspicions."

"Tell me about it," Joe said.

"You use what you have," Amanda retorted.

Donelli, as always, seemed singularly unimpressed by her reportorial ingenuity.

"You have any friends who'll talk to us despite our shady career histories?" he asked Willie with an unmistakable touch of irony that apparently went over the young man's head.

Rocking back on his sturdy gray metal chair, Willie

seemed to be giving the question serious thought. Either he had too many friends to count or almost no one at all he could trust. Amanda suspected the latter to be the case.

"Man, I really don't like the idea of getting my friends mixed up in this," he said finally.

Loyalty wasn't a possibility Amanda had considered at all. "Look, Willie, you're in a real tight spot here. Surely a friend would understand and try to help. I'll do whatever I can to protect their confidence."

The young man, who looked to be no more than twenty-five, studied Amanda and Donelli as if trying to determine their trustworthiness. "You'll keep it off the record?" he said at last. He glanced pointedly at Joe. "No official follow-ups from the cops?"

Amanda awaited Donelli's answer almost as anxiously as Willie.

"Unless they happen to be guilty of this particular murder, their other crimes are irrelevant to this investigation," Joe said after an all-too-apparent struggle with his conscience.

The front two legs of Willie's chair thunked onto the floor and he held out a hand. Donelli shook it solemnly, gazing straight into those piercing eyes. Only as Willie's eyes brightened did Amanda realize that they had been shadowed by a fear he had fought valiantly to hide when greeting them.

He leaned forward and asked earnestly, "Okay, what do you need to know?"

"Names," Donelli said.

"Exactly what happened the day the Revenue agent was shot," Amanda added.

Willie grinned. "Which one of you guys is in charge?"

"We're working on that," Amanda informed him, just as Donelli said adamantly, "I am."

"If I weren't in such a heap of shit, I'd enjoy watching the two of you work it out," Willie said.

He gave a slight nod in Amanda's direction. She took it as an indication that chivalry wasn't quite dead.

"It all started about six weeks ago," he said. "This black guy—I found out later his name was Frank Jefferson—started snooping around, asking questions, turning up in all sorts of places he didn't belong. If there's one thing I learned from my daddy besides makin' whiskey, it was to spot a revenuer. This Jefferson character had it written all over him. I closed down operations, tucked away my equipment in a nice, safe place, and sold down my inventory to a few hand-picked shot houses in Atlanta until what I had left fell within the legal limits for personal use."

"Did he back off?" Joe asked.

"He didn't budge from the county as far as I could tell."

"Maybe he was investigating somebody else," Amanda suggested. "Any other stills in the area?"

"None like mine," Willie said with a touch of pride. "The rest are all small potatoes. Going after them would be a waste of his time."

"Did you ever have a conversation with this guy?" Joe asked.

Willie nodded. "I gave him directions once when I found him at the end of my driveway. He claimed he was looking for my neighbor."

"Couldn't that have been true?" Amanda asked.

"If it was, this guy had a real bad sense of direction. The nearest neighbor, a fellow by the name of Kenny Loftis, is close to a mile down the road." He shrugged at Amanda's expression of amazement. "Daddy and Granddaddy liked their privacy. Over time they bought just about everything within a square mile just to live on. They added acres more, scattered here and there, to drive the revenuers crazy. Most of it's growing wild. Some of it is so dark and overgrown it gives me the creeps. You couldn't get me back in there if a pack of blood hounds was after me."

"Where's your operation?"

Willie gave a faintly self-deprecating smile. "You see, that's the thing. Granddaddy liked it close by. He figured he could protect it better, I guess. When Daddy took over, he felt a whole lot better knowing it wasn't where the revenuers would expect to find it. Said it would make it easier for Ma to say she had no idea what was going on."

"So it wasn't on your land?" Joe surmised.

"Sure it was," Willie said. "Just not close to home. It's real easy to buy up land in the name of some company or other and hide the real ownership. We moved operations once a year whether we thought anybody was onto us or not. If things heated up at one place, we could change locations faster than an ole hound dog could tree a squirrel. All we needed was access to a stream or some other water supply. Daddy always said there might come a day when bootleg whiskey would go out of favor, but we could retire in comfort by selling off all that land."

"Quite a pension plan," Donelli observed.

"But didn't the Department of Revenue figure out that the moonshine operation wasn't back in the woods somewhere near your home?" Amanda wondered.

Willie shook his head. "Daddy used to drive 'em wild. He just plain loved to drop hints that would lead 'em straight to the house. He'd sit on the front porch and laugh his head off while they swarmed through all that underbrush and got their clothes and their lily-white skin all torn up. He was especially fond of watching them rip right through the poison ivy without paying it no mind."

So this was the sort of cat-and-mouse game to which Della had referred, Amanda thought. It sounded downright dangerous to her. Frustrated state officials were sooner or later likely to get supremely irritated, especially once the rash from that poison ivy kicked in. Just the concept of irritated bureaucrats with guns was enough to give her goose bumps.

"What happened the day of the murder?" Amanda prodded.

"Well, this same guy, the one with the lousy sense of direction, parked his car just off the highway about a quarter-mile from my driveway. He'd pulled it into the trees, but there was no mistaking it. That particular shade of green was downright unforgettable. No way I could miss it when I passed by on my way home from a meeting of the local Chamber of Commerce."

He paused, as if to give the two of them time to grasp the irony of his belonging to such a traditional business organization. Amanda couldn't help admiring Willie's sense of the absurd. The young bootlegger's career might be unorthodox, but he was definitely in a line of work he enjoyed, risks and all. He obviously considered himself a vital part of the community's economy.

"Any sign of the Revenue agent?" Joe asked.

Willie shook his head. "Unless he was hiding on the floor, that car was empty."

"What did you do then?" Amanda asked.

"Went home, poured myself a beer—strictly legit, by the way—then settled down on the front porch to see what would happen next."

"Armed?" Joe inquired.

"Daddy's shotgun was propped against the house," he admitted.

"Loaded?"

"I had a few shells in my pocket. Loaded guns make me nervous. That doesn't mean I won't shoot, if the occasion arises. I just don't like to be tempted into settling some little squabble with a gun. Don't forget I never knew my granddaddy outside a jail cell. Learned my lesson from that."

Amanda seized the opening. "Miss Martha is convinced that your grandfather was no more guilty of murder than you are. Is that possible?"

"I wasn't even born when that murder happened," Willie said evasively.

"But surely it was a topic of conversation at home,"

Amanda insisted. "What was your father's opinion? What did your grandfather say when you visited him in jail?"

"By the time I was old enough to ask questions, Granddaddy's mind was wandering. Nothing he said made much sense. As for Daddy, the only time he ever talked about what had happened was when he got a buzz on. Couldn't separate truth from fiction then."

Amanda was convinced Willie was lying. She wasn't about to let the subject drop. "Try," she said.

Willie seemed taken aback by her harsh tone. "Try what?"

"To separate fact from fiction. If you can't, just tell me both and I'll work out the difference."

Willie's expression turned sullen. "I don't see why something that happened more than fifty years ago matters. I thought you were here to help me."

"I'm here at Miss Martha's request," Amanda corrected so there would be no mistaking her intentions. "She wants the record set straight on what happened to your grandfather. If I help you in the process, so much the better. But just so we're clear, my loyalty is to her. If you're not going to be straight with me, I'm out of here. I'll find other sources to tell me what I need to know."

She flipped off her tape recorder, shoved it in her purse, and stood up to emphasize the point. Donelli, she noticed with some dismay, hadn't budged.

"What's it going to be, Willie?" he inquired softly. "Face it. We're your best bet. Miss Martha thinks there's a connection between what happened to your grandfather and what's happening now to you. Could be she's just imagining things. Could be you're guilty as sin."

"I never killed the damned Revenue agent," Willie insisted. He shot a belligerent look at Amanda. "And neither did Granddaddy, if the stories my daddy told were true. He believed that someone had it in for us, someone who knew the moonshine operation and knew how to work the system to get an agent out to our property."

Amanda sat back down again. "A competitor?"

"Doubt it," Willie said. "Like I said before, the other operations around are small potatoes now, just like they were back then."

"But wouldn't they have grown, if they'd put you out of business?"

"I don't think so. I know most of those fellows. There's even one or two that go back to Granddaddy's time. Others are second and third generation, just like me. None of them are especially ambitious. For a lot of 'em, it's just habit. Maybe a source of a little extra off-the-books income."

"Who else would have a stake in closing you down?"

"I suppose you could get some real religious folks who'd go fanatical on you," Willie suggested, but without much conviction. "Can't imagine one of them killing a state official just to put the blame on us. They'd be more inclined to find the still themselves and bash it to pieces, spouting off a lot of pious, self-righteous nonsense while they were at it."

Amanda agreed with his logic. She glanced at Joe. "What else could be behind it? Any ideas?"

"Maybe it had nothing whatsoever to do with the whiskey business," Joe suggested. "Any enemies you know of, Willie? Any personal dealings that turned sour? Anybody openly carrying a grudge against the Ashfords?"

Willie suddenly looked uncomfortable. "There was one thing Daddy mentioned . . ." He shook his head. "I don't think it could have anything to do with what happened last week, though."

"But it might have been related to what happened with your grandfather?" Amanda asked.

"It's possible. Don't know how you'd find out, though. I'm pretty sure old Henry Boggins is dead by now. If he's not, he must be close to a hundred."

Amanda agreed that Henry Boggins sounded like a dead end, no pun intended. Still, she'd learned long ago not to dismiss any possibility until she'd checked it out. "Who is Henry Boggins?"

"I suppose you'd say he was my great-granddaddy. His daughter was married to my granddaddy."

"Laurabel?" Amanda asked, just to be sure she was on the right side of the family tree.

Willie nodded. "Daddy said old Henry went flat-out crazy when Laurabel died. He blamed Granddaddy for killing her. Said he'd been sneaking around behind her back for years and it finally broke her spirit so bad, she just up and died. Apparently there was a pretty nasty scene down at Great-Aunt Emma's on the day of the funeral. Old Henry was waving around a shotgun. Turned out it wasn't loaded, but he scared folks half to death. Some said the display of fatherly devotion came a mite too late. Apparently Granddaddy took his own accusations a step too far. He pointed out to old Henry that he'd abandoned his precious baby and her mother, that he was responsible for the sorry life they'd led. He said Henry could probably share the blame for Laurabel turning to the life of prostitution from which Granddaddy had rescued her."

Amanda winced. It must have been one hell of a send-off for the dearly departed. "How did Henry take the accusations?"

"He vowed he'd get even."

"So he might have done that by setting your grandfather up?" Amanda suggested.

"Might have," Willie agreed. "But he said he was going to do it by destroying the bitch who'd come between Laurabel and Granddaddy."

Amanda and Donelli exchanged a look. "The bitch" was Miss Martha Wellington. What better way to destroy her than to ruin the only man she'd ever loved?

CHAPTER

Five

"That kid is lying," Donelli said before he and Amanda had driven out of the parking lot at the jail.

"Lying?" Amanda said doubtfully. She'd believed most of what Willie Ashford had had to say.

"Okay, holding back."

Amanda thought about the conversation they'd just had. "I know he was being evasive there for a few minutes," she admitted, "but I thought he finally came through with the truth when he realized I was about to abandon him."

"No reflection on your powers of persuasion, Amanda, but the kid told you precisely as much as he figured would keep you in that room. Do you honestly believe some drunken old coot suddenly discovered a deep and abiding love for the daughter he'd abandoned and threatened to destroy Miss Martha for ruining his daughter's life?"

"Stranger things have happened."

"Usually in some TV movie," Joe said dismissively. "Henry Boggins sounds like the type who would be far more likely to blackmail William Ashford or Miss Martha. He'd want money to keep their affair secret."

"There was no affair. They were simply in love," Amanda pointed out. "It was all very discreet."

"Couldn't have been that discreet if Boggins knew about it and thought that widespread gossip was what had killed his daughter."

The comment silenced Amanda temporarily. Finally she said, "We'll just have to ask Miss Martha if Henry Boggins ever threatened her. Do you suppose he's still alive?"

"At a hundred years old? Doubtful. Even if he is, can you see him being in any condition to chase down some able-bodied Revenue agent and kill him? Besides, what would be the motive to frame Willie after all this time? He wasn't even born when all this happened."

"The sins of the father," Amanda suggested. "Or in this case, the grandfather?" Her stomach rumbled, reminding her that it had been a very long time since she'd eaten. "Can we stop for food?"

"There's food at home."

"And there's a McDonald's in the next block. You tell me which is faster."

"One of these days all that cholesterol is going to catch up with you," Donelli said, but he dutifully turned into the drive-through lane. "What do you want?"

"A Big Mac, large fries, and a large Coke," she said, shooting him a defiant look.

Donelli shuddered. "Maybe we'd better go inside. I want to watch as it all settles on your hips."

Amanda scowled at him. "You didn't seem to have a problem with my hips earlier today. Is this an indication of what life is going to be like when I'm old and out of shape? Am I in for an endless stream of snide remarks? Or will you just abandon me for someone who can still wear a size six?"

He grinned at her. "Just trying to keep you healthy long enough to enjoy old age. I have a few interesting plans for our golden years. They require you to be agile."

Inside the brightly-lit restaurant, Donelli continued his war on her food habits by ordering an uncharacteristically saintly salad. There were times—and this was one of them—when Amanda could have cheerfully slugged him. She settled for slapping his hand every time he tried to sneak one of her fries. It was his own damned fault he hadn't gotten the burger and fries he really wanted, just so he could make a point with her.

Chewing thoughtfully on a fry, she went back over the entire interview with Willie Ashford, hoping that some obvious direction for the investigation would jump out at her. She hated to admit it, but she agreed with her husband that Henry Boggins was a pretty weak lead.

More promising were the names of other moonshiners, which Willie had reluctantly coughed up as they were departing. Two of them were old enough, perhaps, to remember what had gone on half a century earlier.

"I think I'll start talking to the people on Willie's list first thing tomorrow," she said finally.

"I don't think so," Donelli contradicted as he successfully speared a cherry tomato with his little plastic fork. Clearly pleased with that triumph, he took aim at Amanda's fries again.

She halfheartedly swatted him away while trying to grasp the significance of his declaration. "You don't think so?" she repeated warily.

"Nope. Not without me. That was the deal."

She was increasingly convinced she had made a very bad bargain. "Miss Martha hasn't officially hired you yet. I could see to it that it doesn't happen."

"Not likely," he said calmly, as his fork skittered off the remaining tomato without even scratching the skin. He frowned, jabbed, and finally got the little sucker, while Amanda stewed over his arrogance.

"She'll listen to me," she insisted. "I'll tell her it will be a waste of her money."

"She also worries about you. Need I remind you that she once hired one of her nephews, a weight-lifting pediatrician of all things, to serve as your bodyguard? I think she'll be relieved to have me on the case, especially since he moved to New Mexico or Arizona or someplace."

"Oh, for heaven's sake, a few hours ago you didn't even want to take the job."

"Now I find that I'm intrigued."

"About as intrigued as I am with aphids."

Donelli grinned. "Fascinating little insects, those aphids. I could tell you stories . . ."

Amanda held up a hand. "Save it, please." Maybe there was another, more subtle way around her husband's protectiveness. "I'd like to leave about eight. How does that sound?"

"Sorry, no can do," he said, clearly amused by her attempt. "I might be able to get away by noon."

"Well, I can't very well waste the entire morning waiting while you drive a tractor around in circles. *Inside Atlanta* has deadlines."

"You should have thought of that before you dragged me into this. If you want something to do, get on the computer and research those names. Pull up files on the murders. Use the phone to call the police and see what they have on Willie. Check out the victims. Talk to the Alcohol–Tobacco Tax guys at the Department of Revenue about the state of moonshining in Georgia today."

"Those are all things I could have Jenny Lee do," she pointed out, referring to her assistant. Jenny Lee Macon was already in a depressed state because she had too little to do and a boyfriend who was shuttling back and forth between Atlanta and his new job in Washington as a photographer for *National Geographic*. Amanda couldn't begin to imagine how Jenny Lee would survive when Larry Carter went off for weeks on end on his first overseas assignment.

For a moment all thoughts of the Ashfords and their history of allegedly killing Revenue agents vanished. She regarded Joe worriedly. "Donelli, what do you think Larry's going to do about Jenny Lee?"

"I think he's already done it. He's taken the job in

D.C. He's commuting on weekends. I'd say he's trying to keep all his options open."

"You don't think he's going to marry her, do you?"

Joe shrugged. "Beats me."

Her husband's indifference irritated her. "Don't you care that she's miserable and he's making the biggest mistake of his life?"

"If it's a mistake, he'll realize it soon enough."

"Jenny Lee may not be waiting around for him then. You know how stubborn she gets when she's miffed."

"Then that will be her choice," Donelli said.

Amanda frowned. "Your pragmatic attitude is very annoying. They worried about us when we split up."

"And in the end it wasn't their worrying that solved our problems, was it?"

Amanda pushed the remains of her hamburger aside. The conversation had ruined her appetite. At least this time she knew the cause of her sudden disinterest in food. She adored and respected Larry. Jenny Lee was a treasure. They belonged together. She sighed. She supposed that Donelli was right. That was something they would just have to figure out for themselves. At least she could keep Jenny Lee occupied in the meantime.

She looked up to find Donelli regarding her with amusement.

"Reach any conclusions?" he inquired in that Brooklyn-tinged accent that was rapidly giving way to a slower and admittedly sexier Southern drawl.

"One," she declared, shooting him a defiant look. "You can pick me up at the office at twelve-thirty on the dot. If you're not there, I'm going after those interviews on my own."

His grin spread. "I'll be there, Amanda. Count on it."

The *Inside Atlanta* offices were housed in a downtown skyscraper. The magazine was only three years old and thriving, thanks to some flashy investigative reporting by Amanda and Jack Davis, the business writer, plus editor Oscar Cates's unerring sense of the region's social and cultural history. Publisher Joel Crenshaw had the good sense to leave them all alone, even on those frequent occasions when business leaders and public officials tried to get him to intercede on their behalf. In fact, Joel seemed to enjoy most the times when he was called on to vigorously defend the First Amendment.

Amanda breezed into the newsroom, which was finally beginning to acquire a suitably lived-in look. She gave wide berth to Oscar's office, hoping he wouldn't notice her and demand to know what she was working on. Unfortunately, one wall of his office was glass. The blinds, usually closed tight, were wide open. Apparently he'd been watching for her.

"Amanda!"

His bellow could have been heard clear out in Gwinnett County. Caught, she sighed and reversed directions. "Yes?" she said, poking her head cautiously through the doorway.

"In," he ordered, removing his hated reading glasses and peering at her. "You okay?"

"I'd be better if you'd leave a vacant spot so a person could sit." She hefted a stack of computer printouts and file folders from a chair and deposited them on the floor, then sat.

Oscar was still regarding her intently. "You look a little green around the gills. Are you sure you shouldn't be back home in bed?"

"I'm fine," she said tersely. She didn't want to acknowledge that the same odd queasiness she'd felt the day before had returned with a vengeance this morning. She was afraid if she acknowledged it, she would also have to admit to the possibility that Miss Martha's diagnosis had been accurate. The next thing she knew she'd be buying one of those home pregnancy tests. And after that, well, she didn't even want to think about what would come after that if the stupid thing turned blue or pink or whatever color indicated positive.

"My wife looked just like that when she was pregnant," Oscar said as if he'd read her mind. His expression brightened. "Hey, that's it, isn't it? You and Donelli are gonna have a kid."

"I have the flu," Amanda said adamantly.

The declaration was greeted with obvious skepticism, but at least he let the matter drop. She hoped he would not share his suspicions with his best buddy Donelli.

"So what were you doing over at Miss Martha's yesterday?" he asked.

This particular ground, while tenuous, was far more to Amanda's liking than the issue of her health. She plunged into the story Miss Martha had told her, then added what little she'd learned from Willie Ashford.

"I have all of her old clippings and the love letters from William Ashford with me," she concluded. "I'm going through those this morning, checking the computer for anything that might tie into it, and then Donelli and I are heading over to talk with some potential sources this afternoon."

Oscar was frowning when she finished. "I don't like it."

Amanda heard something unyielding in his voice she'd never heard before. "You don't like the story?"

"What story? You're doing a favor for an old lady and trying to do it on the magazine's time."

"Oscar, that's not true. If these two murders are connected, it's a great story. It could have a little of everything—scandal, greed, passion," she pointed out, playing to Oscar's subconscious tabloid tendencies.

"Forget it."

She studied him as if his expression might reveal the objections he wasn't willing to state aloud. When that didn't work, she asked, "Why?"

"Because I said so."

"Are you operating a still in your backyard?" she inquired, only half-joking.

"That's not even funny, Amanda."

"I wasn't trying to be funny. I was trying to figure out why you're being so close-minded about this. At least let me check it out for a day or two and see if there's anything to Miss Martha's suspicions."

"Which part of *no* don't you understand?"

Maybe it was because she was feeling lousy. Maybe it was because Oscar's truculent mood had raised her hackles. At any rate, Amanda glared at him and announced, "I want two weeks vacation, starting now."

"No."

"Why not? I haven't had a real vacation since I started here. I didn't even take time off for a real honeymoon when Donelli and I got married."

"That's not my problem. You want vacation, you put in for it in advance like everybody else."

Something was going on here that Amanda couldn't begin to understand. Whatever it was stirred her curiosity. Oscar of all people should know that it was far more dangerous to put roadblocks in front of her than it was to let her do what she wanted in the first place.

Glaring at her boss, she reached down and ripped a piece of paper off the pile she'd removed from the chair. Without even looking to see what it was, she scrawled a note across the inch of white space at the top, then shoved it in Oscar's direction.

"What's that?" he asked without touching it.

"My request for vacation."

Without even looking at it, he balled it up and tossed it in the trash. "Request denied."

"You're being unreasonable."

"I am trying to run a magazine. I can't do that if I have a maverick reporter who thinks she gets to do whatever the hell she wants."

Amanda struggled against a rising tide of fury. Usually Oscar was the first one to defend her against being labeled a maverick.

"Do you have some other article you would prefer that I work on?" she asked. "Maybe menus for Fourth of July backyard barbecues? I could test the recipes at home. If Joe and Pete don't die, we could publish them."

The sarcasm apparently shot straight past him. He didn't react by so much as the blink of an eye.

"Talk to Carol," he said.

"Carol?" she said blankly. "Who the hell is Carol?"

"If you would read the damned memos I write you would know that Carol Fields is the new assignment editor I hired. She started yesterday."

"Assignment editor?" Amanda repeated, thoroughly bemused by the concept that *Inside Atlanta* could possibly need such a person. "Why on earth would we need an assignment editor? Jack and I are the only full-time reporters on staff. Everything else comes in from free-lance contributors."

"Somebody has to coordinate all that, make the free-lance assignments. Did you think every story miraculously appeared on my desk just in time for deadline?"

"No, of course not." Her gaze narrowed. "But why would Joel think we need an assignment editor? You've been managing all that just fine. Better than fine, in fact."

"Thanks," he said grudgingly. He stared at the ceiling, sighed, then finally admitted, "Joel has this crazy idea that he should free up more of my time."

"To do what?"

"Go to a bunch of goddamn luncheons, I suppose. He hasn't exactly made that clear yet."

Amanda's sigh matched his. The picture was finally

becoming clear. She settled back to hear the rest. "Is that what this is really about? You're ticked because Joel is changing your job description, so you feel you have to yank my chain in turn?"

"I am telling you that I don't like this story," he insisted. "I am also telling you that it is no longer my responsibility to oversee your assignments. But just in case you have any notion of trying to coax Carol into okaying this particular assignment, I do oversee her decisions."

His announcement took the wind out of Amanda's sails. She had been hoping to do exactly that, to convince the new and as yet untested assignment editor that this was the story of the century. Well, half-century to be more precise.

"What's she like?"

"Form your own opinion."

"Where is she?"

"At her desk in the newsroom, of course. She's been there since the goddamn crack of dawn. Go on and introduce yourself. She's been very anxious to get acquainted."

Something in Oscar's tone suggested that Carol's interest in meeting Amanda had a whole lot to do with launching a full-scale turf war. Given the way she was feeling, Amanda might very well mark her territory by throwing up on it.

CHAPTER

Six

Amanda took a surreptitious peek at Carol Fields on her way across the newsroom. She could tell at once that they were going to have problems. She wasn't sure she could relate to anyone who didn't have a single blonde hair out of place and who dressed in an expensive black power suit and Tiffany-caliber gold jewelry to run a small, previously friendly, informal magazine newsroom.

The assignment editor's expression as she surveyed Amanda's wind-tossed hairstyle, jeans, silk shirt, and blazer indicated a similar dismay, though obviously for the opposite reason. Still, she managed to plaster a smile on her face as she rose to greet Amanda. Amanda wasn't sure she disguised her own reaction nearly so well.

"You must be Amanda Roberts," Carol Fields said in a perfectly modulated soft voice, holding out a slim, perfectly manicured hand adorned with a perfectly ostentatious diamond and sapphire ring. "Carol Fields."

Amanda thought she detected ice under that syrupy Southern drawl, but she put her gut reaction on hold and tried to warm up to her new boss. "Sorry I wasn't here on your first day," she apologized. "If I'd known you'd been hired, I'd have made more of an effort."

"I heard you were just a teensy bit under the weather," Carol drawled with what seemed to Amanda like feigned concern. "You probably should have stayed home another day. No point in coming in, if you don't feel like working."

"Oh, I'm ready to work," Amanda said, gesturing toward her briefcase. "I brought quite a bit of research for my next piece along with me. I have interviews scheduled this afternoon."

"Oh, that's not possible," Carol said. Her gray eyes turned the steely shade of gunmetal. "You'll obviously have to reschedule."

"Excuse me?"

"Well, of course, you wouldn't know," Carol said apologetically, whipping out a piece of paper from the already impressive array of neatly labeled folders on her desk and shoving it into Amanda's clenched fist. "You weren't here."

"What's this?" Amanda asked suspiciously. She'd found that people who ran a small business by memo generally lacked the skills to deal with others one-on-one. They tended not to trust their own powers of persuasion, relying instead on the force of black-on-white written words.

"We have instituted a dress code for anyone representing the magazine in public," Carol explained.

"A dress code?" Amanda repeated, her voice turning lethal. She slowly and deliberately surveyed the assignment editor's attire. "You mean like little black uniforms with white silk blouses?"

"I mean professional attire," Carol said, not so much as flinching in the face of Amanda's scorn. "A suit would be most appropriate, I believe. Though a well-tailored dress would be acceptable."

The latter was said as if she were granting a great concession. Amanda perched on the edge of the closest desk and slowly swung one jeans-clad leg back and forth. She was fully aware that first Jack Davis and then Jenny Lee had arrived and were watching the exchange with an almost palpable sense of expectation. She suspected Oscar was glued to that office window of his, gleefully taking in the newsroom battle zone.

"Tell me, Carol, when was the last time you reported a story?" she inquired in what she hoped was a deceptively pleasant tone that disguised her annoyance.

"I spent ten years as a reporter before becoming an editor," Carol replied with an obvious touch of pride.

"Covering what? Police? The courts? Breaking news? Washington, perhaps?"

Patches of color flared in the other woman's cheeks. "Actually I was in the feature section of a daily paper in Birmingham."

"Ah, I see." Amanda closed in for the kill, all pretense of congeniality gone. "Then most likely you almost never had to climb over a fence to chase a source or run half a mile to get away from a crazed murderer," she said. "Perhaps in features you could afford to dress in what you refer to as professional attire. No doubt the kind of people you interviewed dressed in power suits of their own. I prefer to dress in clothes that will not impede my progress or intimidate the daylights out of my sources."

Carol, to her credit, still didn't look the least bit daunted. She stared straight into Amanda's eyes. "That assumes that you will continue to be doing stories in which your sources are either nervous or poorly dressed or both. It suggests you might have further occasions on which your progress needs to be excessively fast."

She whipped out another piece of paper from that daunting stack of folders on her desk. Actually, to be more precise, it turned out to be several sheets of paper stapled together. The weight of it gave Amanda chills.

"If you read this, I believe you will see that the new vision I have for *Inside Atlanta* does not include the sort of controversial, depressing material in which you have indulged in the past."

Amanda heard a muffled choking sound behind her and guessed it was Jenny Lee anticipating an explosion. Instead, she held on to her temper by the most fragile of threads. "Indulged?" she repeated softly. "I do not indulge myself when I select my stories. I choose topics that I feel are important to this community. Admittedly, some of them are dark, but the world's not always made up of afternoon teas and coming out parties. I occasionally tread on some very powerful toes, a practice that has made *Inside Atlanta* widely respected in journalistic circles."

"And caused certain advertisers to shy away, from what I hear," Carol shot back. "Joel and Oscar hired me to put some balance back into the magazine."

"Fair enough," Amanda said, trying to behave reasonably when she really wanted to smack this pompous little twerp upside her perfectly coiffed head. "I'm all for balance. Happy little features and freelance puff pieces come in all the time. I'm sure you'll have plenty of material from which to choose."

"But you're on staff. Why should I pay for outside material, when I can assign the same story to you? That certainly isn't very cost-effective, is it? As a business, we do have to keep the bottom line in mind."

Amanda wasn't oblivious to the tenets of those who lived or died by the profit motive. Unfortunately, though, mention of the bottom line tended to be one step ahead of the kind of wimpy journalistic decisions she usually couldn't live with. She moved until she was scant inches from the woman's face to clarify her position.

"Ms. Fields, I don't do frivolous features and I don't do flattering profiles just to feed the ego of some prospective advertiser. I do investigative reporting. That is why Joel hired me."

"Well, obviously, he has had second thoughts," Carol said with an irritating note of triumph.

"Then he'll have to tell me that himself."

The next thing Amanda knew a phone was being shoved into her hand.

"I'll dial," Carol said.

Amanda slammed the receiver back into place. "Save your nails. I'd hate for you to get a nick in your polish. I'll go up and see him in person."

As she strode across the newsroom, Jenny Lee fell into step beside her looking worried. Amanda also noticed that Jenny Lee was wearing a prim little navy blue suit and what appeared to be a pair of expensive and eminently stylish—and, therefore, suitable—Ferragamo pumps. She even had on navy hose.

"Amanda, I'm not so sure it was smart to antagonize her the very first time you met her," Jenny Lee said with a frown.

"No," Amanda corrected. "It was not so smart of her to antagonize me. I will quit or force her to fire me before I'll spend a dime on a corporate uniform or waste my time writing the kind of garbage she obviously has in mind. Where in God's name did Oscar find her?"

"Actually, I think she married Joel's nephew the day after she graduated from some swanky school like Bryn Mawr. She's probably been filling his head with ideas at every family get-together since the wedding. Somewhere along the way he must have decided to take her seriously."

Suddenly Amanda groaned and stopped in her tracks, her head spinning. She swallowed hard against a tide of nausea. Jenny Lee was halfway down the corridor before she realized that Amanda wasn't with her. She came running back when she saw that Amanda was leaning against a wall.

"Amanda, honey, you're white as a sheet. Are you okay?"

"Actually, I'm just a little bit dizzy. I guess I'm not over that flu after all."

"I'm calling Joe."

"Don't you dare!"

"But you need to go home and I don't think you have any business driving. I'd take you myself, but Carol's started this policy . . ."

Amanda groaned and this time it had nothing to do with the state of her stomach. "Don't even tell me. I don't want to know." She squeezed Jenny Lee's hand. "Don't worry. I'll be fine. Joe's coming to pick me up at lunchtime, anyway. Just walk with me to the restroom. I'll stay on the sofa in there for a few minutes until this passes."

Clucking like a mother hen, Jenny Lee settled her on the sofa in the white-tiled ladies' room. The lights were so bright, Amanda promptly closed her eyes to shut out the glare.

"What can I get you?" Jenny Lee asked. "How 'bout a ginger ale to settle your stomach?"

"That sounds good." As Jenny Lee turned to go, she added, "Hey, promise me you won't say anything about this to the barracuda in there."

"But she's going to want to know where you are."

"Tell her I'm in a closed-door meeting with Joel. That ought to give her something to think about."

* * *

Amanda awoke from a sound sleep to find her husband hovering over her, his expression anxious. Of course, it was possible he was just worried about being discovered in the ladies' room.

"We're going to the doctor," he announced.

"Why?" she asked groggily.

"Because I don't like what I see."

She scowled at him. "You have an unusual way of trying to perk up a woman's spirits."

"Flattery seems pretty pointless under the circumstances." He studied her thoughtfully. "Can you manage to stand on your own two feet or should I carry you?"

"When the time comes, I can walk."

"Then let's move it."

He held out his hand to help her up. Amanda ignored it. She wanted to buy a little time until her head stopped spinning.

"I'll make you a deal," she offered. "First, we do the interviews. Then I'll go to the doctor's."

"What interviews? Jenny Lee said some woman's in charge and she hasn't even given you your first assignment."

"And, God willing, she never will," Amanda said, getting to her feet on her own.

"Meaning?" Joe inquired suspiciously.

"I'm working this story, either for *Inside Atlanta* or on my own. If they don't like it, they can fire me. I was on my way to tell Joel just that when I got sick."

Joe shot her a disbelieving look. "Is it really so important to you?"

"This particular story? Maybe not, except for its

importance to Miss Martha. It's the principle. If this magazine is going to turn into a bastion of safe, marshmallow journalism, I don't want any part of it anyway."

She shot a glare in the direction of the newsroom as they passed by. She would find Joel first thing tomorrow, when she'd had time to think up even more ammunition, and explain why he'd made a terrible mistake in hiring a woman with no vision for the assignment desk.

Amanda was still expounding on the same theme when she and Donelli crossed the county line and entered Ashford's territory north of the city. Willie had given them very clear directions to his property.

They found the narrow dirt track to his place with surprisingly little difficulty. Donelli turned in. Suddenly it seemed they were in the wilderness. The rutted road passed between huge, centuries-old trees. Branches met overhead, creating a canopy that shut out sunlight, leaving the road in shadows.

"Eerie," Amanda declared.

Donelli slowed the car and glanced around. "I don't know about you, but I expect a pack of unfriendly Dobermans to greet us at any second."

As if the remark had been overheard, a dog howled in the distance.

"Amanda, maybe we should just get the hell out of here."

"Come on, Donelli, don't chicken out now. Remember, nobody's home. The owner's in jail. I want to see what kind of arsenal he kept here. I also want to see if he was telling the truth about keeping his moonshine operation somewhere else."

"And how do you intend to go about getting your answers? I doubt he left the house unlocked. Nor do I suppose that the still is set up in the backyard."

"The house probably has windows," she reminded him, cautioning herself not to admit that she had been entertaining thoughts of jimmying the lock. Joe tended to give dull little speeches about the sanctity of private property whenever she got such urges. "As for the still, there would have to be some kind of path, right?"

"The whole point of hiding the still would be lost, if the path were in plain sight."

She scowled at him. "Stop throwing up roadblocks. Let's just see what we find when we get there, okay?"

"Whatever you say, dear."

The compliant tone didn't exactly ring with sincerity, but Amanda was willing to take whatever cooperation she could get.

"How far have we driven from the highway?" she asked a few minutes later.

"Not quite a mile. I'm afraid if I go any faster these ruts will jar every single part of the car loose."

"Surely we must be getting close to the house," she said, searching unsuccessfully for some sign of a break in the dense forest.

Then, just when she was certain that they were on a road leading nowhere, they rounded a sharp curve and entered a clearing scattered with pink and white dogwood trees that were just beginning to bloom. Ahead of them stood a huge fieldstone house, a porch stretching across the front, planters of bright red geraniums beneath the sill of every window.

The house wasn't particularly fancy. In fact, based on the varying shades of the gray stone, it looked as if it had been built piecemeal over time. Chimneys rose at both ends and in the middle, suggesting an old-fashioned kind of coziness indoors. A single rocking chair, its once-white paint chipped and weathered, sat on the porch. Sitting there all by itself, it suggested a certain loneliness for the home's occupant.

Though the house appealed to Amanda, for the life of her she could not imagine Miss Martha ever living there or desiring to live with the man who built such a haphazardly-designed home. Nor could she picture the socially active woman she knew being content in this quiet, out-of-the-way environment.

Donelli met her gaze. "Hard to imagine her here, isn't it?"

Amanda had no doubt that he, too, was thinking of Miss Martha. "I wonder if she ever even saw it? After all, he could hardly have brought her by while his wife was alive. And it's not like she could ever sneak a drive through the neighborhood to take a peek."

Joe shut off the engine. "Well, shall we take a look around?"

Amanda exited the car eagerly. She was partway across the yard, when another bout of queasiness struck. To cover the way she was feeling, she turned back for her briefcase. At Donelli's puzzled look, she shrugged. "I've been putting off reading William's letters. Somehow this seems like the right place."

"Yes," he said softly, pausing to give her a tender kiss. "I think maybe it would."

Amanda wasn't surprised that he understood. Donelli, for all his stubborn pragmatism, occasionally displayed the heart of a true romantic.

Of course, it was entirely possible he was merely glad to have her out of his way, while he snooped in search of clues he might or might not decide to share with her. And if she hadn't felt as if she were within seconds of passing out cold, there was no way in hell she'd be giving him this chance to search on his own. Five minutes in a rocker on the porch and she was bound to be feeling well enough to join him inside. At least in the meantime, William's letters promised to be a fascinating distraction.

CHAPTER
Seven

The lilacs bloomed today, filling the air with their delicate, sweet scent. With every breath I took, I thought of you. Love, William

Amanda read the note, charmed by its sentiment, awed that Miss Martha's renegade bootlegger had captured his emotions with such brevity and such clarity. Apparently he'd had the soul of a poet to go along with the daring of a professional lawbreaker.

All of the notes were similar, brief to the point of terseness, yet sweetly tender or illuminating. None was longer than a single page of the heavy cream vellum, but his bold handwriting covered the paper.

The notes began in 1935, sporadically at first, perhaps once a month. Some were no more than hurriedly scrawled suggestions for a meeting time and place. A country inn. A tearoom. In warmer weather, the bank of a creek or a shaded picnic area. All secluded. All romantic.

At first the notes hinted of insecurity, a faint disbelief that she would come. As time passed, they seemed to grow more confident and, for a while, almost desperate. Based on the tone and the postmarks on the envelopes of the last few, Amanda guessed that they must have been written during the darkest hours of his wife's illness.

The ailing Laurabel was never mentioned. Nor was his son. Nor was the danger inherent in his work. Nor the future, not until the very last slim packet of letters. In those, at last, Amanda found her first hint that William Ashford believed that he and his beloved Martha would soon be together forever.

The seasons, which have passed so slowly, endlessly until now, show signs of promise. With the turning of the leaves this fall, or the first gentle flakes of snow, perhaps at last I will hold you in my arms. It is the moment I long for. With love eternal, William

There was only one more. This time the paper was cheaper, William's handwriting shakier. The postmark, Amanda saw, was September 23, 1942, two days after the murder that had sent him to jail, the murder that had ruined a lifetime of dreams.

By now you will have heard about the charges against me. Please believe that I am innocent and that I will fight. Still, you must wait for me no longer. I have stolen too much of your life, kept you from too many adventures. Bless you for the years you have devoted to a man not worthy of your love. Live happily, my love, and think of me from time to time, as I will always think of you, the sweet angel of my soul. William

Amanda let the letter slip from her fingers and flutter to her lap with all the others. A single tear crept down her cheek, followed by a silent flood. She let them flow unchecked, caught up in the sorrow, touched by William's determination to set the woman he loved free. He should have known, though, that it would never work. Miss Martha might have stayed away, as he requested, but a love that deep didn't fade away on command. It had lasted a lifetime.

Amanda heard Joe's footsteps on the porch. He hunkered down in front of her, his hands resting on her knees. "You okay?"

"Just sad," she said, brushing ineffectively at the tears.

"I might be able to brighten your mood," he said softly.

"How?"

He grinned. "The back door's unlocked."

She stared at her husband in astonishment. "You're giving me permission to break in?"

"I'm telling you that the door is open for any stranger to wander through. Might as well be you."

"Have you been inside?"

"Nope. I thought I'd wait for you. Just don't . . ."

". . . touch anything," she concluded, giving him a wry look. "Please, I know the rules."

"I know you know them. Your tendency to break them is what worries me. Besides, since William gave us permission to be here, I'm less concerned about your touching anything than I am about any inclination you might get to take a few things along for further perusal at your leisure."

Amanda hurriedly gathered up the letters and put them back into her briefcase. Then she followed Donelli around to the back of the house. At the kitchen door, she paused.

"Is there anything in particular we should be looking for?"

"A motive for murder."

"Well, that certainly narrows it down."

"Investigating a crime is not exactly a predictable science," he reminded her. "If it were, the police would solve more of them."

Amanda turned the doorknob and stepped inside the kitchen. Logs waited in the fireplace for the touch of a match. Clean dishes had been left by the sink to dry. A bouquet of lilacs had dried out and turned brown in a vase in the middle of the kitchen table.

Lilacs, Amanda thought with a smile. Apparently Willie had a penchant for them as his grandfather had. She was about to move on, when she was struck by a thought.

"Donelli?"

"Hmm?" His distracted reply came from what appeared to be a pantry.

"Come here a second."

He poked his head around the door. "What?"

"Does this seem out of character to you?"

"What?"

"A vase of lilacs on the kitchen table. Can you see

Willie picking flowers just to brighten up the place for himself?"

"Now that you mention it, no."

"But nobody's said a thing about a woman. He never once mentioned a girlfriend. The cops said he hadn't had a single visitor until we showed up, except for the attorney Miss Martha hired for him."

"Maybe he just had the guys over for poker."

"And put flowers on the table? Please. A bowl of onion dip and some chips maybe. A sack of pork rinds would be more likely." Amanda shook her head. "Wouldn't it be something if it turned out Willie's been sneaking around seeing someone, just like his granddaddy was?"

"Willie's not married," Donelli pointed out. "What's the harm?"

"Maybe her family wouldn't consider him suitable. Maybe she's married. What an ironic twist that would be."

"Maybe she doesn't even exist."

"The lilacs, Donelli. There's the proof right there. If we find the woman, I bet we'll find the answers."

Unfortunately, there were no women on the list of names Willie had given them. Nor was there any further evidence of a female's presence anywhere in the house, not even so much as a stray pair of pantyhose or a lace-edged hankie. She even checked the back of the bathroom door, hoping to find a nightie hanging on a hook. Nothing.

Amanda eventually returned to the kitchen, where she waited impatiently for what seemed to be an eternity.

When she could stand it no longer, she went in search of her husband. She found him sorting through papers in what appeared to be a very modern, very well equipped office. It had a computer with all the bells and whistles, a copy machine, a fax. It was awfully fancy for a man who professed to be nothing more than a fourth-generation bootlegger.

"Find anything?"

"Evidence that Willie was holding out on us," he said.

"More illegal activities?" Amanda asked hopefully.

"Nope, real estate."

"That's no surprise. He told us they owned property for miles around."

"He didn't mention that he is one of the primary partners in a development company that has aspirations for getting a Disney-caliber amusement park built within the next five years. All that land the family has been buying up? It's smack in the middle of the area being proposed for the park. It would probably triple or quadruple in value if the deal goes through."

"So what's the connection to the murder?"

Donelli shrugged. "Maybe none. Or maybe somebody got the bright idea of framing Willie so he'd have to sell out cheap to pay his legal expenses. Or maybe someone is just jealous enough to frame him."

"Sounds like a stretch to me."

"Nothing's a stretch if the stakes are high enough."

"Okay, make some copies of the papers and let's get out of here."

Donelli regarded her as if she'd suggested he steal the crown jewels. Amanda shook her head and held out her hand. "Want me to do it, so you can remain lily pure?"

He sighed. "I suppose making a few copies wouldn't exactly break any laws."

Amanda grinned. "Hurry, though. I want to actually talk to some people before nightfall. The idea of roaming around in these backwoods after dark gives me the creeps."

"I'll second that," Donelli concurred. "Just give me a minute. Go on out to the car, if you want to."

Amanda retreated outside. As she leaned against the car's front fender, she decided maybe the isolation out here wouldn't be so terrible after all. The filtered sun was just strong enough to splash warmth across her shoulders. She could hear the distinctive chirps and coos of several types of birds. The clean air was scented with lilacs and pine. Squirrels chattered incessantly. It all seemed terribly bucolic in the nicest sense of the word.

Maybe the atmosphere of pure tranquility was what threw her. Maybe that was why the sharp crack seemed at first no more than the snap of a tree branch. The second crack, however, shattered the window in the car's passenger door, no more than an inch to the left of her. Shards of glass flew. One nicked her cheek. As she hit the ground, she could feel the warm trail of blood, smell the faintly metallic scent. Her stomach churned.

Donelli tore from the house. His own gun, which she hadn't even realized he was carrying, was drawn. His face was the color of the sheet flapping on the line in the side yard. His gaze swept the woods with professional intensity.

"You okay?" he called out.

"Fine."

"Which direction did the shot come from?"

She gestured toward the woods to his left.

"Don't budge. I'm going to check it out."

She opened her mouth to protest, but before the words could form, he had slipped into the tangle of undergrowth. Amanda's heart seemed to have lodged in her throat, choking off breath. It stayed there until she finally caught a glimpse of him several minutes later.

"Did you see anybody?" she hollered.

"Not a soul," he said, brushing leaves and spiderwebs from his clothes as he came toward her. "Just these." He held out two shell casings, then tucked them into his pocket. "Pure luck, too. I stepped right on them. If I'd been looking, it would have been like trying to find a needle in a haystack."

He reached out then and helped her to her feet. "What's this?" He brushed his fingers gently along her cheek. They came away bloody. "Dear heaven, Amanda, I thought you said you weren't hit."

She had forgotten about the nick. Definitely a mistake. Donelli's expression had turned dark. Amanda recognized that look. In another minute or two he'd start insisting she belonged in bed, at home, for the rest of her natural life. "I wasn't, not by the gunman anyway. Maybe a piece of glass."

"That does it," he said grimly. "Get in the car."

"Donelli, the car is filled with shattered glass." He was so absorbed with the implications of her injury he obviously hadn't thought beyond that.

"Sorry. I'll have that cleaned up in a second." He took the car-vac from the trunk, plugged it into the lighter, and sucked up most of the glass. "That ought to do it until I can get to one of those gas stations that have the more powerful vacuums. Just watch yourself, okay?"

He'd barely turned onto the highway before he was punching out a number on his cellular phone.

Amanda's gaze narrowed. "Who are you calling?"

"The doctor Miss Martha recommended when I talked to her about taking on the investigation this morning. I want to be sure he waits for us. That cut probably needs stitches."

Amanda doubted it. There hadn't been that much blood. She snatched the phone. "Not yet. I'm not leaving here until we talk to at least one person on that list."

"One person?"

"At least one," she corrected.

He sighed. "Okay, which one?"

Amanda studied the piece of paper Willie had given them. "Let's start with Kenny Loftis."

"Why him?"

"Because he owns the piece of property east of this one."

"And that was the direction from which the gunshot came," Donelli concluded, making a squealing U-turn in the middle of the highway.

Amanda grinned at her normally cautious husband. "I'll make a decent driver out of you yet, Donelli."

He eyed her balefully. "Don't get your hopes up."

She reached over and patted his hand. "Where you're concerned, my hopes know no bounds."

CHAPTER
Eight

Kenny Loftis was obviously not in the same financial league as Willie Ashford. His ramshackle cabin was set maybe fifty feet back from the highway in a clearing that gave him little more than walking space around the exterior. A stack of firewood had been piled up to the windowsills on one side of the front door. An overweight hound dog basked in the last patch of sunlight on the other side. A man armed with a shotgun stood in the doorway, his expression less jovial than that of the classic farming couple in Grant Wood's famed *American Gothic* painting.

"Almost looks as if he was expecting company," Donelli commented.

"Not too excited about the prospect, is he?" Amanda observed. "Think he's our sniper?"

"No."

Amanda stared at her husband. "You sound awfully

confident for someone who's looking at an unfriendly man holding a shotgun right after someone shot at me."

"How far do you suppose we are from Willie's property, even allowing for a shortcut of some kind?"

"A mile, maybe a little more."

"And how long did it take us to get here after the shooting?"

"The drive didn't take long, but you spent what seemed like an eternity tromping through the woods in search of a suspect," Amanda said.

"True, but we're still talking a half hour tops. I guarantee you that nobody could cut through that wilderness back in there in that time unless it was Arnold Schwarzenegger or Sly Stallone armed with a machete." He gestured toward the man whose chilly gaze remained fixed on them. "This old geezer has to be at least seventy."

"Hey, Jack LaLanne is no spring chicken and look at the shape he's in." At Donelli's look of disbelief, she shrugged. "Okay, more than likely this guy isn't the sniper. Go on and introduce yourself. If he doesn't put a bullet through you, I'll follow."

"Amanda, you're all heart." He winked at her as he exited the car. "Try not to antagonize him until I get him to put that shotgun down."

"Not one word will cross my lips," she promised.

"Don't make promises you can't keep."

Actually, she tried really hard to keep this one. She sat perfectly still and silent for at least ninety seconds, according to the exceedingly slow sweep of the second hand on her watch. Then it became clear that Donelli was actually engaged in a conversation, not a confrontation, with a man who was most likely Loftis. She wasn't about to be left out of the first real interview since the investigation had begun.

Slipping cautiously from the car, she took her time meandering up the path, just in case the old man decided to change his mind about the degree of hospitality he was offering.

"Nope," he said to whatever Donelli had asked before Amanda was within hearing.

"You've been here all afternoon, Mr. Loftis?" Donelli inquired.

"Yessir."

"See anybody sneaking through the woods?"

"Nope."

Amanda had the feeling she would not be printing a lot of quotes from Kenny Loftis.

"You've lived here a long time, though," Donelli said.

"My whole life."

"And that would be how long?"

"I'll be seventy-four next fall."

"Then you must have been acquainted with Mr. William Ashford and his wife, Laurabel."

"Yessir."

Donelli seemed content with the terse replies. The slow pace of the conversation was making Amanda jittery. She knew better, however, than to interrupt the weird rapport the two men had achieved. At least Loftis hadn't chased them off his property or shot them point-blank. Maybe he would actually dribble out some information eventually.

In the meantime, she leaned down to pet the old hound that was sniffing at her shoes.

"Careful," Loftis warned. "Daisy bites."

A low growl confirmed the dog's antisocial attitude. Amanda resigned herself to standing still and surviving boredom.

"Do you recall much about the murder of that revenuer back in '42?" Donelli asked.

"Nope."

Amanda's gaze shot to the older man's face. Her adrenaline kicked in. He had to be lying. How could he not recall something that must have been hot news in these parts?

"Wasn't here," he volunteered, apparently reading the disbelief in her expression. "Fighting in Europe."

"So, by the time you got back from the war, William was in jail?" Donelli concluded.

"Yessir."

"Word was that he was innocent," Donelli suggested. "Do you think that was possible?"

"More 'n likely."

"Who might have set him up?"

"Don't know."

"How about last week? You around when that revenuer got shot?"

"Can't say."

Amanda was getting tired of the reticence. "Surely you must have heard the shot?"

He kept his gaze on Donelli, as if Amanda hadn't spoken. "Folks shoot all the time in these parts," he said, responding to her question without acknowledging her presence. "Squirrels, deer, beer cans. In season. Out of season. Don't pay no attention to it."

Donelli jumped back in. "Had you seen the Revenue agent in the area?"

"Yessir."

"Were people talking about him? Maybe worrying about what he'd find?"

"No more 'n usual. Strangers draw attention, 'specially black folks sneakin' where they don't belong."

"Were there any other strangers here around the same time?" Amanda asked.

"Nope. Just the one fella. Lotta folks since. The police. You two. Some guy in a fancy suit."

Amanda seized on the last comment. Who would be tromping around way out here in a fancy suit? Some Department of Revenue bureaucrat? A police official? A real estate developer?

"Did you happen to talk to the guy in the suit?" she asked.

"Nope."

Amanda sighed. This was getting them nowhere. Just when she was about to drag Donelli away, Loftis added, " 'Course, ain't no need for a guy like that to talk to me. Everybody in these parts knows I ain't gonna sell this place."

"So the guy was a real estate developer," Amanda said. "You know that for sure?"

He nodded. "Seen him with Willie half a dozen times,

maybe more. Don't know what the two of them had up their sleeves, but more 'n likely they was up to no good. That Willie has big ideas. He ain't satisfied with the moonshine, like his daddy and granddaddy was." He turned his watery blue eyes on Amanda at last. "Just lookit where them big ideas landed him."

He picked up his shotgun and gestured with it. "You two git on out of here. Said too much as it is."

Amanda might have been inclined to try for one last question since they seemed to finally be getting somewhere, but Donelli clamped a hand around her wrist and led her away.

"He's just getting started," she muttered under her breath, dragging her heels to try to slow her husband down.

"Amanda, he tolerated us for a while because it suited his purposes. When he picked up that gun again, I took that to mean that his patience was at an end. I'd prefer not to stick around long enough to find out if he would really blast us to kingdom come with the thing."

He glanced at his watch. "Besides, we really have to get to Doc Flanders' office before he closes up for the night."

"There's no rush. We could see him in the morning," she suggested hopefully.

"Tonight, Amanda. That was the deal. Besides, Miss Martha said she'd call him and tell him we'd be stopping by."

"But I'm feeling terrific now. Never better."

"Then do it to humor me."

It wasn't so much a concerned request, as a veiled

order. She sighed heavily and tried to force herself to relax. Obviously he'd made up his mind. One thing she'd learned since she'd first met her husband: Changing his mind once it was made up was like trying to send a bull to the barn once he'd spotted the flash of a red cape.

Dr. Wendell Flanders was an old-fashioned family practitioner, who'd been treating Miss Martha for most of her adult life. She had apparently been more than pleased to recommend him when Joe had spoken to her about whether she'd like him to officially join the murder investigation.

After trips to sterile, impersonal doctors' offices in Manhattan skyscrapers, Amanda felt as if she'd stepped back in time as she studied his office. It was on one side of what looked like a small white clapboard duplex with weathered urns of just-budding flowers on the front porch. A white shingle with his name neatly painted in dark green to match the shutters swung from a post near the curb. A smaller sign with an arrow pointing the way to the office door was attached to the front of the house.

"It's awfully late," Amanda said. "He's probably gone for the day."

"Miss Martha said if he wasn't in the office to buzz him at home. He lives in the other half of the house."

"Oh."

"Amanda, do you have a thing about doctors I ought to know about?"

"Not really." What she had was a thing about pregnancy. She wasn't ready. She'd had enough trouble deciding that she and Donelli should adopt Pete—and he was way past diapers and formula and the terrible twos.

"You probably just need a shot of vitamin B^{12} or something," Donelli consoled her. "We'll be out of here in no time."

A simple shot. Now there was a thought. Maybe she could just ask for one, have that cut on her cheek doctored, and slip away without ever having to describe her symptoms. Unfortunately, if she was pregnant, getting a shot now would only postpone the inevitable revelation and would fly in the face of all that well-publicized advice about the importance of early prenatal care. She'd read all the articles. Hell, she'd even written one about the traumas suffered by babies of poor mothers who continued to smoke, do drugs, drink, and ignore prenatal visits to their doctors.

A bell tinkled overhead as Amanda reluctantly opened the door. She stepped into an outer office that was decorated with comfortable, if slightly worn, furniture, stacks of astonishingly up-to-date magazines, and a kiddie corner filled with toys and children's books atop a scaled-down table surrounded by colorful chairs. A reception desk sat near a hallway entrance. Down the hall Amanda could see a half dozen doorways to what most likely were examining rooms.

No sooner had she and Donelli stepped inside than a white-haired man wearing a lab coat over a red plaid shirt emerged from the room closest to the front, a fishing magazine in hand.

"Ah, you must be the Donellis. Miss Martha told me

you'd be stopping by," he said, dropping the magazine on the table with the others. "Wendell Flanders. Come on back and set a spell. Let's see if we can't find out what's making you feel so punk."

At a panicked look from Amanda, Donelli said, "I'll wait out here, if you like. Or would you rather I come along?"

"No, you can wait here," she said, forcing a smile. "I'll be fine."

Dr. Flanders led the way to his office and closed the door. He gestured toward a chair, then perched on a corner of his desk. "So, young lady, what's been going on with you? Where'd you get that cut on your cheek?"

Amanda figured explaining the source of that would arouse questions she didn't care to answer. She stuck to her overall health. "The cut's nothing. A little peroxide ought to fix it right up. Actually, I think I'm probably just a little run down. And ever since I went to see Miss Martha, I've been worried about her. How's she doing?"

If he guessed that she was trying to maneuver the conversation away from her own condition, he never let on. "As well as can be expected, I suppose."

"I understand she's dying. Something about her heart failing."

He seemed oddly surprised. "Is that what she told you?" he asked.

Something in his voice, a faint wariness, alerted Amanda that perhaps all was not exactly as Miss Martha had described it. "That is precisely what she said. Is she exaggerating?"

He sighed, suddenly looking a dozen years older

than he had just seconds earlier. "You know, Mrs. Donelli . . ."

"Actually, it's Ms. Roberts. I kept my name for professional reasons when Joe and I got married."

He shook his head. "I just can't keep up with all these modern ideas. Okay, Ms. Roberts it is. As I was saying, there's an amazing connection between what goes on in the head and what happens to the body. It's been proven time and again. Positive thinking can work miracles."

"And negative thinking can kill?"

"In a manner of speaking."

Amanda thought she saw where he was going with this. "Are you suggesting that Miss Martha has made up her mind to die? That she's going to will herself into her grave?"

"Oh, she's sick all right, but if she'd agree to treatment, I have some hope that it could be quite effective."

"Then she's not terminally ill?"

"If her condition is left untreated . . ." He shrugged and his expression turned somber. "Ethically you know I can't discuss the specifics of Miss Martha's situation with you. In fact, I've probably already said far too much. However, if you are her friend, I would ask that you do what you can to encourage her, to lift her spirits. Talk to her before she comes to a decision that will be irreversible."

"A decision," Amanda repeated slowly. What kind of decision might Miss Martha be weighing about death?

As the answer slowly formed in her head, she found that she wasn't nearly as shocked as Dr. Flanders no doubt expected her to be. If she was reaching the right conclusion about his very circumspect hints, then Miss Martha was not only anticipating her death as a result of her deteriorating health, she was planning it. It was the second time Amanda had reached that conclusion.

She thought back over a couple of seemingly innocuous comments Della and Miss Martha had made, comments about plans and surreptitious conversations with the doctor that had Della in a tizzy. It didn't strike Amanda as uncharacteristic at all that Miss Martha would choose suicide for ending her life. If her illness was terminal, she would want the closing chapter of her time on earth to be as dignified as her life had been.

"She feels her condition is terminal and she's been asking about suicide, hasn't she?" she inquired bluntly. "Assisted suicide, perhaps? Is she in pain? Are we talking about cancer, rather than her heart?"

Dr. Flanders' face remained totally expressionless, as if he'd anticipated the barrage of questions and braced himself for them. "Talk to her, young lady. That's all I have to say on the subject." He reached over and patted Amanda's hand. "Now let's see what's going on with you, why don't we?"

Amanda could think of at least a hundred things she'd rather do, up to and including shopping for one of those disgustingly proper suits Carol Fields thought all good little journalists should wear. Unfortunately, though, it appeared she was going to be examined by a doctor instead and, if her best guess was right, she was going to be shopping for maternity clothes.

CHAPTER

Nine

As it turned out, Amanda was so engrossed in thinking about what might be going on in Miss Martha's head that she was practically oblivious to the doctor's exam. She was startled when Dr. Flanders told her to get dressed and meet him back in his office. She tarried as long as she could before joining him, once more considering the benefits of an emergency trip to the mall. When she finally slipped into the chair opposite his desk, he was jotting notes onto a medical record form in her new patient folder. When he'd signed and dated it, he lifted his gaze to hers.

"Maybe you'd like to bring your husband in here for this," he suggested.

Amanda swallowed hard. She didn't need to be smacked upside the head to figure out the diagnosis. The pleased expression on the doctor's face was a dead giveaway. "So it's true, then. I'm pregnant."

He smiled. "I won't have the blood test back until morning, but all the preliminary tests do indicate that you are pregnant. Congratulations!"

Even though she'd been expecting the news, Amanda felt the blood drain from her face. "Pregnant," she repeated as if it were a foreign word. "I'm going to have a baby."

"Unless I'm very much mistaken, you are."

She regarded him hopefully. "Have you ever been mistaken?"

"Not once in forty-five years of practicing medicine." His brow creased with a worried frown. "Aren't you pleased by the news?"

"Stunned by it would be more accurate," she said. "I mean I'd guessed, obviously, but we just hadn't planned . . ." Now her cheeks flushed. "Isn't that absurd? I'm an intelligent woman. I have a college degree, plus a law degree. You'd think I could do something as simple as protecting myself from pregnancy."

"It's been my experience that no method is absolutely foolproof. And sometimes God just takes the decision out of our hands. I like to believe He knows what He's doing. How will your husband feel?"

She grinned ruefully. "He'll be ecstatic. There's never been a single doubt in his mind about children. And our recently adopted teenager has been pleading for a baby brother or sister. I'm the one who wanted to wait until everything was just perfect."

He regarded her with obvious curiosity. "How did you plan to tell when that time had come?"

"Signs and portents, I suppose."

There was a twinkle in Dr. Flanders' eyes when he said, "I think you have your sign."

"Yes," she said, unconsciously resting her hand on her stomach. "Yes, I suppose there's no mistaking this one."

"Shall I tell Mr. Donelli?"

"No, please. I'll tell him when the time is right."

"Soon, Ms. Roberts. It's not the kind of happy news you should keep to yourself. It's the kind best shared with someone who loves you. When I spoke with Miss Martha earlier today, there wasn't a doubt in her mind about his feelings for you. She said he was deeply concerned about your health."

Amanda was certain that was true. Joe's emotions were always close to the surface, easily visible to the naked eye. Maybe it was his Italian heritage. Maybe he simply saw no reason to be guarded about something so basic.

She, to the contrary, hid what she was feeling beneath a cover of intellectual analysis. Professionally, she prided herself on her gut-level reactions to people and situations. But when it came to herself, she tended to rely on facts, on closely studied options.

She hadn't always been that way. But sometime during her divorce from Mack Roberts she had stopped listening to her heart and started counting on her brain to protect her from further emotional hurt. Then Donelli himself had taken a sledgehammer to her fragile trust and it had taken months for her to overcome that sense of betrayal.

Now, though, their relationship was solid. She knew

that. She knew they could handle a baby's demands. She knew, too, that when she faltered as a parent, Donelli would be right there to take up the slack. Patience and nurturing were his greatest strengths. Their marriage was living proof of that. He'd believed in the two of them, when she'd been neck-deep in doubts.

Acting on impulse, she borrowed Dr. Flanders' phone so Joe wouldn't overhear her conversation. She made a quick call to make arrangements for Pete for the night, then called for dinner reservations. Her head was still spinning with the news when she went back into the reception area to meet Donelli. He studied her intently, apparently didn't find what he was looking for, and turned to Dr. Flanders. "She's okay?"

"Better than okay," the doctor informed him. "Don't worry about your wife. She's perfectly healthy."

"Then why . . .?"

"I'll explain," Amanda promised. "Let's let Dr. Flanders get home to his dinner."

"Don't forget to call for an appointment in the morning. I'll want to see you again in a month," the doctor called after them.

Donelli stopped in his tracks. "You have to come back? Why?"

"Stop asking so many questions and get me to a restaurant. I'm starving."

"Not fast food again. I refuse," he said, but he did leave the office and head for the car.

"I was thinking about that romantic little inn over toward Athens."

"Amanda, that's fifty miles in the wrong direction. They're usually booked weeks in advance. There are perfectly good restaurants closer to home."

"I came to the doctor to humor you. Now it's your turn. Besides, I've already booked a table."

"Oh, for heaven's sake."

She grinned. "I swear to you it will be worth it."

His expression turned resigned, then brightened. "Of course, they do have rooms right upstairs."

"Now you're catching on."

"But Pete . . ."

"He's staying with a friend. I called from Dr. Flanders' office. Mike's mom is driving over to pick him up."

He glanced over at her. "You constantly amaze me."

"That is certainly my goal."

They actually almost made it. Amanda could see the soft pools of light from the lanterns on the inn's front lawn. When her cellular phone rang, she was tempted to ignore it. She was thoroughly tantalized by visions of candlelight and romantic music, down pillows and a feather bed. And, amid that setting, an appropriately dramatic revelation that they were going to have a baby.

"You're not going to answer it?" Donelli asked, sounding astonished.

"Just this once, I'm not," she said decisively.

The ringing stopped. Thirty seconds later, it started again. Amanda sighed. Back-to-back calls implied a certain urgency. She dug the phone out of her purse and answered it.

"Amanda?" Jenny Lee's voice was hushed.

"What? Speak up. I can hardly hear you."

"Where are you? Carol's been flipping out because you disappeared. She's threatening to go to Joel and have you fired for insubordination if she finds out you've been out interviewing sources without an assignment and without adhering to the new dress code."

Amanda saw red. "You tell Carol. . . . Oh, never mind. It's not your fight. I'll tell her myself."

"When?"

"In the morning."

"If you're planning to get into a huge brouhaha first thing tomorrow, maybe you'd better do this one teensy interview tonight before she pulls your plug."

"What interview?"

"I was checking out those murders, like you told me to. I found out that that one old guy, Boggins, is still alive, but barely. He's in Grady Memorial right now. Nobody's expecting him to make it out."

"But he's conscious now?"

"That's what the head nurse on his unit told me when I said I was his niece from Mississippi. She says he pinches every fanny that passes by his bed, then wheezes so bad they're certain he won't live out the hour. So far he's kept surprising them. She did say if I wanted to see dear old Uncle Henry, I'd better hightail it on over to Atlanta, though."

"Thanks, Jenny Lee, you're terrific!"

"I've been telling you that for months now."

"See you in the morning."

"Don't start the battle until I get there. I don't want to miss a word of the newsroom showdown. Jack Davis and I have started a pool on which one of you will strike the first blow."

"I assume you bet on me," Amanda said wryly. "I'll try not to let you down." She turned off the phone and faced Donelli.

"Just how terrific is Jenny Lee?" he inquired. "So terrific that we're going to have to forget all about that romantic tryst at the inn?"

"I'm afraid so."

He uttered a sigh of resignation, but he dutifully pulled out of the inn's driveway and back onto the highway. "Where are we going?"

"To Grady Memorial. Boggins is alive, but they're afraid the stress of pinching all the nurses' fannies might kill him any minute now."

"I can hardly wait to meet him."

"Just don't go getting any ideas."

"Come a little closer, honey."

The old man's voice creaked and groaned like a rusty hinge, but his seductive intent was unmistakable. Amanda knew at once that she'd found Henry Boggins' room.

Faded, watery blue eyes gazed up at her when she warily approached the bedside, staying just out of reach. Donelli had agreed to wait in the corridor, figuring an old man with a penchant for pinching bottoms would be more inclined to bare his soul to a female.

"Do I know you?"

"I'm Amanda Roberts," she told him as she studied his wizened, nut-brown face. She wondered if it had been weathered that shade by a century in the Southern sun or if his heritage was mixed, maybe part African-American, maybe part Cherokee. "I'm a reporter with *Inside Atlanta*."

"*Inside Atlanta*? What's that? Some leftie publication written by a bunch of Yankee carpetbaggers?"

Given her own New York background and accent, Amanda couldn't offer a thoroughly credible denial of all the charges he'd managed to level in that one damning question. "My bosses are both from the South," she said, which was about as much of a disclaimer as she could make.

"What do you want with me?"

"I thought maybe we could chat a little, if you feel up to it."

He chuckled, but the laugh turned into a violent spasm of coughing that shook his entire body. Amanda was about to press the bell for the nurse, but he latched onto her hand with a surprisingly firm grip. He shook his head frantically.

"Be . . . okay. Give . . . me a . . . minute."

"Would water help?"

"Nothing . . . helps."

The terrible, wracking sound finally eased. "If I'd known I was going to go out like this, I'd have blown my brains out years ago," he said matter-of-factly in that strange, creaky voice. He surveyed Amanda intently. "Pretty little thing, but you're too skinny."

Amanda warmed up to him at once. After Donelli's fears that her taste for hamburgers and fries was going to add pounds of fat to her hips, she felt like kissing someone who actually thought she was skinny.

"What're you doing here? Only folks who come to see me these days are social workers and lawyers. Don't suppose one of them sent you over here to see what I really intend to do with my estate?"

"Nope. You could be dirt poor for all I know."

"Well, I ain't about to tell you any different. So, what do you want?"

"I want you to tell me about your daughter."

His gaze shifted away. He began fiddling with the thin white blanket on the bed, picking at a tiny three-cornered rip. Amanda thought he'd drifted off into some other place until she saw a tear spill down his cheek.

"Mr. Boggins? Are you okay?"

"It's been years and years, but just thinking back on my Laurabel still makes me cry. She was a beauty, sweet and sensitive. That dirty, thieving Ashford fella destroyed her, sent her to an early grave."

Sweet? *Sensitive*? It sounded to Amanda as if Henry Boggins had rewritten history just a bit. Those weren't words usually associated with a madam, especially one who'd reportedly turned mean and arrogant the instant she got out of the business. Apparently he'd convinced himself of his own devotion to her as well.

"You blamed William Ashford for killing your daughter?"

"He did it, sure as I'm here in this bed. I vowed I'd make him pay, too. Ruined his life, I did, and took pride in it."

Amanda wished she could pull out her tape recorder and get Boggins' confession on tape. Even if his story never made it into print, it might bring Miss Martha some measure of peace.

"Exactly how did you ruin his life?" she prodded cautiously.

"Found those stills of his. He thought he had 'em hidden out of the way, thought he'd fooled everyone in town into thinking he was a legitimate businessman with not a care in the world, but I knew better. Once a man starts relying on the vices of others to make his way in the world, he ain't likely to give it up. Searched high and low, until I tracked 'em down. Then I reported him, led the Department of Revenue straight to 'em. Stood there and watched while they bashed 'em to bits. I gotta say there hasn't been much in life before or since that I enjoyed more."

Amanda thoughtfully considered what he was saying. It didn't make sense. She'd been convinced by what she'd read in those old clippings that William Ashford had shot the revenuer while he was in the act of trying to close down his moonshine operation. This sounded more as if the murder had been committed in retaliation for something that had already happened.

"Were you there when the shooting took place?" she asked Boggins.

He managed what passed for a weak slap on his thigh. "No, indeed. That was just the icing on the cake. Ashford must have come back after I'd gone, taken one look at the mess and shot the guy they'd left around to wait for him. They figured he'd turn up sooner or later to check his operation. He probably wouldn't have got much more than a slap on the wrist for operating them stills, but murder? They threw the book at him for that. Can't say I was one bit sorry, except for the family of the poor victim, of course. Alcott's kids took it real hard. Daughter ended up moving away, as a matter of fact."

"Why are you so certain Ashford killed the man, if you didn't see it yourself?"

"Who else could it have been?"

Amanda regarded him pointedly. "Someone who had it in for him. Someone who hoped to frame him for the murder."

"Me?" He sounded genuinely incredulous. "Honey, I might have been angry at Ashford, but I wasn't no damned fool. I draw the line at murder."

That sounded like a fairly lax ethical code to Amanda. Sometimes folks whose values permitted everything just short of pointing a gun and pulling the trigger slipped up and crossed that fine line in the blink of an eye. At a hundred years old and laid up in a hospital bed, Henry Boggins might seem like an unlikely murder suspect, but fifty years ago with vengeance on his mind? She wouldn't have put it past the wily old codger at all.

CHAPTER Ten

Amanda heard the hospital room door inch open and guessed she had about another thirty seconds before a nurse or Donelli or her own suspicious nature destroyed her rapport with Henry Boggins.

"One last thing," she said hurriedly. "Can you think of anyone at all who hated William Ashford as much as you did?"

"What're you getting at?"

Hearing the sudden wariness in his voice, she proceeded cautiously. Because the footsteps she'd heard had stopped just inside the door, she guessed it was Donelli who'd entered and had quickly taken in the fact that she was right at the heart of her interview. He might wait patiently in the room's shadows, but there clearly wasn't much time to elicit this one last piece of critical information.

Keeping her voice confiding, she leveled a look

straight into Boggins' eyes. "I just meant that men who are as evil as you say Ashford was don't usually have just one enemy. They attract them like flies."

"I suppose that's true enough," he conceded. "Ashford got pretty big for his britches. Started thinking he was part of corporate America or something. That's when he took up with that fancy lady over to Gwinnett. Guess he wanted more than what my Laurabel could give him. Must have figured a high-society type and bigger business would bring him respectability."

Amanda didn't want to get back on that particular track. "Who did he antagonize in the process?"

"He ran a few moonshiners out of the business by selling cheap so they couldn't afford to compete. I suppose they didn't like him much."

"His grandson—your great-grandson—says most of those guys were small potatoes compared to Ashford."

"I suppose to a man selling bootleg whiskey by the caseload, a few gallons here and there wouldn't seem like much," he said, apparently paying little mind to the mention of Willie. Rather he laid the insensitive opinion directly at the door of his old enemy. "But to a man barely scraping out a living for his family, especially during the Depression or when times were tough after the war, every extra dime mighta meant the difference between survival and starvation."

Was that a strong enough motivation to try to frame Ashford for murder? Amanda doubted she would know that until she'd talked to some of his victims. "Who, for instance? Can you remember any specific families who were hurt?"

He closed his eyes and for an instant, Amanda thought he might have drifted off. Then his eyes snapped open and he said, "Salty Tufts. Lordy, but I ain't thought of that old coot in years. Got his name 'cause he went off to sea to become a fisherman. Turned out he threw up his guts every time the boat rocked. Came home and got back into the whiskey trade with his pappy." He gazed at Amanda with apparent regret. " 'Course, he's dead now."

"Does anyone in his family still live around here?"

"His daughter, I believe. What was her name? Something Frenchified, because Salty's wife thought it sounded grand. Suzanne? No, Suzette. That was it, Suzette Tufts. Believe she married a Babcock, over to Dahlonega."

Amanda recalled the list of names Willie had given them. There was a Steven Babcock on that list. Suzette's husband? Or perhaps a son? Amanda moved him to the top of her schedule. Maybe she'd even interview him first thing in the morning before going into the office to deal with Carol Fields once and for all. Of course, that assumed she could shake her protective husband.

"Anyone else you can recall?" she asked.

"Honey, there's times I can't even remember my own name. You caught me in a good spell."

Impulsively she reached out and patted Henry Boggins' huge, weathered hand. "Thank you. You've been a big help."

He scanned her face intently. "You never did say exactly what kind of story you're looking to write."

"Sometimes I don't know that until I sit down in

front of the computer," she said, skirting the truth. "For the moment, I'm just hoping to ease a friend's mind by gathering a few facts."

"Not many folks who'd go to this much trouble for a friend." He lifted his hand in a weak wave. "You stop by and see me again, if you're of a mind to. Maybe I'll recollect something else."

The man's loneliness was almost palpable. Even though she was halfway convinced that he'd shot that revenuer himself fifty years ago, sending Ashford to prison and causing Miss Martha all that pain, Amanda couldn't help feeling a little saddened by his current plight. At his age there weren't a lot of contemporaries left to stop by for a chat.

"Maybe I will be back one of these days," she said softly and rose to leave.

No sooner had she turned her back, though, than she felt a sharp little pinch on her fanny. If it had been any male other than a dying old man, she would have slugged him or, at the very least, delivered a blistering lecture on respect for women. As it was, she just hid a smile and joined Donelli, who'd exited to wait for her in the corridor.

"He got you, didn't he?" he said, plainly amused as she rubbed her injured backside. "You should have known better than to turn your back on him."

She grinned. "What makes you think I didn't do it on purpose?"

His eyebrows climbed a disbelieving notch. "Why, Amanda, honey, I had no idea you were that desperate for cheap thrills."

"If you find me a Dahlonega phone directory, I'll teach you a thing or two about thrills."

"You can do something interesting with a phone book?" he said, feigning bafflement, but clearly willing to play along.

"Try me."

"Would you settle for Steven Babcock's phone number?" he inquired as they exited the hospital through the chaos of the emergency room and headed for the car.

She stared at him in amazement. "How did you know?"

"What you wanted or the number?"

"Both."

"You didn't corner the market on intuition, Amanda. I got my share."

"Intuition didn't have a damned thing to do with it," she said, putting together the facts for herself. "You were listening to every word I said in there, weren't you? Even before you snuck in the door."

He shrugged. "You I couldn't hear so well, but that croaking voice of Boggins could have been heard in the next county. And I spent my time in the hall tracking down phone numbers and addresses for everyone on that list Willie gave us." He waved what looked like a hospital medical record form under her nose. Numbers were scrawled all over it. "Pay up. You promised interesting rewards just for the Babcock number. I can hardly wait to see what you have in mind for the entire list."

Amanda stopped under the glare of a mercury vapor light in the hospital parking lot. Grady Memorial, Atlanta's primary hospital for the indigent, sat in the shadow of a freeway and cheek-by-jowl with public housing. Still, it suddenly seemed like as good a place as any to break the news about her pregnancy. Her original plan would have been far too ordinary. This particular setting was one Donelli was never likely to forget. And as a reward for information, this would be a doozy.

"Why are you stopping?" Donelli asked.

"You wanted me to pay up."

He glanced around. "Here?"

"Don't go all shy on me now, Donelli."

He stood stock still and held out his hands in a gesture of surrender. "Okay, have your way with me."

"Much as I'd like to, I had something else in mind."

"I'm not sure anything else you could come up with would be sufficient payoff for that list."

"How about a baby?"

"A baby?" he repeated, staring at her blankly.

"As in yours and mine," she prodded, since he didn't seem to be getting it. Either that or he was too dumbfounded by the possibility to believe it might actually be true.

"Yours and mine?"

"Donelli, snap out of it." She put her hands on either side of his face and gazed straight into his dark brown eyes. "We're having a baby," she said, spelling the news out slowly.

With that her brawny, tough ex-cop looked as if he were about to cry. "You're pregnant?" he asked, his voice filled with a note of awe.

Amanda nodded. "It's official."

"Dr. Flanders," he began, obviously finally doing the correct mental addition. "And that's what the inn and the romantic dinner were all about? You were going to break the news there?"

"I thought I should make a big deal out of the announcement."

"Oh, baby," he said, sweeping her into a tight embrace, then releasing her almost as quickly. His gaze swept over her warily. "Are you okay? Did I hurt you?"

"I'm not breakable all of a sudden."

"You're sure?"

"Donelli, don't do this to me," she warned. "Don't you dare start treating me as if I were some fragile piece of glass or I will regret not waiting to tell you until I am on the way to the delivery room."

"I'm a pretty observant kind of guy. I might have figured it out for myself before then."

He pulled her back into his arms and folded her close. Amanda could feel the steady beat of his heart, the reassuring warmth of his body, the powerful strength of his love. The last of whatever doubts she'd been harboring about the wisdom of the pregnancy disappeared. She knew they would come back time and again over the months to come, but for now, for this moment, she felt happier and more complete than she had ever felt in her life.

The depth of her contentment shocked her. She'd always thought of herself as self-contained, independent to a fault. Now there were two people in her life who needed her, people whom she needed just as badly. And a baby was on the way.

What an incredible, unexpected merry-go-round she had climbed aboard when she'd looked into Joe Donelli's wicked eyes and fallen desperately in love!

The message light on their answering machine was blinking like crazy by the time Amanda and Joe got back to the farm. They'd been delayed by stops at a half dozen stores to search for a bottle of nonalcoholic champagne with which to celebrate.

While Donelli popped the cork and poured, Amanda listened to the messages. Seven of the ten were from Miss Martha, berating her for missing their nine A.M. appointment. Apparently her conversation with Donelli earlier hadn't been enough to appease her. She demanded to know the status of the investigation.

"Call the minute you get this message. I don't care how late it is," she ordered, then succumbed to a fit of coughing every bit as wracking as the one Henry Boggins had had while Amanda was in the room.

Two of the remaining messages were from telemarketers cheerfully promising to call back tomorrow. The last one was from Pete wanting to know where the hell they were at midnight. Amanda suddenly felt as if she were the one who was thirteen, a kid who'd stayed out past curfew.

"Anything important?" Joe asked when he returned from the kitchen with two glasses and the champagne.

"We've been missed," she said, summing up the messages. Those from Miss Martha lingered in her mind. She thought about what she'd learned from Dr. Flanders about Miss Martha's state of mind. On the tape, however, she hadn't sounded depressed. She'd sounded anxious for answers. "Joe, listen to these messages from Miss Martha."

He regarded her curiously as she rewound the tape and played it through again. "What am I listening for?"

"Just listen."

When the tape concluded, she said, "How does she sound?"

"Mad as a wet hen. Imperious. The way she always sounds, when she's got a bee in her bonnet. Why?"

"I was just thinking about something Dr. Flanders hinted at earlier. He thinks she's suicidal."

Donelli's expression turned incredulous. "Miss Martha? No way. Why would he say something like that?"

"He didn't say it, not in so many words. I mean, he couldn't break a confidence." She explained what Della had said to her earlier about overhearing a conversation between Miss Martha and the doctor. "And Miss Martha herself told me she was in a hurry to get this over with because she had plans to make."

"But why jump to the conclusion of suicide? Maybe she wants to go on a trip."

"Donelli, she's bedridden. From what I understand, her heart's getting weaker by the day and Dr. Flanders all but said she had cancer and won't accept treatment. You know how a woman like Miss Martha would hate being incapacitated for the rest of her life. She brushed aside Della's fears that the stress of this investigation might kill her. I think she might not care if it did."

Joe sat back, his expression thoughtful. "Okay, I can buy that she might not go out of her way to pamper herself, but suicide? How would she do it?"

"An overdose, maybe. Or if she could get Dr. Flanders to help, maybe a lethal injection."

"That's illegal," he said flatly. In other words, a black and white issue to a cop.

"But not unheard of," Amanda argued. "I'm not just talking about that doctor up in Michigan. He's made headlines because he's gone public when he's helped people commit suicide. But how many times has a compassionate doctor made it easy for a terminally ill patient to get the drugs they'd need to end their lives? How many times has someone given just a little too much painkiller? Or pulled the plug on a respirator just long enough to allow a patient to die with dignity?"

He frowned. "Are you saying you think it's right?"

Deeply troubled by the entire concept, Amanda sighed and began to pace as she mentally weighed the pros and cons. "I don't know what I think," she admitted eventually. "I know I wouldn't want to live for months or years in terrible pain. I would hate to see one of my parents suffering. Shouldn't there be a safe, compassionate way for a rational person to make a conscious choice to end his life, rather than spend his final days hooked to machines or living on massive doses of painkillers?"

Donelli shook his head. "This conversation is depressing the shit out of me. We're supposed to be celebrating a baby, a new life, not talking about suicide and dying. Besides, you're just speculating about Miss

Martha. You don't really know if that's what she's thinking at all, do you?"

"No."

"Then go see her in the morning. Ask her point-blank."

Amanda was doubtful about the advisability of that. "She'll be furious that I'm invading her privacy, especially if she's considering a decision as personal and potentially explosive as this one."

"She might be grateful to have someone with whom she can talk about it objectively."

Amanda halted her pacing beside Donelli's chair and regarded him worriedly. "If I find out she is considering that option, do you want to know? Or would you feel you had to report her to the cops or something?"

He reached for her hand and tugged her into his lap. "I always want to know about anything that matters to you, Amanda. Even when we disagree, okay? And you should know by now that I won't betray a confidence."

"Even if what she's planning is illegal?"

"I'm not a cop anymore. As for my conscience, I'll deal with that. It's not your concern." He tapped his champagne glass to hers. "A toast, okay?"

"To?"

"The baby, of course. A sweet, beautiful girl, who looks exactly like her mama."

"Or a handsome, rugged boy with his daddy's sensitivity and compassion," Amanda countered. "Have I mentioned lately that I love you, Joe Donelli?"

"On occasion," he said, clinking his glass to hers

again. "But that is something worth toasting, Amanda. To a love that will last a lifetime."

"To a love that will be as strong fifty years from now, as Miss Martha's is for her beloved William."

CHAPTER
Eleven

Amanda stood at the kitchen door just after sunrise the following morning, a cup of coffee in hand, and gazed toward the fields where Donelli was already at work, his tractor kicking up a fine red dust. She scowled at him and wondered if he'd intentionally stranded her on the farm this morning. Why the hell hadn't she remembered last night that her car was parked in a downtown Atlanta garage? Maybe because she'd had more important things on her mind, such as the baby growing inside her.

She rested her free hand on her stomach and tried to imagine what it would be like a few months from now. How long would it be before she could feel the baby moving? Hear its heartbeat?

All at once her journalistic training kicked in, her compulsive need for information went into overdrive. She needed books on pregnancy, books on parenting. A few days of research in a library wouldn't hurt either. She could track down articles on the latest information that had been published in mass-market magazines and medical journals. She might be scared to death, but she would be the best-informed mother-to-be in Georgia.

In the meantime, though, she had to get over to Miss Martha's. Even more problematic, she had to get to Steven Babcock up in Dahlonega. She weighed her options. None of the logistics were exactly simple.

She could have Jenny Lee come and pick her up, but that would involve her in Amanda's planned disobedience of Carol Fields's edicts. Though Jenny Lee would be a more-than-willing accomplice, Amanda wouldn't risk Jenny Lee's career.

She could ask Miss Martha to send a driver for her, then maybe borrow a car to take into town. Miss Martha had several. She'd even lent one to Amanda's visiting mother a while back. But that would mean she'd wind up with two cars in Atlanta eventually.

She glanced outside at Donelli's car with the shattered passenger window. She supposed she could drive that to Miss Martha's, then return to pick up her husband for the trip to Dahlonega. He could deposit her at the *InsideAtlanta* building after they'd interviewed Babcock and anyone else on Willie's list they could find. Or they could drop his car at a repair shop and drive hers home. Then he'd be stranded, which would probably suit him just fine. He'd be perfectly content with his seeds and his neatly plowed fields.

The last plan sounded like the best. She had her purse and Donelli's spare keys in hand and was halfway out the door, when the phone rang. She ran back and grabbed it.

''Where were you guys at midnight?'' Pete demanded irritably.

''Why aren't you in school?''

''It's too early. Where were you?'' he repeated, his tone intractable.

''I told you we might not be home until very late, and possibly not at all. That's why you're staying with your friend, remember?''

''I just figured you wanted me out of the house so you two could have some privacy for a change,'' Pete said.

Amanda thought she heard something in his voice, a note of uncertainty. ''What's this really about?''

Silence greeted the question. Finally, he said, ''Maybe it's not working out so good for us, after all. Maybe you're tired of me being in the way.''

She felt a rush of guilt. She'd forgotten how insecure their newly adopted son was. Normally, he acted far older and wiser than his years, the product of life on the streets and a teenager's natural arrogance. That made it easy to forget he was just a kid with a very troubled past. ''Oh, Pete, that's not it. Joe and I love you. You're our son now.''

''But you could un-adopt me.''

''Never. Get that thought right out of your mind.'' She reached a sudden decision. Maybe she should wait until they were all together, but she had a feeling Pete needed to hear this now. ''Besides, we're really going to need you around here.''

"You mean because summer's coming and Joe needs help in the fields and running the vegetable stand and stuff."

"No, I mean to help us take care of your new brother or sister."

"We're having a baby?"

Excitement sent Pete's adolescent voice skittering over several octaves. He was much quicker catching on than Donelli had been.

"I mean *you're* having a baby?" he amended hurriedly.

"I may be the one who's pregnant, but this family is having a baby," Amanda corrected, chuckling over his attempt to be politically correct.

"All right! Wait till I tell the guys I'm gonna be a big brother. Can I tell 'em now?"

Amanda wondered if they shouldn't just take out an ad on one of the local TV stations. It seemed unlikely that she and Joe were going to keep the pregnancy secret for long. It seemed important, though, for Pete to share in the excitement, to feel it was his news to impart to his friends.

"Sure, tell anyone you'd like."

"How long before the baby gets here?"

"Several months." She hadn't even done the addition herself. She counted on her fingers. "October sometime."

"That's so long," he protested.

"Sorry, kid, that's the way it works. I can't do a thing to speed up the process. Besides it'll probably take me that long just to pick out wallpaper for the nursery."

He laughed. "Guess your patience is gonna get tested, too, huh?"

"It is, indeed. See you, sweetie. Have a good day in school."

"Jeez, Amanda, don't call me that. Somebody might hear."

"Not unless the phone is tapped."

"With you, that's always a possibility," he said in a cynical way that sounded exactly like Donelli. "Bye."

She was still thinking about how quickly Pete had picked up his adoptive father's mannerisms and jaded outlook when she reached Miss Martha's shortly after nine A.M. Della opened the door, took one look at her, and practically slammed the door in her face. Fortunately, years of interviewing reluctant sources had made Amanda very quick. She was able to jam her foot inside just in the nick of time. She'd worry about her crushed arch later.

"Della, what's wrong?"

Della glowered. "What do you care?"

"That's not fair. You know I care about Miss Martha or I wouldn't be working on this investigation for her. Now, tell me what happened."

"She's had a spell, that's what's happened. The doctor is with her now. It's all because of you and this ridiculous investigation she's so set on." She shook her head. "You think you're doing her a favor. What you're doing is sending her straight to her grave."

Amanda would have preferred to have the rest of this discussion inside, but Della clearly wasn't budging. She resigned herself to eking out information with her foot wedged in the doorway. "What happened exactly?"

"When you didn't show up yesterday like you was supposed to, she got herself agitated," Della said accusingly. "Every time she called and got that answer machine of yours, she got more and more upset. Next thing I know, she can't breathe. She was clutching her chest, like she was gonna die right then and there. Those teeny little pills she's supposed to take, nitro-something, didn't do a lick of good. I had the doctor here twice. First time was going on midnight. Last time was in the middle of the night. She wouldn't go to the hospital, like he wanted. He's been up there with her since three in the morning."

"How is she now?"

Della placed her hands on her hips and glared. "How do you suppose she is after that close a brush with death?"

"May I see her? Maybe it would reassure her to hear what I've found out."

"You got an answer for her?"

"If you mean do I know who killed that Revenue agent, no, not yet."

"Then there's nothing you could say that would give her any peace." She shooed Amanda away from the door. "I'll tell her you was by, that you'll be back when you know something."

Amanda started to leave, then turned back. "Tell her one more thing for me, will you? Tell her I'm in a pack of trouble for doing this investigation for her. If she dies before I'm done, I'll never forgive her."

A reluctant smile tugged at the corners of Della's grim, down-turned mouth. "I suppose that might get to her, all right. I'll let her know."

On her way back to the farm, Amanda drove at a more leisurely pace than usual. While she was at it, she risked a call to Jenny Lee at the magazine.

"Are you out of your mind? You said you'd be here first thing this morning," Jenny Lee whispered the second she heard Amanda's voice. "Carol's flipping out. She's been yelling at Oscar and you know how he hates that. He told me the very minute I heard from you to tell you to call him on the double or he won't be responsible for your fate. He'll throw you to that she-wolf. And that's a direct quote." She paused, then added, "I don't think he likes her much."

"He hired her," Amanda reminded Jenny Lee.

"Well, officially he did, of course, but face it, Joel forced him to."

"Jenny Lee, this dissection of office politics is all very fascinating, but I am working a story."

"Unofficially," Jenny Lee reminded her.

"Yes, well, there is that. Does that mean you don't want to help?"

"Don't be ridiculous."

"Okay, then, how about digging around for information on the two murdered Department of Revenue agents? I guess it's the Alcohol-Tobacco Tax unit or something like that. I want to know everything from their shoe size to their marital status. A personnel folder would be a real help."

"Like they're going to give me that," Jenny Lee said with a note of disgust. "Any other impossible requests?"

"This one's easier. Find a source for me over there who can fill me in on procedures, the amount of moonshine activity there is in Georgia today, etcetera."

"Find a source for you?" Jenny Lee echoed, sounding prickly. "How many times have I heard those words?"

"Too often, I suppose. Okay, arrange an interview and we'll both go. I really want to see the guy face to face or I'd let you do it for me, okay?"

"I suppose."

"Stop sounding like a martyr. You signed on to be my assistant," Amanda reminded her. "And if things keep going the way they have been, you can probably snatch my job when I'm fired."

"I'm sorry," Jenny Lee said, immediately contrite. "I know I'm too impatient about moving up, but I don't want to do it because you're gone. I don't know what I'd do if you left, too."

There was no mistaking the woebegone note in her voice. Nor was it too difficult to guess its cause. "How's Larry?" Amanda asked.

"Having a ball," she confessed. "He's not even complaining about the commute yet. I figure it's just a matter of time before he realizes he's got his professional life and his social life separated by several hundred miles and decides to do something about it."

"Which could mean marrying you," Amanda pointed out.

"Or dumping me."

"Jenny Lee, that's enough negative thinking. If you don't believe in the feelings you and Larry share, why should he? Now perk up and get to work. We have murderers to catch."

"Do you suppose anybody really cares?"

"I do. Miss Martha does. And Willie Ashford, who's being held in jail for a crime he says he didn't commit, cares a whole lot."

"Okay, okay, I'll get to work. Where are you gonna be?"

"As soon as I pick up Donelli, we're going over to Dahlonega to talk to a guy named Steven Babcock. Willie mentioned him and Henry Boggins told me about a woman named Suzette Babcock, whose family might have had a grudge against the Ashfords. I want to see if she's any kin."

"What should I tell Oscar if he asks if I've heard from you?"

"Tell him you have a sneaking suspicion I've taken off for Tahiti."

Just then she heard Oscar bellowing across the newsroom. "Jenny Lee Macon, is that Amanda on the phone? Didn't I make it clear that I wanted to talk to her?"

A very irritated feminine voice chimed in. "Which line, Jenny Lee?"

Amanda did not intend to stick around until either Oscar or the she-wolf got on the line. "Bye-bye, Jenny Lee. Gotta run." She doubted if Jenny Lee even heard her. The phone clicked off while she was still in mid-sentence. Obviously Jenny Lee figured they were both better off if Oscar and Carol couldn't prove it had been Amanda on the line.

Ten seconds later the beeper at the bottom of her purse went off. She ignored it. Almost simultaneously the cellular phone began to ring. She stuffed that into her purse as well, then turned on the car radio, tuning the volume on the country music station up to a decibel level that would drown out all those beeps and rings.

Maybe it was sheer coincidence. Maybe it was a sign. But the song blasting over the airwaves at that precise moment suggested exactly what she felt like telling Oscar and Carol they could do with her job: shove it.

CHAPTER

Twelve

It didn't take long for Amanda to discover that Steven Babcock was several slices short of a full loaf. In his mid-twenties, he had the empty, nobody's-home stare of someone who'd been doing drugs or exorbitant amounts of booze for too long. His blond hair hadn't been washed, combed, or cut in ages. It straggled around his pinched face and skimmed his narrow shoulders. His clothes—torn jeans and a once-white T-shirt—were covered with stains of dubious origins. His snarling pit bull, barely restrained by an awfully flimsy-looking leash, added to Amanda's sense that she'd rather be in Kansas.

Donelli, oddly enough, seemed fascinated and more than willing to chat the afternoon away, even if most of what Babcock had to say sounded like it was an old 78-rpm record being played on slow speed.

"Your grandfather was Salty Tufts?" Donelli asked patiently.

Babcock gave the matter some consideration, then nodded. "On my mama's side."

"And your mother, is her name Suzette?"

"Yep. That's mama."

"Is she home now?"

"Mama don't take to strangers," he said flatly.

"But she is here?"

"She's here," Steven conceded.

"Perhaps you could ask her if we could visit with her for just a moment," Donelli suggested.

"No."

So much for that, Amanda thought.

"Did you know your grandfather?" Donelli inquired, clearly regrouping after his attempt to get to Suzette was rebuffed.

"Saw him some when I was a kid." Steven paused again, as if he were thinking hard about something, then a faint spark of understanding glinted for the space of a heartbeat. He nodded, as if to acknowledge that he'd gotten the message from some unseen force. "After that, he died," he said. There wasn't a trace of emotion in his voice.

Clearly Steven Babcock would not be regaling them with insightful family anecdotes, Amanda thought with some regret. Somehow she was having great difficulty imagining this young man and the far wittier Willie Ashford as friends.

"What do you remember about him?" Donelli asked in a low, coaxing tone.

"Peppermints," Babcock replied with surprising alacrity. "Always had a fistful in his pocket. Mama said he kept 'em so grandma wouldn't smell the likker on his breath."

"He liked to take a drink now and again?" Donelli asked.

"Drunk as a skunk from morning till night." He said it with an odd note of pride. "Occupational hazard, Mama said."

"What did he do?" Donelli inquired, as if he didn't know perfectly well that old Salty had been mixed up in moonshining.

"Made corn likker. Used to sell enough to bring in a decent living till somebody run him out of business."

"Who?"

Babcock looked as if the strain of dredging up all of these answers was giving him a headache. "Don't know," he said, beginning to sound disgruntled. "Maybe you'd better be going now."

Amanda didn't have to be asked twice. She whirled around and headed for the car. Donelli exchanged a few more words with the young man, then started after her.

Suddenly there was the distinctive sharp crack of a shotgun blast, a sound with which she had recently become all too familiar. Dust rose not three inches from Donelli's feet. Amanda's pulse took off like a train trying to make up time as she waited for the next shot to hit its mark. She heard Donelli's muttered string of oaths as he made a break for the car with shotgun blasts spraying a pattern just behind him.

Once a quick glance assured her he wasn't hit, just

exasperated by the local tendency to shoo folks away with firearms, Amanda became far more fascinated by the shout she heard from inside the house.

"Dammit, Mama, why'd you have to go and do that for?" Steven Babcock lamented after a few curses of his own.

Donelli apparently heard Babcock's remark as well. He opened the door on the driver's side and hunkered down behind it. "Amanda, slide over here."

The request hinted that he had plans of his own, plans from which she was to be excluded. "Why?" she asked suspiciously.

"I want you to drive out to the highway, park on the side of the road, and wait for me."

She stared at him incredulously. "Where the hell are you going to be?"

"I'm going to slip around to the back of the house and have a few words with *Mama*."

"She's got a damned shotgun. Her son has already told us she doesn't like strangers. Are you out of your mind?"

"I can't stay here arguing with you about this. Just do it," he ordered, then snuck off around the back of the car. It provided ample cover until he vanished into the neighboring stand of trees.

"I don't like this," Amanda muttered under her breath. If she'd had a gun herself, she would have gone after him, but she hated the damned things. She refused to carry the one she owned except in the most dire emergencies. Donelli, she consoled herself, had no such qualms.

He was probably armed. He was an excellent shot. Working the streets of Brooklyn had seen to that. He could take care of himself.

Her fingers shook as she started the engine, then backed the car down the narrow dirt lane to the highway. She was trembling so badly it was a wonder she didn't back straight into a tree.

"If you get yourself shot to death before this baby is born, I will never forgive you, Joe Donelli," she said, staring in the general direction of the house. "I am not qualified to raise a child alone. Just think about that, while you're risking your neck, why don't you? You'll be leaving your innocent little baby with someone who can't even boil water, much less make formula or strain peas."

She continued to rattle on as she waited. The sound of her own voice, echoing in the otherwise empty car, kept her from completely losing it. The more time that passed, the more dire her proclamations. A half hour later, she was threatening to kill Donelli herself.

"That's it," she said, when she could stand the waiting no longer. "I'm going after him." She hadn't heard another shot, so presumably he wasn't already dead. That didn't mean he wasn't tied to a kitchen chair with a shotgun poked in his stomach.

"And what do you propose to do if he is?" she asked herself dryly.

She didn't have an answer for that, at least not the proactive sort of answer she might have liked. She did have a cellular phone, however. She could always call the sheriff. It wouldn't be as dramatic as storming the place and rescuing Donelli herself, but it would get the job done.

She slipped out of the car, quietly closed the door, but left it unlocked in case they needed to flee in a hurry. She was rather proud of her precautions. She even had a game plan, for once, instead of rushing off impulsively.

She'd taken approximately a dozen steps into the woods, when a hand clamped over her mouth and someone lifted her off her feet. It was Babcock judging from the sour, sweaty smell of him, though she was surprised that he had the strength to get her off the ground. So much for precautions.

"You don't want to be going no farther," he said in that distinctively slow speech pattern.

It seemed like good advice to Amanda. Slowly he lowered her feet to the ground. His hand remained clamped over her mouth, which prevented her from contradicting him, even if she'd been of a mind to. He twisted her around until she could look into his eyes. Big mistake. The odd, feral gleam she saw there was not reassuring.

"If I let you go, will you git on out of here?" he asked, a faintly plaintive note in his voice.

Amanda nodded emphatically.

He released her.

"Where's my husband?" she demanded.

"Ain't he with you?" There was no mistaking the genuine expression of confusion that spread over his face.

Amanda decided now was not the time to enlighten

him about Donelli's desire to have a talk with his mama. Besides, even now Donelli might have made his way back to the car, where he would be mad as hell at not finding her. Somehow they must have crossed paths in the woods.

"He's probably waiting for me out on the highway," she said. "See you."

She scrambled through the thick underbrush as rapidly as she could. Not until she got back to the still-empty car did she stop to wonder why Babcock had been lurking in the woods in the first place. Had he suspected they would try to return? Was he protecting the house? Or, more likely, was he guarding a moonshine operation? She hadn't seen the supposedly necessary stream, but given the tangled undergrowth one could have been just yards away. It seemed entirely possible that Steven had gotten back into the family business that William Ashford had driven his granddaddy out of.

Amanda was still pondering the alternatives when she spotted Donelli emerging from the woods, a thunderous expression on his face. At the sight of her, relief flickered in his eyes for barely a second before the scowl settled in more deeply.

"In the car, Amanda."

It didn't seem like an opportune time to argue. She got in. Donelli, however, did not start the car. In fact, his white-knuckled grip on the steering wheel struck her as an obvious attempt to keep himself from strangling her.

"Which part of what I asked you to do was too complicated?" he inquired eventually. "The car's on the highway like I asked, so that couldn't have been it.

Must have been staying in the car. Did you mistake my meaning?"

"You don't have to be so sarcastic. I was worried about you."

"Then you should have called the sheriff. You should not, under any circumstances, have come dashing through the woods after me. I get back here. You're gone. I didn't know what the hell to think. It occurred to me that my pregnant wife might have been captured by a lunatic." His complexion was still ashen when he finally looked directly into her eyes. "It was not a comforting thought."

"I'm sorry, but I was scared out of my wits, too," she informed him huffily. "The last I saw of you, you were planning to face down some woman with a shotgun who'd already taken aim at you more than once."

He sighed and rubbed his hands over his face. "Amanda, this has to stop."

"What?"

"You risking your neck. It's not just you anymore. There's a baby to consider."

She opened her mouth, but he held up a silencing hand.

"Just wait a minute. I'm not treating you like some fragile doll. I know you have a job to do, but couldn't you, just for the next few months, let me be the one who takes the risks? Is that so unreasonable? Is that compromising your integrity or your independence or whatever? It's what I'm trained to do. And you, for all your daring, are not."

For once in her life, she couldn't argue with him.

Pointing out that she didn't want her baby's father to get himself killed might logically be counterpointed by a reminder that first the baby had to survive if the question of the father's fate was to come up at all. She clamped a lid on her instinctive desire to protest.

"Okay," she said.

"I spent a lot of years as a cop. I know how to handle a gun." He seemed prepared to continue the litany of his skills, but apparently her single-word response finally registered. "Okay?"

"That's what I said. I will try my damnedest to stay out of harm's way for the next seven months."

Still looking taken aback by her easy acquiescence, Donelli muttered something about miracles.

"In return, you have to do something for me."

"Anything."

"Come back after sundown and see if Babcock is operating a still back in these woods."

His gaze narrowed. "What makes you think he is?"

"It's the only thing that makes sense. Why else would his mama be so trigger-happy? Why else would he be lurking around to make sure we didn't circle back to check out the property?"

All the color drained out of her husband's face for the second time in the past ten minutes. "You ran into him in the woods?"

Whoops! "Briefly," she said, trying her best to sound blasé. "He sent me on my way. He seemed more anxious about where you'd disappeared to."

"Jesus, Amanda. Keep this up and my hair's going to turn pure white before this kid of ours is born."

"You'll look very distinguished," she reassured him. "Could we go somewhere for dinner? I'm starved."

"Again?"

"I've searched the bottom of my purse for jelly beans and there's not a one left. We're talking desperate."

"It's only five o'clock. How about a candy bar?"

"I was thinking more on the order of meatloaf and mashed potatoes."

He regarded her with sudden suspicion. "I suppose you have a place in mind, too."

"Actually I did see this cute little truck stop as we were driving over. It even had curtains hanging in the windows. It looked friendly and quaint."

"If it was called Mom's, I'm not going anywhere near it."

"Actually, it was called Babcock's Cafe."

A glint of fascination sparked in his eyes. He reached down and turned the key in the ignition. "Wonder if we can get a drink with our meal."

"I was wondering the exact same thing."

The cafe was about two miles away and practically blocked from view by the collection of semis in the parking lot. A couple of the huge rigs were parked at the very old-fashioned gas pumps out front, but most had been left helter-skelter over the rectangle of pavement that stretched for a hundred yards or so to the east.

A handful of exiting truckers shouted farewells as they headed for their rigs. Joe caught up with one of them. Amanda followed just closely enough to overhear the conversation.

"Say, can I ask you a question?" he asked the burly, bearded man in his path.

The man extracted a toothpick from his mouth. "I suppose. Depends on the question whether you'll get an answer."

"I was wondering about this place. My lady and I are dry as a bone after eighteen hours on the road. We were wondering what the possibilities might be of getting a drink inside."

The trucker regarded Donelli closely from head to toe, then subjected Amanda to the same scrutiny. "No liquor by the drink," he said flatly.

"I know. That's the problem. But I heard there were places that kept a supply of hard stuff on hand for folks they know. Thought maybe this was one of 'em."

"Like you said, places like that only serve to folks they know. These people don't know you."

Amanda gathered from his rather oblique comment that the liquor was on hand. It was just a matter now of getting well enough acquainted with the owner to get served.

"How 'bout an introduction then?" Donelli suggested.

"Eighteen hours with no sleep," the man said doubtfully. "You ain't planning to drink and get back on the road, are you? There are enough crazy fools out there as it is."

"Tell me about it," Donelli said with heartfelt sincerity. "No, we thought we'd rest up a bit after dinner, then take off about midnight."

"Well, you look honest enough. I suppose it can't hurt nothing to tell you the code. If they get suspicious, though, don't you go telling 'em where you got it."

"Not a word," Donelli vowed.

"Ask for a creme soda," the trucker advised. "They'll bring it to you straight up. You want ice, you gotta mention it. They ain't cheap. Five bucks a pop. Guess they're saving up for the day when they're arrested and have to pay some fancy lawyer to get 'em off."

"Who runs the place?"

"Just like it says in the window. Fellow name of Babcock. Has himself some crazy son and a wife who waits tables now and again. Mostly, though, it's just him and his daughter. She's a right pretty little thing. Try the chicken potpie. You won't find a better one in all the South."

"Thank you. I'll do that," Donelli said. "I'm mighty obliged."

After the trucker had walked on, Amanda linked her arm through her husband's. "If that accent of yours gets much thicker, you'll qualify for Georgia Cracker of the Year."

"Whatever works, Amanda. Isn't that your credo?"

She grinned at him. "Indeed. I just wasn't aware you'd been taking notes."

CHAPTER
Thirteen

It didn't take more than five minutes from the time Amanda and Donelli slid into a booth with a blue checked tablecloth and blue vinyl seats to discover that Babcock's name was Tommy and his daughter's name was Suzi. The latter was more than likely a diminutive of her mother's "Frenchified" *Suzette*.

Conversation flowed among the booths and tables. Truckers shouted orders to the harried girl, who looked to be no more than eighteen. Tommy, whose paunch hung over a belt that seemed in danger of cascading straight to his ankles, mingled. He poured coffee, frequently pausing to sit a spell before moving on. All in all, Babcock's Cafe appeared to be a friendly stopover for a gathering of regulars, mostly men. If anyone was on the way to rowdy drunkenness, Amanda couldn't spot him.

Suzi finally swung by their table, order pad in hand.

She had the same blonde hair as her brother, but hers was shining clean and swept up into a careless ponytail. Her jeans and T-shirt were decidedly cleaner as well. And rather than looking pinched, her face simply had the kind of well-defined bone structure a camera would love.

"You two need a menu? The specials are on the chalkboard." She gestured over her shoulder to a sign by the cash register. There wasn't a meal listed for over five dollars. Good, filling country cooking at a reasonable price. No wonder the place was packed.

"I heard the chicken potpie is terrific. I'll have that," Amanda said.

"I'll have the same," Donelli said.

"Anything to drink?"

"Just water," Amanda said.

"I was thinking a creme soda might taste good," Donelli said. "A tall one over ice."

Suzi didn't even blink. "Sure thing. I'll have your drinks here in a minute. The potpies will take a little longer. We don't pop 'em into the oven until we get an order. Daddy insists we serve everything nice and fresh from the oven. Keeps these guys coming back."

A young man dressed in a red plaid flannel shirt, his long black hair caught at the nape of his neck with a leather thong, apparently overheard her. "Don't be so modest, Suzi. Everybody knows you're the reason we keep stopping here." He grinned at Joe and Amanda. "Cutest little butt in ten counties. I ain't never seen a woman sashay across a room like our Suzi here."

Amanda's hackles rose on the teen's behalf. Suzi,

however, apparently needed no protection. She calmly retrieved a glass of ice water from her admirer's table and dumped it over his head. "Cool down, Sonny. I'm out of your league."

Sonny goodnaturedly laughed right along with everyone else. Amanda got the feeling it was not the first time that he and Suzi had tangled over his amorous intentions. In fact, they both seemed comfortable with the routine.

"One of these days you're gonna wake up and see me for the treasure I am," he called after her.

"In your dreams," she shouted right back.

Sonny's grin widened. He looked over at Joe and Amanda again. "I think she's beginning to weaken."

"How can you tell?" Amanda inquired.

"Last week, she whapped me upside the head when I riled her. Week before that she mashed a whole pie in my face. Lemon meringue. She knows I hate it. Her daddy flipped out. Made me pay for it."

Amanda laughed. "Then this was definitely a marked improvement."

Suzi reappeared with their drinks, setting the brown plastic glasses on the table and skirting Sonny's irrepressible, groping hands. Amanda studied those tinted glasses in which water was indistinguishable from creme soda or whatever, then glanced at her husband.

"Good way to camouflage a drink, huh?"

He nodded and took a sip, sputtered, then looked at Amanda with obvious astonishment. "It's creme soda."

Suzi apparently overheard the comment. She hurried back, a frown on her face. "Isn't that what you ordered?"

Donelli nodded. "Absolutely," he said at once. "It's

just been so long since I tasted a good creme soda, it kinda took me by surprise."

When Suzi had retreated to the kitchen, Amanda leaned across the table. "Guess that drawl didn't fool our friend outside, after all."

"You know the worst part of all this?"

"What?"

"Now I have to drink the damned stuff."

Tommy Babcock appeared just then, coffee pot in hand. "You two ready for some coffee to go along with the potpies? They should be out shortly."

"I'd love some," Donelli said at once.

Apparently her husband was not one whit suspicious of the timing. Amanda, however, thought Tommy just might have been waiting for his chance to get a chuckle over the trap he'd sprung. Maybe "creme soda" was the right code, but only when uttered by a trusted customer.

Her suspicions grew when Tommy devoted a lot of time to chatting them up as they ate, apparently trying to keep them around until the place emptied out about six-thirty. She was ready to panic when he told the cook and Suzi to take off for the night.

"You get on home, babycakes. I'll close up," he told his daughter, then flipped the CLOSED sign on the door and turned the lock. The sound of that key turning gave Amanda goosebumps.

When the place was secure, Babcock pulled up a chair and settled in at the end of Joe and Amanda's table. "How was your dinner?"

"Terrific," Amanda said honestly. As long as dinner

remained the topic, she had nothing but positive things to say. "I can't tell you the last time I had a potpie that good."

"That's my wife's recipe. Not a trucker that passes by doesn't go away raving about those potpies." He studied them a minute. "Ain't seen the two of you in here before."

"We don't get over to this part of the state all that often," Donelli said. "I've got a little farm over near Athens."

Tommy didn't look as if he believed that for a minute, but he seemed willing enough to play along. "What brings you over here?"

"We've been looking up some people for a friend," Donelli told him.

"Is that right?" Tommy nodded slowly. "Must be why you were out at my place earlier. You looking my boy up for your friend?"

Obviously the jig was up. Maybe it was time for a little straightforward honesty. "Actually, your wife is the one we probably should have spoken to," Amanda said. "Apparently she wasn't available."

His expression darkened. "Who's this friend of yours?"

"I'd rather not say," Amanda said.

Babcock didn't seem to take offense. He simply scooted his chair back and stood up. "Then I guess we got nothing further to talk about."

"In that case, I might have a few things to mention to the sheriff," Donelli told him.

Tommy blinked at the sudden turn from friendly chat to ominous threats. Amanda could see him visibly recalculating.

"Now why would you want to be doing a thing like that?" he asked with feigned innocence.

"For one thing, your wife, who supposedly wasn't available to company, shot at me today." Donelli continued to tick off the reasons. "For another, your son attacked my wife in the woods. And for a third, I suspect you're making moonshine at home and selling it here."

Babcock was obviously more concerned about the last charge than the first two. In fact the talk of shots fired and an attack by his son didn't even cause him to blink. The mention of moonshine brought beads of sweat to his brow.

"You got no proof of that," he said with a touch of belligerence.

Donelli nodded agreeably. "Just suspicions."

"Can't put a man in jail for some stranger's suspicions."

"But I can stir up a pack of trouble, now can't I?"

Apparently convinced, Tommy sat back down. "Okay, let's get down to brass tacks here. You two some kind of cops or something?"

"I'm a reporter," Amanda said. "My husband is a private investigator. And we're both over here on behalf of a friend, just like we said."

"Why should I believe that? You got *trouble* practically branded across your foreheads. The minute you asked for a creme soda, I knew something was funny."

"Why?" Amanda asked. "Isn't that your code for asking for a drink?"

Tommy shook his head as if to say he found them pitiful. "Do I look stupid enough to serve liquor to folks I don't know, assuming I had it available in the first place?"

"No, you look like a man who's been in business a long time and knows how to avoid suspicion," Donelli said. "Let's forget about the creme soda for a minute and get back to our original reason for wanting to talk to your wife."

"Which is?"

"We wanted to know about something that happened to her family a long time back."

"Then you're fresh out of luck. Suzette's memory faded a long time ago. They say she has that old-timer's disease."

"You mean Alzheimer's," Amanda said.

Tommy nodded. "Have to keep someone in the house with her all the time. Otherwise, she wanders off and gets lost."

"She's still one hell of a shot," Donelli attested.

"I'm right sorry about that. Sometimes Stevie forgets to lock away his gun when he comes back to the house. I've told him and told him, but you know how kids are."

For some reason Amanda didn't buy Tommy's ingenuous demeanor. She suspected the sudden burst of frankness was riddled with lies that suited his purpose. Maybe all this talk about poor, forgetful Suzette was simply meant to persuade them they had no reason whatsoever to return to his property. Of course, it was possible he was trying to protect his sick wife, but Amanda had a feeling it was to keep them from finding whatever he was hiding out in those woods. Or possibly he intended to keep them from trying to learn whatever secrets might be locked away in Suzette's brain.

"Tell us about Salty Tufts," Amanda suggested.

There was the faintest flicker of caution in Tommy's eyes, but he spoke up readily enough. "Old Salty was a character, all right. A legend around these parts."

"Why is that?" Donelli asked.

"Word was that Salty had developed a process for making moonshine that would revolutionize the business. Of course, folks had to take Salty's word for that. Nobody could get within firing distance of those old stills of his without getting a load of buckshot in the butt."

Apparently being gun-happy was a family trait, Amanda thought.

"I heard there was another big moonshiner around these parts back then, a guy by the name of Ashford," Donelli said.

Tommy shook his head. "I don't believe I recollect that name."

Amanda knew damned well he was bluffing. Even if for some reason he hadn't known William Ashford, she knew for certain that he was acquainted with Willie, if only as a buddy of his son's. The name shouldn't have made him go as blank as he was pretending. She was about to call him on it, but Donelli apparently read her mind. He jumped in.

"So what happened to Salty? Did he make a fortune on his process?"

"Who was going to buy it? It's not like he could take it to some big old trade show. If you ask me, he just liked to talk about it, make himself feel important. Probably didn't amount to much more than not using something contaminated with lead. Wasn't so long ago that a guy name of Fat Hardy killed thirty or forty people with lead-poisoned moonshine. Folks who don't know what they're doing try using old radiator coils. Damn things are filled with lead."

"Was Salty always in the moonshine trade?" Amanda asked. She'd gotten Donelli's hint to keep Ashford out of the conversation for the time being.

"All the time I knew him." He paused. "Now wait a second. Now that I think about it, there was a time when he got out."

"And when was that?" she asked.

His expression turned thoughtful. "I'd have to say it was back around '39, maybe '40," he said eventually. "Suzette wasn't even born yet, but she used to tell me about how bad things were for her ma and pa right around then. She came along in '45 and by then her folks were doing just fine. In fact, Salty was pretty much the moonshine king in these parts."

"Who would you say holds that title now?" Amanda asked.

Tommy grinned and stared her straight in the eye. "I wouldn't have the vaguest idea."

Amanda might have pressed him, but Donelli slid out of the booth and held out his hand.

"Thanks for your time."

"My pleasure," Tommy said, looking pleased as punch, probably because he thought he'd fooled them. "Y'all come back anytime."

He walked them to the door, then watched until they had backed up and pulled their car onto the highway. Amanda noticed that the second he could, Tommy turned around and headed straight for the pay phone on the wall beside the cash register.

"Now who do you suppose he's calling?" she wondered.

"My guess would be Stevie. I suspect he wants to make very sure that someone's standing guard in case we try to go snooping around back there tonight."

Unfortunately, that was Amanda's guess as well. "Which means you're not going to want to risk it, are you?"

"Sorry, sweetheart. I'd sooner stare a rattler in the eye than take on Stevie in the dark on his own turf, especially without the element of surprise on our side."

"But how are we supposed to find out if there is a still back in there?"

"Patience, Amanda. We'll find out, just as soon as they let their guard down."

"By then, they will have dismantled it and moved the whole damned thing to some other location."

Donelli shook his head. "Stevie's not bright enough to think of doing that and his daddy's got an arrogant streak. He figures he's already taken us for fools once. He'll be sure he can do it again."

"What do we do in the meantime?"

"Pick up your car. Go home and see our son. Have a quiet family evening for a change. Say a little prayer of thanks that we are not related to the dysfunctional Babcocks."

"What a disgustingly normal plan," Amanda said, then smiled. "I can't wait."

The words were no sooner out of her mouth than she panicked. Normal? What if she really was losing her edge? What if she was about to turn into some safe, contented little feature writer just as Carol Fields wanted?

"Donelli, if you ever hear that I am willingly going out to cover quilting bees, will you slap me upside the head and remind me why I became a journalist?"

"It will be my pleasure, Amanda."

It wasn't so much his words, as the gleam in his eyes that worried her. He seemed to be anticipating the prospect with an inordinate amount of glee.

CHAPTER
Fourteen

"Della, if that's Amanda, you send her right up here. If you don't, so help me I'll fire you."

Miss Martha's shout echoed down the staircase. For a woman who'd just had a close call with death, she sounded surprisingly strong and very capable of inflicting her will on her protective housekeeper.

"You might's well go on up," Della told Amanda, after heaving a sigh of resignation. "She's got half the county up there as it is. Ain't nothing I can do with her, if she wants to kill herself."

Given what Amanda suspected about Miss Martha's intentions, Della's offhand comment sent a chill chasing down her spine. "Did you mean that literally?" she finally dared to ask the worried-looking housekeeper.

Della regarded her suspiciously. "Mean what?"

Still wondering if she was making a terrible mistake by getting into her suspicions with Della, Amanda took a deep breath and blurted it out. "About Miss Martha killing herself."

Unfortunately shock did not spread across Della's face. "You didn't hear that from me," she said with a weak attempt at indignation. "What I said just now, it was a figure of speech."

Tears had gathered in the old woman's eyes. Amanda ignored her obvious distress and pressed harder for a straight answer. "Okay, maybe just now it was, but Della, if she is depressed about her health, if she is thinking about suicide, please tell me. Maybe she can still be talked out of it."

Della's expression set stubbornly. She folded her arms across her chest. "I don't go blabbing what I hear in this house. And if you're as smart as she thinks you are, you won't go meddling in things that are none of your concern. She's determined not to talk about her health. Won't even tell me straight out what the doctor says. What I know I have to guess from the bits and pieces I overhear around here."

Amanda read between the lines and heard a vague, unwilling confirmation that Della had indeed heard talk of suicide, perhaps, as she had hinted earlier, between Miss Martha and Dr. Flanders.

Almost wishing she'd left the subject unspoken, Amanda slowly climbed the stairs. With only vague remarks to go on, did she dare bring up the subject with Miss Martha? How would the proud old woman respond to having been found out? And what could Amanda say to her anyway? Should she try to persuade her one way or the other? Or simply listen, as Joe had suggested?

Fortunately, any decision about that particular topic was delayed by the presence of several of Miss Martha's friends from her historic preservation society. Most of them Amanda recognized. Her arrival immediately set off a buzz of fond recollections of Amanda's recovery of some of their most prized Civil War antiques. The half-dozen white-haired ladies, all smelling of lily-of-the-valley cologne and wearing similar flowered silk dresses they'd probably owned for thirty years, clustered around Amanda.

"We heard about the baby, dear. How wonderful for you and Joe!" Eleanor Mae Taylor said in her frail, quavery voice.

"Oh, yes, it's splendid," Henrietta Cosgrove declared, bobbing her head so hard that the white curls on top threatened to come loose from the pins holding them in place. "We're so delighted that you and that nice detective are starting a family of your own. It's about time, too. Neither of you is getting any younger."

Amanda gazed at them in astonishment. "How on earth . . ."

"I told 'em," Miss Martha declared, sounding disgruntled at being ignored.

"But I hadn't told you a thing. I didn't even know myself the last time we talked."

"It was plain as day when you were here the other day," Miss Martha said airily. "Besides, I can read Dr. Flanders like a book. When I asked him straight out, he hemmed and hawed around the answer, which was tantamount to confirming it. That old man never could play a decent game of cards. He couldn't bluff if his life depended on it. Playing gin rummy with him is a waste of my time."

She glanced at her friends. "Ladies, if you don't mind, I have some private matters to discuss with Amanda. Thank you all for coming."

The abrupt, imperious dismissal was so typical of Miss Martha that not one of the visitors batted an eye. The ladies dutifully left amid a flurry of promises to return soon, good wishes for Amanda, and pecks on the cheek for Miss Martha.

"I declare they wear me out," Miss Martha said when they had gone.

"But your color's better," Amanda said. "Have you all been plotting some historic preservation scheme?"

"Oh, they were talking about some house or other that's destined for a wrecking ball, but I wasn't paying 'em much mind. I have more important matters to think about." Her gaze fixed avidly on Amanda. "What have you found out? I want to hear everything. Have you seen Willie? What's he like? Does he look anything like his grandfather? What took you so long to get back over here? And why the devil didn't you answer any of my messages?"

Amanda used her own judgment about which question to answer. She couldn't see any benefit to defending her tardiness in getting back to Miss Martha. She was here now. "I did meet Willie," she said. "And, yes, he does bear a striking resemblance to the picture I saw of his grandfather. He's very grateful to you for coming to his assistance."

Miss Martha sighed. "I do so hope I have the chance to meet him."

"Of course, you will," Amanda said.

"Nothing in life is that certain," Miss Martha admonished her. "Now what else have you discovered?"

"So far I haven't come up with anything that makes much sense," Amanda admitted. "I do have a couple of names to run by you. Does Henry Boggins mean anything to you?"

Miss Martha's eyes sparkled dangerously at the mention of the name. "That old coot?" she said derisively. "He must be dead by now. Good riddance, I say."

"He's not dead, though he is in the hospital in Atlanta."

"You've seen him?"

Amanda nodded.

"Then you know how he felt about William. He blamed him for Laurabel's death or so he said to anyone who'd listen."

"What do you mean, *so he said*?"

"He was a greedy old son of a gun. Carried on about poor, sweet Laurabel like he'd doted on her since birth. I'd be willing to bet that's exactly the kind of pitiful tale he spun for you."

"It went along those lines," Amanda conceded.

"Well, the truth of it was, he hadn't even seen her since she was a toddler. He ran out on her and her mother. Couldn't take the pressure of marriage, poor thing. I doubt he ever did an honest day's work in his life. That's why Laurabel's mama turned to making a living on her back, if you know what I mean. Laurabel just followed in her footsteps until William came along and saved her from that life."

"Why would Boggins make such a big deal out of Laurabel dying, if he wasn't sincerely grieving? Maybe he regretted all those lost years. Maybe he felt bad about the life Laurabel and her mother had been forced to lead."

"Hogwash!" Miss Martha declared. "He was after money, of course. First he tried to blackmail William. Said he owed him for sending his beloved child to her grave with his carrying-on. When that didn't work, he came to me. He knew practically down to the penny what my family was worth. He figured I wouldn't want my reputation sullied. I told him what he could do with his threats and insinuations."

Well, well, well, Amanda thought. Donelli's guess had been right on target. Henry Boggins had attempted to blackmail William and Miss Martha. Despite her devil's-advocate defense of him, somehow she wasn't all that surprised. "How did he take being turned down?"

"Called me every name in the book. Threatened again to expose our tawdry little affair, first to my family, then to the world. Told me he'd make me a laughingstock. You know the sort of thing a person of that class says."

"Was he angry enough over having his plans foiled to commit murder and frame William for it?"

"He was angry enough, but I doubt he had the gumption. Besides, the way he'd messed up everything else in his life, he would have botched that too. They would have caught him for sure."

Amanda wasn't so convinced that Boggins wasn't wily enough to pull it off, but she clung tenaciously to her journalistic objectivity for the time being. She'd find out the truth when she paid another call on dear old Henry to confront him about his behavior back then.

"How about a man named Salty Tufts?"

To her astonishment, Miss Martha laughed, her expression brightening. "Old Salty. Goodness, I haven't thought about him in years. Now, I know he's dead, because I watched them put him in the ground."

"You went to his funeral?"

"Of course I did. He and William were best friends. Salty was practically the only person around who knew how we felt about each other. I'd have trusted that man with just about any secret."

"Then there wasn't bad blood between him and William?"

"Never."

Miss Martha sounded so certain that Amanda couldn't doubt her. Why then had Henry Boggins tried to make it seem that William had run Salty out of the moonshine business? And why would Tommy Babcock claim never to have heard of Ashford, if William and his father-in-law had been so close? Were those just more lies to throw Amanda off the scent? Obviously she had a lot more digging to do.

"Who else is on your list?" Miss Martha demanded.

"Salty's daughter, Suzette. She took some shots at Donelli yesterday. After that we had a long conversation with her husband. He was lying through his teeth."

"Why did you go to see them in the first place?"

"Both Boggins and Willie sent us in that direction."

"False leads," Miss Martha said succinctly. "What else?"

"Kenny Loftis." At Miss Martha's blank expression, Amanda added, "He had a place next door to the Ashford property."

"Don't recall William ever talking about him. How old a person is he?"

"Seventy-four. He remembered William and Laurabel, though I hardly got the feeling they were all bosom buddies."

Miss Martha waved him off as being of no consequence. "Okay, then. It's not much, but it's a start. What's your theory?"

"Theory? I don't have one. We've only been at it a couple of days," Amanda reminded her a bit defensively.

"Don't get all riled up, Amanda. I was just hoping, I suppose. You're usually quick to draw conclusions."

"So I've been told," Amanda said dryly.

Miss Martha regarded her worriedly. "What's this I hear about Oscar threatening to pull you off the story? Della said you'd mentioned something about being in trouble at the magazine for following up on this for me."

"Oscar didn't threaten. He flat out told me not to do it."

"Do I need to call him?" She was already reaching for the bedside phone.

Amanda would have enjoyed that, but with Carol Fields as the real problem she couldn't imagine what good a call to Oscar would do. "No," she said with some reluctance. "I'll handle things at work."

"I want you on this full time," Miss Martha commanded. "There's no time to waste."

"Why do you say that?" Amanda asked cautiously. There was an opening here, but she wasn't sure she could take it. "You're looking and sounding much stronger today."

Miss Martha waved off the compliment. "I'm not going to get better, Amanda. That's the truth of it. Every day my heart gets a little weaker and the pain gets a little more unbearable. And I do not intend to linger here waiting to shrivel up and die or doped up on the kind of pain medication Dr. Flanders would have me take."

So, Amanda thought, there it was. Miss Martha couldn't have spelled out her intentions any more clearly. Still, she wanted to hear the words cross the older woman's lips. "What are you saying?"

Miss Martha reached for a photograph that had been turned down on her bedside table, probably to keep it from the view of her visitors. She gazed at William Ashford's portrait for a long time, her expression nostalgic. Her eyes were misty when she finally turned her attention back to Amanda.

"I mean that when the time comes, I will go quietly to my reward," she said with soft, but unmistakable determination. "I've made all the arrangements."

"What arrangements?" Amanda persisted.

Miss Martha scowled at her. Her grip on the silver-framed photo tightened. "Why are you asking all these questions?"

"Because I want to know if you intend to kill yourself the minute I tell you who was responsible for these murders," Amanda said bluntly. "Are you just waiting for answers so you can rest in peace?"

"I told you that from the beginning," Miss Martha said querulously. "Why are you acting as if it's some sort of sneaky plan I intended to put over on you?"

"I was under the impression that you were figuring to die of natural causes, not to help yourself along," she said more angrily than she'd intended. Apparently her feelings about assisted suicide were stronger and more conflicted than she'd realized.

Miss Martha leveled a look straight at her. "So what if I do? That's nobody's business but mine."

Amanda wasn't daunted. In fact, she was building up a full head of steam. "Really? What about Della?"

"She's been provided for."

"I was referring to the pain she's in every single day because she suspects what you intend to do. And how about your nephews?" She had no idea what the pediatrician would think, but Amanda could just imagine what Donald Wellington would have to say if he discovered his aunt's intentions. As a lawyer and former senator, he would be all over the legalities.

When Miss Martha said nothing, Amanda continued the list of people who would be affected by her decision. "What about Dr. Flanders? You're putting him in a terrible position. He's caught between his concern for you and the law. On top of that, he says you could be treated, but you're not even willing to try."

"I will not spend my last days or weeks or whatever I have left sick as a dog from chemotherapy. At my age with my heart that would likely kill me quicker than the cancer. I won't do it and that's final, so you might's well save your breath. Besides, Amanda, you're young yet. You're not ready to face death, so you can't understand my willingness to do it."

That might be true enough, Amanda thought. And she hadn't had to face the inevitable pain and progression of terminal cancer. But right now, Miss Martha's decision to simply give up, in fact to embrace death at a time of her own choosing, simply made her mad. It seemed like a selfish act. She thought of yet more people who would be affected by Miss Martha's decision.

"What about those ladies who just left here? They admire you. They expect you to set an example. What about the preservationists who count on you to lead their fight? What about all the poor people whose lives you touch with your generosity?" Finally she got to the heart of her dismay. Her voice dropped as she asked bleakly, "What about Joe and me?"

Miss Martha heard her tirade out without a word. But when Amanda was finished, Miss Martha regarded her wearily. "And what about me?" she asked quietly. "Do I not have the right to die with dignity, rather than submitting to the tortures of the medical profession just so the rest of you will feel you've done your best by me?"

Tears gathered in Amanda's eyes as Miss Martha lovingly stood the photo on her bedside table and reached for Amanda's hand. "Don't cry, dear," Miss Martha said. "I'm ready to go. I'm ready to be with William again. I just want to take him good news, when I go."

"You've given me a lousy incentive to finish this investigation," Amanda protested. "I don't want to lose you."

"It was bound to happen sooner or later," Miss Martha reminded her. "You're a young woman and I'm a very old lady."

"But this way? It seems wrong, like you're giving up."

"I'm not giving up. Faced with the inevitable, I'm making a choice." She patted Amanda's hand. "And it's my choice to make, no one else's. Please, try to understand."

"Intellectually, I suppose I do," Amanda said, swiping at her tears. "Emotionally, I'm not ready to let go. The others will feel the same way."

"The others won't know, unless you tell them."

"Della knows," Amanda insisted.

Miss Martha smiled. "Ah, yes, Della. She's been my right hand, my friend, my conscience all these years. But when the time comes, she will grant me this one last selfish whim, as will Dr. Flanders. I will go quietly into the night, Amanda. Just the way we were all meant to do in a compassionate world."

She suddenly seemed to tire right before Amanda's eyes. The color washed out of her face. Her hand in Amanda's turned icy. "Dear, if you don't mind, I believe I'd like to take a little nap. Call me the minute you have any news."

Impulsively, Amanda leaned down and kissed her cheek, then rushed from the room to allow her pent-up tears to spill over. She was still leaning against the wall when Della trudged up the stairs and paused in front of her.

"She told you, didn't she? She admitted she's going to take a whole handful of pills or something."

Amanda could only nod.

Della clasped a hand to her chest. "Sweet Jesus, I thought it was my imagination. It ain't right what she's thinking. It ain't the Lord's way."

Amanda was no less troubled by the concept and yet she couldn't forget Miss Martha's plea for compassion and dignity in death, as in life.

"Who are we to say?" she asked Della softly. "Who are we to say?"

CHAPTER

Fifteen

Amanda took her time as she walked down the hallway at Grady Memorial Hospital to see Henry Boggins again. She had a whole long list of questions for the old reprobate, most of them focusing on his attempts at blackmail. If it had been anyone else, she would have gone in, reportorial guns blazing, filled with righteous indignation over being lied to. She would have pinned his weathered hide to the wall.

As it was, she was afraid that too violent a confrontation might silence him for good. No one had told her exactly what was wrong with him, but that wracking cough of his sounded like a death knell.

She sighed. If she had to tiptoe around many more sources in fragile health, she thought with disgust, she really would be good for nothing but syrupy features. Carol Fields would win by default.

She opened the door to Boggins' room, stepped inside,

and saw at once that the bed was occupied by someone she had never seen before in her life. Looking panicked by the intrusion, the battered young black woman stared back at her through eyes that were almost swollen shut.

"I'm not talking to any social worker, so you can get on out of here," the patient warned, sounding frightened and defiant at the same time.

"Then you'll be relieved to know that I'm not a social worker," Amanda said. "I'm just a reporter who's apparently wandered into the wrong room by mistake. I was looking for Henry Boggins. I'm sorry to have disturbed you."

The young woman's anger deflated like a week-old balloon, sapping every last bit of animation out of her. Compassion welled up inside Amanda. Warning herself that she couldn't take on the world's problems, she forced herself out the door. Grady Memorial was probably filled with cases that could tap her emotions. It was a hospital of last resort for the indigent, a trauma center for victims of street violence and domestic wars. If she wrote stories from now until retirement, she couldn't begin to scratch the surface.

Safely back in the hallway, her detachment hard-won, she took note of the room number. She hadn't been mistaken. It was exactly the same room she had visited before when Henry Boggins had occupied it. She wandered off toward the nurses' station in search of answers.

It took longer than she would have imagined possible in a place crammed with so many people just to get one of them to look her way. She supposed there was some sort of organization to the chaos, but it escaped her.

Finally a harried-looking clerk came back to answer one of the ringing phones. She signaled to Amanda that she'd be right with her, then proceeded to take half a dozen calls about missing lab reports, missing doctors and at least one about an urgent need for the chaplain who was reportedly making rounds on the unit.

The clerk—Debbie, according to her nametag—sighed heavily and put the caller on hold. "Anybody around here seen a chaplain?" she shouted into the crowd behind her. "I don't even care what denomination."

"I saw that guy who's filling in about twenty minutes ago," one nurse called back.

"He was getting on the elevator when I came on duty," another chimed in. "But that was hours ago, six-thirty, six-forty-five, maybe."

"Up or down?" Debbie asked. "Maybe they can still catch him."

"I was coming up and he got on, so I guess he was heading up."

Debbie forwarded that information to the caller, then hung up and looked at Amanda. "Sorry. It's nuts around here when the docs finish making rounds. They're writing up orders, talking to the nurses, shouting for meds they ordered not five minutes ago. Heaven forbid they should grab a phone and call the pharmacy themselves." She grinned, displaying a dream set of shining white teeth, the product of excellent bridgework or expensive orthodontia. "At least it's not dull, right? What can I do for you?"

"I seem to have misplaced a patient, Henry Boggins."

Debbie's previously animated features shifted into a polite, sympathetic mask. "You a relative?"

"No, a friend. I was here to visit with him night before last." Debbie's increasingly somber expression and the note of unspoken condolence in her voice alerted Amanda that something was seriously wrong. "Did he take a turn for the worse?"

"I'm not supposed to give out information on the patients' conditions. Maybe you should talk to his doctor." She turned around. "Hey, Paltrow, over here."

An astonishingly tall young man who looked as if he ought to be playing high school basketball, not treating patients, separated himself from the crowd and walked over. His lab coat pockets were bulging with papers, prescription pads, pens, and a stethoscope. He regarded Amanda with open curiosity as Debbie explained that she was there to see Henry Boggins.

"You say you're a friend?" he said, running his fingers through short brown hair that already stood on end.

Amanda nodded.

"I'm Ryan Paltrow. Mr. Boggins was my patient. Perhaps we should talk in the lounge."

His voice had dropped to a somber tone that matched Debbie's expression. He looked as if he'd rather be anywhere on earth but Grady Memorial. Amanda got the picture. "You can tell me here. I won't keel over on you. He's dead, isn't he?"

Paltrow nodded, looking so guilty Amanda found herself wanting to comfort him.

"About five this morning," he said.

"It's not like it wasn't expected," she consoled him and herself.

"That's what I keep trying to tell myself," he said, then shook his head. "I don't know, though. Yesterday he was in good spirits. He seemed stable. I checked him myself about two A.M., right before I went to catch a couple hours of sleep. I just can't figure it."

"He was old, wasn't he? About a hundred?" Amanda reminded him.

Paltrow didn't looked reassured. "If he'd died from complications from the pneumonia that brought him in here, it would have made sense, but he was just about recovered. Then, *bam*, his heart blows. Full cardiac arrest faster than you can spit. If I didn't know better, I'd . . ." He cut himself off as if he'd been spooked by the sight of a circling covey of malpractice attorneys.

The start of that sentence, however, was just enough to intrigue Amanda. "You'd what?" she prodded.

"I'd say somebody helped him along," he said. He had lowered his voice to a whisper. "At his age it wouldn't have taken much. A little extra potassium in his IV would probably have done the trick."

"Can that be detected by an autopsy?"

"No autopsy was ordered. Like you said, he was a hundred. He died of a cardiac arrest while he was in the hospital for treatment. Shit like that happens."

"Can you still order one?"

Ryan Paltrow looked as if she'd asked him to perform

surgery on the President of the United States. His expression was a fascinating combination of excitement, guilt, terror, and dismay.

"His body has already been released for burial. I signed the death certificate. There weren't any family members to give instructions, so we just did what he'd asked us to do when he first came in. Is there some kind of problem I should know about?"

"Could a family member get that burial stopped?" Amanda persisted, ignoring his question. She was thinking of Willie, whose fate might depend on discovering whether his great-grandfather had died of natural causes or had been helped along by someone who feared he knew too much about some murder conspiracy that had happened decades earlier.

"I suppose. My residency just started a few months ago. I haven't lived in Georgia all that long, so I don't know the rules for stuff like that." He studied Amanda with renewed curiosity. "You must have been close to the old guy to want to go to all this trouble."

"Actually I hardly knew him, but he was a key source on a story I'm working and it makes me very nervous when my sources start turning up dead."

Ryan Paltrow turned positively pale. "He was some kind of witness or something?"

"That's the big question," Amanda said. "And I would very much like to know the answer."

Unfortunately, if it were up to Oscar Cates and Carol Fields, the only answers Amanda was likely to be getting for the rest of her career were the dates of society events for *Inside Atlanta*'s calendar section. The two of them advanced on her the second she emerged from the elevator. She almost wondered if they'd stationed a lookout in the building's downstairs lobby. For a fleeting instant she regretted her decision to stop by the office.

The impulse to flee passed, though, and she decided a good battle would really get her adrenaline flowing. She popped a couple of lemon Jelly Bellies from her fresh supply just to get a head start on the tart exchange that was clearly in store.

"My office. Now!" Oscar said, gesturing in the general direction as if Amanda might have forgotten it during her absence.

A bright gleam of triumph shone in Carol's eyes. As Amanda strode past her, she paused just long enough to whisper to the new assignment editor, "It ain't over till it's over, sweet pea."

The declaration didn't do much to wipe the smug look off of Carol's face, but it made Amanda feel infinitely better. She gave a thumbs-up gesture of encouragement to a very pale Jenny Lee, who was anxiously watching the little parade.

As if they'd been preparing for her return for quite some time, Oscar's office had been swept free of debris. Another of Carol's domestic touches, perhaps? At any rate, there were actually chairs on which to sit. Amanda chose to stand. It might give her only a tiny psychological advantage, but she wanted it nonetheless.

"So, guys, what's happening?" she inquired cheerfully.

"Cut the shit, Amanda," Oscar intoned, oblivious to

the patches of indignant color that immediately rose in Carol's cheeks as she frowned at him. He must have missed her memo on appropriate office language. "Where the hell have you been?"

"Working a story."

"Not for us," Carol interjected. "I have assigned you nothing."

"Some of us don't wait around to be told what to do," Amanda informed her. "It's called initiative."

"It's called insubordination," Carol shot back.

"Ladies, that's enough!" Oscar roared.

Amanda turned a wide-eyed gaze on him. "So you are still in charge around here? For a minute there I wondered."

"Amanda!" he warned.

"Sorry."

"Now let's discuss this in a calm, reasonable manner," he suggested. He seemed to have great difficulty with the words and concept, probably because no one had ever applied them to his management style.

Carol's smug expression returned. Oscar seemed to be struggling to recall what he should say next. Obviously they hadn't rehearsed this part enough. Amanda regarded the two of them expectantly.

"Why don't you tell us about the story?" Oscar finally suggested.

"There is no story!" Carol insisted, just as Amanda said, "I went over that with you the other day."

Oscar shot them both a quelling look. "I'd like to hear it again."

Sensing an unexpected openness that hadn't been

there earlier, Amanda dutifully summarized the two murders. She lingered over the poignant attempt by Miss Martha to right an injustice from her deathbed, sensing that the more she said about the society grande dame, the more open-minded Oscar was likely to become. She carefully avoided so much as a hint about Miss Martha's intentions to hurry along her own demise. There was no way she intended to lay that open for public dissection, no matter how topical and controversial the subject might be.

"Now, just this morning, there's been another death," she concluded.

Oscar at least recognized her cautious wording and seized on it. "A death, not a murder?"

"I don't have all the facts yet. It could be a homicide. And if I don't get busy right away, the guy will be buried before we get any answers. I need to call Jim Harrison over at Atlanta PD and see what the procedure is for blocking a burial and ordering an autopsy."

Carol looked as if she'd just stepped in a pile of manure. "I really find this entire subject distasteful. It's another example of the sort of sensationalistic stories that are totally inappropriate for this magazine. We are hoping to capture wealthy, refined readers. We should not be setting out to offend their sensibilities by writing about such morbid subjects."

"The wealthy and refined, that's our new target audience?" Amanda said, ignoring for a moment the sensationalistic label Carol had tacked on to describe her story. If it weren't so ludicrous, she might have laughed in the woman's face.

"Naturally, we want a cultured, well-bred readership," Carol insisted. "That will appeal to upscale advertisers."

"I wasn't aware there were enough of them to keep our circulation above the bankruptcy level," Amanda said. "But if that's your focus, then what could appeal to them more than a story about one of their own? You are aware that Miss Martha Wellington can assemble more movers and shakers with the blink of an eye than just about anybody else in the state, including the governor. She could probably buy up the entire print-run and hand it out at her next party and reach the very people you claim to want as subscribers."

"She's Old South," Carol said dismissively. "There's an entire new generation . . ."

Amanda interrupted. "Whose parents still control the purse strings on their family fortunes."

"But you will be writing about convicted murderers," Carol protested with a delicate shudder. "It's sensationalism, pure and simple."

"Unjustly convicted murderers," Amanda reminded her. "There's nothing sensational about this. It's damned good journalism. Think of the awards we could win if we managed to clear two innocent men. JOURNALISTS DO WHAT THE JUSTICE SYSTEM COULD NOT. It would be banner headlines around the country. We might even get featured on *Sixty Minutes*."

Carol opened her mouth for another counterargument, but Oscar had apparently had enough.

"Do it," he said.

"But . . ." Reddening, Carol began to sputter.

Amanda winked at Oscar. "Thanks." She scooted out the door just as Carol launched into a tirade about having her authority undermined.

"I'll back up your decisions when you develop some news sense," he shot back. "And if you don't like that, go crying to your cousin or uncle-in-law or whatever the heck Crenshaw is."

"Way to go, Oscar," Amanda murmured as she raced into the newsroom, grabbed Jenny Lee by the elbow, and practically dragged her to the elevator. "Let's get out of here, before one of them draws blood."

Only after they were out of the range of fire did she grin at her assistant. She offered Jenny Lee a few piña colada jelly beans for a triumphant toast of sorts. "Score one for our side. Now, do you have that information I asked for?"

"Of course I do," Jenny Lee said indignantly. "It's right smack in the middle of your desk, which I could have told you if you'd given me two seconds before hauling me out of the newsroom."

Amanda gave her a chagrined smile. "Sorry. Go back and get it. I'll get the car and pick you up at the Peachtree entrance in five minutes."

She exited on the garage level and waved as the elevator doors started to close. Jenny Lee stepped between them and held them open.

"Hey, Amanda," Jenny Lee called after her.

"What?"

Jenny Lee grinned. "I think it's fantastic about the baby."

She stepped out of the way and let the elevator doors

slide closed before Amanda could ask how the devil she had found out. If Jenny Lee knew, though, then so did Oscar, which might have been why he'd suddenly turned indulgent.

That, or he'd finally given free rein to his previously repressed hostility toward Carol Fields. Either way, Amanda got to do the story and get Carol's goat at the same time. Life was good.

CHAPTER
Sixteen

One of the things Amanda liked most about her research assistant was Jenny Lee's willingness to take any risk without asking questions. For a genuine Southern belle, Jenny Lee had turned out okay. She reminded Amanda of the way she herself had always approached her job. Of course, the impulsive, daredevil attitude Amanda had employed might have to disappear not just while she was pregnant, but forever after, once the baby was born.

With a child to consider, she couldn't be cavalierly putting her life at risk as she had in the past. And she couldn't leave raising the baby entirely to Donelli, while she chased the bad guys, journalistically speaking. She would have to budget in more time at home, settle into some sort of routine that accommodated regular meal-times, PTA meetings—the list went on and on.

The thought of the changes she would have to make

in her journalistic nature were too troublesome to deal with now, however. Besides, she was starved. Again. Apparently she was going to be one of those fortunate women whose bouts of morning sickness turned out to be little more than the occasional flash of queasiness. Of course, at the rate she was eating, she might also be one of those who blew up to the size of a blimp.

That particular prospect didn't daunt her. She turned the car into the first fast-food restaurant she spotted.

"You are not feeding that baby junk," Jenny Lee protested. "You drive right back out of here, Amanda."

"But I'm hungry."

"There's a nice, healthy restaurant about six blocks from here."

"Healthy?" Amanda said dubiously. "I'm not eating sprouts, Jenny Lee. Not for you. Not even for the baby."

"I'm sure you'll be able to find something on the menu that won't make your poor, mistreated arteries scream out in frustration at not getting their daily quota of grease."

"Then what's the point? A hamburger is a hamburger."

"That's a matter of opinion," Jenny Lee retorted. "Six blocks, Amanda. On the left. And we need to start thinking about getting you back on an exercise program."

Healthy food? Exercise? She knew from personal experience how enthusiastic Jenny Lee could get about those two topics. With a baby as the incentive, she'd probably get downright compulsive. Amanda's gaze narrowed as she inched back out into the mid-morning traffic.

"I'm pretty sure it's not recommended that a woman start exercising when she's pregnant, if she hasn't been doing it all along," Amanda said, trying to keep a note of triumph from her voice.

"You can walk," Jenny Lee countered. "Or swim. I checked it out this morning."

"Checked it out with whom?"

"I found this terrific informational service on the computer. I asked some questions and an obstetrician gave the answers."

"You've already had time to do all that? When did you find out about the baby, anyway?"

"First thing this morning from Joe. He wanted Oscar and me to keep an eye on you. He doesn't seem to think you've grasped the concept of taking good care of yourself—an opinion held by many, I might add."

"If you intend to spend the next seven months lecturing me, you can get on back to the office and answer the phones," Amanda warned.

Jenny Lee grinned. "I don't think so. Oscar wants me to stick to you like glue."

Amanda sighed. With all this hovering, it was promising to be a very long seven months. And if the Natural Grains restaurant to which Jenny Lee was directing her was where she was doomed to eat, it was going to seem like even longer.

Inside, surrounded by more pine boards and thriving ferns than she'd ever before seen assembled in one place outside of a forest, she searched the menu for some sign of something edible. Oat bran, berries, and lettuce leaves seemed to be the staples of the chef's repertoire.

"I'm not a horse or a rabbit," she muttered under her breath.

"Try the burger," Jenny Lee said.

She searched the menu hopefully, figuring she must have missed it. She finally spotted it under the poultry offerings. She scowled at Jenny Lee. "It's made out of turkey, for God's sake."

"Try it," Jenny Lee insisted.

Amanda sighed and gave in. Maybe Jenny Lee's report on the murdered Revenue agents would be juicy enough to make up for the lack of the inch-high beef patty topped with cheddar cheese she had been craving. Before that, though, she had to talk to Jim Harrison about getting that burial stopped. She grabbed her cellular phone and dialed the Atlanta Police Department. The detective groaned when he heard her voice. It was a common enough reaction that it didn't offend her.

"What now, Amanda?"

"How do I get a burial stopped and an autopsy ordered?" she asked straight out, since he didn't seem in the mood for banter.

His sigh of resignation could probably be heard all the way to the chief's office. "Explain."

She made the story as concise and compelling as possible.

"He was *how* old?" Harrison demanded incredulously.

"A hundred, I think, but that's not important."

"It will be to the medical examiner. Forget it, Amanda. The doctor on duty filled out a death certificate. What more do you want?"

"Even he had his suspicions. Try, please. It could be critical to Willie Ashford's case. If you need an okay from the next of kin, I'm sure Willie would give it."

Probably because he knew her persistence so well, Harrison relented. "I'll make a call, but I'm not making any promises, Amanda. In fact, if I were you, I'd forget all about this angle. I doubt it will be worth all the paperwork Willie's lawyer would have to file."

"Just do what you can. You're a sweetheart, detective."

"Yeah, right. I'll be in touch."

After he'd hung up, Amanda turned her attention to Jenny Lee. "Tell me what you found," she instructed, when the round-cheeked farm girl who waited on them had taken their order.

"Don't you want to read this stuff yourself?" Jenny Lee asked, pulling out several folders.

"No. My eyes are so tired, I doubt they can focus," she admitted.

Jenny Lee instantly looked concerned. Her mother-hen instincts clearly went into overdrive. "But you're okay? You're sure?"

"Fine," Amanda reassured her before Jenny Lee insisted on calling the doctor or, worse, the rescue squad. "My energy just seems to come and go in waves."

Jenny Lee looked doubtful, but she finally relented,

"Okay, then." She opened the first folder. "I'll start with Randy Blaine Alcott. He was the agent shot back in '42."

Amanda was suddenly struck by the fact that she was already days deep into an investigation and this was the first time she had given serious thought to the victims.

Randy Blaine Alcott. She'd read right over his name in the original clippings. She'd barely listened when Boggins had mentioned his name. She had dismissed him because, thanks to Miss Martha's fervor, her focus was entirely on William Ashford. She couldn't even dredge up a mental picture of him, she realized guiltily.

"Tell me about him," she told Jenny Lee.

"He was forty-six, had a wife and two grown kids. One of them, a girl named Katherine, was studying law at the time. She dropped out and moved away after her daddy died."

That confirmed what Boggins had recalled.

"His son, Randy Junior, was working at the Department of Revenue just like his daddy," Jenny Lee went on. "He quit after his father was shot. He was quoted as saying his mother was too distraught over his father's death to be able to cope with having her son in the same kind of danger."

"What kind of agent was Randy Senior? Were you able to get his personnel records?"

"The papers had most of that stuff. He was dedicated and driven, spurred on by his personal beliefs as well as his job description. The dream agent, according to his superiors. Seemed he didn't believe in quote demon rum unquote, no matter who put it out, a moonshiner or Seagrams."

"The perfect match of obsession and career," Amanda summarized. "So why was he so against alcohol? Any clues? Religious beliefs, maybe?"

Jenny Lee shook her head. "That's the odd thing. He was Catholic. For the most part Catholics were never as opposed to drinking as some other religions."

"What about drinking problems in his family? A parent? His wife? Himself, for that matter?"

"If so, it wasn't in any of the material I could gather."

"Where's Randy Junior these days? He should be able to tell us that and a whole lot more."

"Such as?"

"Whether or not his daddy's career was as exemplary as was reported."

Jenny Lee regarded her with puzzlement. "Why would you even suggest such a thing? There wasn't a bad word printed about him when he died, not so much as a hint of scandal."

A theory about that popped into Amanda's head at once. "If one of your agents were taking bribes, would you talk about it after he'd been shot?" Amanda speculated, warming up to the scenario that had just begun to form. Donelli, of course, would suggest the theory was just another example of liberal media bias that attempted to turn the victim into the criminal, while exonerating the person responsible. Jenny Lee, however, appeared willing to test the idea.

"Who was bribing him?" she asked.

"Maybe William," Amanda speculated as she tried her hamburger. "Maybe he'd convinced Alcott to turn a blind eye to his particular moonshine operation by giving him enough money to send Katherine to law school. William could have seen to it that Randy's record looked impressive by feeding him information about the smaller operations in the area. A bust now and then would have kept everyone at the Department happy. If a dwindling supply of moonshine kept William's business booming, so much the better."

"Okay, say I buy that for the moment," Jenny Lee conceded. "Who killed him?"

"Obviously not William, if I'm right that Randy was taking bribes to protect him. Could have been one of the angry competitors who saw it as a way to kill two birds with one stone, get rid of a Revenue agent and shut down William's business at the same time. The perfect revenge."

Jenny Lee nodded thoughtfully. "Or, if that scenario you've just created is true, it could have been Randy Junior."

Now it was Amanda's turn to look skeptical. "Why would he shoot his own father?"

"Because from all I found, Randy Junior was even more fanatical than his daddy. If he discovered that daddy had gone over to the enemy . . ." She shrugged.

"He would have been disillusioned, betrayed, and furious."

"Exactly," Jenny Lee said.

"An interesting suspect," Amanda agreed. "Better than any I've come up with. Is he still around these parts?"

"Sure is. I have his address right here."

"What's he doing now?"

Jenny Lee looked like the cat that swallowed the canary. "Now that's the interesting thing. He's a preacher." She paused dramatically to let that little tidbit sink in, then added, "He went off to seminary right after he left the Department of Revenue. Graduated top of his class. Then he organized his own little splinter group that's not affiliated with any particular church. He's very big on hellfire and damnation."

"I can hardly wait to meet him," Amanda said with a certain amount of undisguised glee.

Of course, all she had at the moment was wild speculation, but every once in a while, her intuition proved to be smack on target. Randy Blaine Alcott, however, was only part of the story.

"Tell me about the agent Willie supposedly shot ten days ago," she requested.

Jenny Lee picked up the second folder she'd brought along and opened it to the neatly typed page she'd put on top of the printouts and clippings she'd found. "Franklin Jefferson was a twenty-nine-year-old agent. African-American. He'd only been with the Department for two years, mostly working a desk. Nobody seemed quite sure what he was doing out in the field, except maybe bucking for promotion by making a big bust all on his own."

"Any family?"

"A wife, Sandra Mayotte-Jefferson. She's a nurse . . ."

Before Jenny Lee could complete the sentence, Amanda's pulse started racing. She jumped in. "At Grady Memorial."

"How'd you know that?" Jenny Lee asked in a way that confirmed it.

"Lucky guess. Which unit is she on?"

Jenny Lee shook her head. "It didn't say."

"I'll bet I know. I'd be willing to lay odds that she's on the same unit where Henry Boggins was until he died this morning at five A.M. Which shift does Mrs. Mayotte-Jefferson work?"

"Nights."

Amanda grinned at Jenny Lee. "Bingo," she said softly, shoving aside the remains of the tasteless burger. As a reward, she dug a handful of chocolate jelly beans out of her purse for dessert. She waved them under Jenny Lee's nose. "Fat-free. Any objections?"

Jenny Lee rolled her eyes heavenward. "No, Amanda. Have a ball. Just remember that you should be limiting your sugar, too. There's such a thing as gestational diabetes. Or you could make the baby all hyper."

"Oh, for pity's sake, it's one jelly bean, Jenny Lee." Amanda popped the single jelly bean into her mouth, savored the rich chocolate taste, then stood up. "Let's go."

"I'm still eating," Jenny Lee pointed out, indicating the bowlful of salad she'd barely had time to touch.

"Have 'em pack it to go. You can eat in the car."

Sighing dramatically, Jenny Lee dutifully did just that as Amanda paid the check.

"Where the hell are we going in such an all-fired hurry?" she asked as she scrambled to catch up with Amanda.

"To see Mrs. Mayotte-Jefferson, of course. I assume you have her home address."

"Of course. She's probably sound asleep, though, since she didn't get off work till seven this morning."

Amanda grinned. "I know. All the better to get nice, uncensored, self-incriminating responses."

CHAPTER
Seventeen

Sandra Mayotte-Jefferson was every bit as sleepy-eyed and befuddled after being awakened as Amanda had hoped. She clutched a navy blue terry-cloth robe tightly around her middle. It looked as if it might once have belonged to a much bigger person, namely her late husband. Silent, she stared at Amanda and Jenny Lee through the narrow crack of space that a hefty-looking chain permitted.

Taking advantage of the woman's less-than-alert state of mind, Amanda waved a press pass before her just long enough to give an impression of officialdom, but not so long that the woman could tell for certain whether she was dealing with the police. Amanda hoped that shadow of doubt would get her in the door. After that, she'd explain her presence in a more leisurely fashion.

"What's this about?" Mrs. Mayotte-Jefferson asked eventually, probably after a few more brain cells had awakened and kicked in. "Can't it wait? I just got off work a couple of hours ago. I was just getting to bed."

"I know," Amanda apologized. "But this really is important, if we're to track down the person who murdered your husband."

With obvious reluctance, the exhausted woman removed the chain and opened the door to admit them. With a halfhearted gesture, she waved them toward a living room that was so sterile looking, Amanda wondered if she wiped it down daily with antiseptic. If there was a speck of dust anywhere on those gleaming glass and chrome surfaces, it was an endangered species. Every gray pillow had been plumped and arranged precisely against the sofa's spotless white.

"You'll have to excuse me for a minute," the recent widow mumbled, finally tying the robe's belt in a manner that implied resignation to their continued presence. "If you want me to say anything that makes sense, I'll need coffee."

Amanda had no desire to sit in the cold, functional room that had been indicated. Beckoning to Jenny Lee, she tagged along behind their hostess through a dining room barely big enough for its drop-leaf table and four chairs to the doorway to the kitchen.

If Mrs. Mayotte-Jefferson was aware of their presence, she gave no indication. Mechanically, she scooped up coffee, dumped it into its filter-lined canister, shoved it into the electric coffeemaker, and flipped the switch. Only then did she turn back and spot Jenny Lee and Amanda waiting nearby, closely observing her.

"You might as well sit in here," she said grudgingly.

The kitchen was a vast improvement over the living room, although Amanda doubted that Sandra Mayotte-Jefferson had had much to do with it. The house itself had been built with a huge window over the sink and a bay window on the south side. An antique oak breakfast table and chairs sat in that sunny alcove. The bright, airy ambience and warm wood were sufficient to counteract the cold sterility of pristine white tile countertops, a gleaming linoleum floor without so much as a smudge on it, and a white porcelain sink that looked as if no dirty dish had ever been stacked there. Maybe Mrs. Mayotte-Jefferson's career as a nurse had given her a thing about germs, Amanda decided in an attempt to be charitable.

She did, however, make a decent cup of coffee. Rich and dark. Hazelnut, perhaps. Amanda sipped it gratefully, as she studied Sandra Mayotte-Jefferson's face. She had a light brown complexion, delicate features, big brown eyes, and full lips that might have been seductive, if there hadn't been such a sour downturn to them. Of course, having her twenty-nine-year-old husband killed recently might tend to make a woman bitter.

Finally she put down her cup and looked square at Amanda. "Okay, what's this all about? I thought Frank's killer was locked away."

"Maybe not," Amanda said. She repeated her identification and explained the story she was working on.

Anger flashed in the nurse's eyes. "I thought you were with the police."

"I never said that. I said I was looking into your husband's murder."

Clutching her robe together in front as if she didn't

trust the belt to hold it closed, Mrs. Mayotte-Jefferson stood up. "I want the two of you out of here now. My husband's dead. The police have the killer. That's all that matters to me. I have nothing to say to some media vulture trying to clear the man accused of the crime." She was practically quivering with rage.

An immediate expression of compassion on her face, Jenny Lee jumped up and put her arm around the woman's tensed shoulders. "I'm so sorry for your loss," she said softly, playing good cop to Amanda's typically assertive bad cop deportment. "May I call you Sandra?"

After some sort of internal tug-of-war, Mrs. Mayotte-Jefferson's stiff posture began to relax. She gave a curt, obviously reluctant nod.

"Sandra, I can understand your wanting to forget all about what happened, but you wouldn't want an innocent man to be convicted, would you?" Jenny Lee said in a low, coaxing drawl. "That's not what Frank would have wanted, is it?"

At the mention of her husband, the woman's face crumpled. She covered it with both hands, whispering, "Oh, God, oh, God, oh, God."

Jenny Lee guided her back into her chair. She poured her more coffee, added a heavy dollop of cream and two teaspoons of sugar. "Here, drink this."

Amanda thought a shot of Kahlúa might have been more effective, but the sweetened coffee seemed to settle down their very reluctant source. Since Jenny Lee appeared to be on a roll, Amanda sat back and waited to see what tactic her assistant had up her sleeve to get the woman talking.

"You know," Jenny Lee began softly, "I was real impressed with how brave Frank was going out there all alone."

Sandra's head snapped up, her expression incredulous. "Brave? He got himself shot. We've got a baby due in six months and now my husband is dead, because he wanted to play hero." Her escalating indignation quickly gave way to another bout of heaving sobs.

Listening to her, Amanda's hand instinctively went to her own belly. She thought of that instant at the Babcocks' when a shotgun blast had come within inches of her husband. Suddenly she thought she knew exactly how Sandra Mayotte-Jefferson must be feeling—the anger, the grief, the bitterness, all warring inside her. Impulsively, she reached for the other woman's hand and held it tightly. To her surprise Sandra didn't pull away. Maybe she sensed that Amanda was an unexpected ally.

"I'm expecting a baby, too," Amanda explained. "I can imagine how alone and furious you must be feeling."

The other woman's gaze homed in on her. "When?" she asked, her voice still choked.

"When what?"

"When is your baby due?"

"October, a month after yours."

The nurse sighed. "It's so hard. We'd tried before. I've had two miscarriages. This time, though, everything seems to be going smoothly. The doctor's very encouraged, especially since I didn't lose the baby after Frank was killed. He feels if I didn't miscarry during all that stress, then I probably won't."

"Then I'm very sorry I've added to the stress," Amanda said with complete sincerity. "But something went terribly wrong that day and I want to know what it was. I've talked to Willie Ashford. He swears he was nowhere near his property when the shooting took place."

"Of course, he would say that," the other woman retorted. "You don't think his attorney is going to let him admit it, do you? Besides, I know all about that grandfather of his. He did the same thing, picked off a Revenue agent as if he were no more than an irritating nuisance."

She sounded as if she thought there were some sort of genetic explanation for the two incidents. "There's some question about that case as well," Amanda countered.

"Not according to the police or the Department of Revenue. The story's a legend around there."

"Maybe they were a little too anxious to wrap things up," she said, hoping that the woman would catch the implication that she, too, was too eager to lay blame and put what had happened to her husband behind her. "Couldn't you answer just a few questions for me? See where the answers lead us?"

Sandra scanned Amanda's face. "You really believe they have the wrong man?"

Amanda nodded.

With a weary sigh, Sandra turned to Jenny. "Make another pot of coffee, will you? It looks like we're going to be here a while."

Jenny Lee beamed at her approvingly and set out to

make the coffee, while Amanda began asking questions. She began with the most innocuous.

"I read that Frank had mostly been working a desk job. Is that right?"

"Yes, but he wanted field work in the worst way."

"How was he going about getting it?"

The question seemed to puzzle the other woman. "By doing his job, I suppose, and then some."

"Was he spending a lot of spare time working? Maybe going out to hunt for stills? Or following up on leads he should have turned over to someone else?"

"He worked all the time. Nights. Weekends. As for going out to hunt for stills, if he was, he didn't admit it to me. I would have told him he was playing with fire. Everybody knows what happens when a black man gets too uppity. Frank knew it better than most."

"Meaning?" Amanda prodded. "Had he had trouble at work?"

"Trouble? That's putting it mildly. Frank had a boss who had flat-out told him he would make it into the field over his dead body. He said a lot more, the usual racial slurs when nobody was likely to overhear, but that was the gist of it."

"What's his name?"

"Cutter Haines," Sandra said. "The most obnoxious SOB I've ever run across. I told Frank as long as Haines was in charge, he might as well forget all about a promotion or field work. I wanted him to get out, but Frank wanted to succeed right where he was. He said if he quit just because his boss didn't like him, he'd spend the rest of his life running from tough situations."

"He sounds like a man of conviction," Amanda said. "I would have liked him."

"What good are those fine convictions now?" his wife shot back. "He's a dead man."

The anger and indignation suggested to Amanda that Sandra Mayotte-Jefferson might easily get riled enough to take justice into her own hands if she felt Henry Boggins had had something to do with her husband's death. So far, though, nothing she'd said so much as hinted of a connection.

"May I run some names past you?" Amanda asked. "Maybe you'll recognize somebody your husband might have mentioned."

"You can try, but I doubt it will do any good. Frank kept his work pretty confidential. He was very sensitive to the possibility that he could be accused of leaking word of impending busts. He wouldn't have put it past Cutter Haines to frame him."

Cutter Haines was beginning to sound like the South's worst nightmare, a bigoted good ole boy who hadn't realized that times had changed. Amanda edged him to the top of her interview list. Meanwhile, she wanted Sandra's reaction to the other players, particularly Boggins.

She began with the least likely names. "Salty Tufts?"

"Never heard of him," Sandra said at once.

"Babcock? Steven, maybe? Or Tommy?"

Sandra slowly shook her head. "I don't think so."

"You sound as if you're not certain. Could you have heard those names?"

"No," she said slowly, then added more emphatically, "No, I'd never heard Frank mention them."

"How about Henry Boggins?"

A flicker of recognition flashed in Sandra's brown eyes, immediately followed by alarm. "What does Henry Boggins have to do with this?"

"Then you do know him?"

"He was a patient at Grady. He died this morning."

"Was he your patient?"

She shook her head. "He was for the first few weeks he was in the hospital, but I was switched to the other end of the unit last night. I heard about his death when we gave report this morning just before going off duty." She leveled a puzzled look straight at Amanda. "You didn't answer me before. What does he have to do with this?"

"Willie Ashford . . ."

"The man accused of killing Frank?"

"Exactly. Willie was Henry's great-grandson. Henry hated Willie's grandfather. There is a very good possibility that Henry framed William Ashford for that murder more than fifty years ago. And I can't help but wondering if he might not have had something to do with Frank's death as well."

Amanda watched Sandra's reaction closely. She saw the precise moment when the woman made the connection between that theory and Jenny Lee and Amanda's presence in her kitchen.

"You think I knew about some connection and that

I had something to do with that old man's dying?" she said, looking shocked. Then suddenly a smile spread across her face and then she was laughing.

Hysterical laughter? Amanda wondered. A guilty overreaction?

"Oh, you must be kidding," she said at last. When neither of them joined in her amusement, she insisted, "I had no idea about his connection to Willie Ashford. He was quick-witted and lonelier than any man should be at his age. I sat in his room night after night when he couldn't sleep and played checkers with him. This morning when I heard he'd died, I cried. Ask anyone on the unit."

"When you were playing checkers with him, did he ever talk about moonshine or the past or his family?"

"Not really. He used to talk to me about the baby and about Frank. He was real sweet that way."

Amanda seized on that. "He was asking about Frank before your husband's death? Could he have been pumping you for information?"

"Absolutely not. It wasn't that way at all. He was not pumping me for information," Sandra said adamantly. "He was a kind, lonely old man who liked to talk, especially in the middle of the night when he couldn't sleep. Do you think he conspired to get onto my unit at the hospital? That pneumonia of his wasn't faked, I can tell you that. He was in ICU for days before we got him on our floor. He never had any visitors that I heard about, so I don't know how he could have passed along this information you say he was pumping me for. The truth of it was that I felt sorry for him."

"Look, I know this is painful for you to consider, but please don't dismiss the possibility of his involvement too lightly," Amanda pleaded. "How did he act after Frank's death?"

"Like I said, when I got back from funeral leave yesterday I was assigned to the other end of the unit. I had one very sick patient over there that I couldn't leave. I only saw Henry for about five minutes when I was on break. He said he was sorry about my loss." She glared at Amanda as if to dare her to contradict Henry's sincerity. "I believed him."

"What time was this?"

"About two-fifteen in the morning," she said without hesitation.

"He died at five," Amanda reminded her. She allowed the implication to hang in the air for a minute. Two minutes. Nothing. Sandra Mayotte-Jefferson was either telling the truth or she was one tough cookie. She never so much as blinked. Her hands, lightly clasped around her coffee cup, were steady as a rock. It seemed unlikely they were going to shake her story with further questioning, at least not without evidence.

Amanda stood up. "Thank you for your time. I know this wasn't easy for you. I hope you understand why I had to ask these questions."

"Everybody's got a job to do," Sandra conceded. "Maybe you hate asking lousy questions almost as much as I hate giving shots. Will you let me know if you find out anything?"

"I will call you before one word gets into print," Amanda promised. "One last thing, how easy would it have been for an outsider to get onto the unit in the middle of the night? Is there much security?"

"It would have been easy enough to walk onto the floor, but chances are somebody would have noticed a stranger who was around for long."

"How long would it take to tamper with an IV?"

"Less than a minute, if they knew what they were doing."

"Thanks, again. You've been a big help," Amanda said.

At the front door, Sandra Mayotte-Jefferson's strength seemed to falter. Tears once again sprang up in her eyes, but she lifted her chin a defiant notch. "You know, Ms. Roberts, it wouldn't break my heart if you found some way to nail Cutter Haines."

Amanda winked at her. "He's my next stop."

CHAPTER

Eighteen

"What did you think of Sandra?" Jenny Lee asked the minute they were back in the car. "I thought she was sweet."

Amanda shrugged. "Sweet might be a stretch, but I believed her. I believed she had no idea that Boggins might be connected to the case. I believed her when she said she liked him. And, to my everlasting regret, I believed her when she swore she didn't kill him." She glanced over at Jenny Lee. "What about you? Did you pick up on any vibes?"

"I believe she's got one nasty grudge against Cutter Haines. Is it possible for any man in a state position like his to be as deep-down rotten as she painted him?"

"I imagine it is," Amanda said. "Some people are naturally good at covering their biases when it counts. They pick their targets, counting on the fact that the person won't fight back. Racial harassment isn't so different from sexual harassment, and we know how often that goes on with nobody taking action."

An hour later, after being detained by a thick-necked drill sergeant of a secretary, they were ushered into Cutter Haines's office at the Alcohol–Tobacco Tax unit of the Georgia Department of Revenue on Washington Street. A more unlikely good ole boy stereotype Amanda had never met.

No more than forty, with just the first faint touches of silver in his neatly-trimmed, dark brown hair, he was handsome, tanned, and fit. He wore a suit that Amanda would have bet cost upwards of five hundred dollars and had some Italian designer label stitched in the back. An embroidered monogram on his expensive-looking white shirt peeked out from beneath the jacket's cuff. A gold Rolex—or an outstanding knockoff—circled his wrist. State salaries must have improved since the last time Amanda had examined the budget. Either that or Cutter Haines had few other living expenses, which permitted him to indulge his taste in fancy clothes.

He nodded politely as Amanda and Jenny Lee introduced themselves, lingered a little too long over his handshake with Jenny Lee, then ushered them into chairs in front of his desk. Then, rather than retreating to his position of power behind that desk, he perched on its corner, his knees scant inches from Jenny Lee's. No doubt he meant to imply openness and informality. Jenny Lee looked as if she wanted to squirm out of his way.

"What can I do for you ladies?" he drawled as if they'd come for tea and a chat, rather than information.

"It was good of you to see us without an appointment," Amanda said.

"Always happy to oblige the media."

Amanda figured he probably would have preferred a TV camera, but maybe getting to ogle Jenny Lee was a satisfactory trade-off in his view. "First, I'd like a little background on moonshining in Georgia these days," she said. "Is it considered a big problem?"

He seemed disappointed that the question wasn't a little more personal. Or perhaps he was just sorry that he and Jenny Lee weren't alone. At any rate, he responded a bit grudgingly.

"I wouldn't call it significant. Moderate's more like it. It happens." Responding to their attention, he warmed to his topic. "And since the price of sugar dropped and the tax on alcohol went up, it's been increasing. Naturally the government disapproves of any level of activity that cuts into the state's rightful revenues." He beamed as if he'd just completed a talk to a class of enthusiastic sixth-graders. He glanced at the two of them as if awaiting applause.

"How interesting," Jenny Lee murmured dutifully and twisted to the side in an attempt to put a little space between their knees.

Almost as if he were unconscious of the action, Cutter Haines shifted right along with her. Check. And checkmate. Amanda figured it would take perhaps two more moves in their minuet before Jenny Lee hauled off and slugged him.

"Mr. Haines," Amanda began, hoping to draw his

attention away from her assistant before the interview got sidetracked by a brawl.

"Cutter," he drawled automatically, barely looking at her as he said it. His gaze had locked on Jenny Lee's mouth and showed no signs of straying.

"Mr. Haines," she repeated, then waited until she had his full attention again. "Exactly how much revenue are we talking here?"

"The Georgia tax on liquor is round about two dollars and sixty cents a gallon. The federal government's is twelve-fifty. You got a two-thousand-gallon still making moonshine in the woods, it adds up."

"How many stills do you suppose there are?"

"No way I can give you a precise count. If we knew about all of 'em, we'd blow 'em up. A year or so back we took out thirty-nine the whole fiscal year, nowhere near the days when we were taking out a hundred to two hundred a month."

He glanced at Jenny Lee, probably hoping for some hint that he'd impressed her. She nodded politely.

Amanda used his latest distraction to suggest a new topic. "Tell me a little about Frank Jefferson," she said.

That got his attention. "An unfortunate tragedy," he said, turning her way and gazing directly into her eyes. "A terrible loss."

Amanda thought the sudden sincerity appeared feigned, but maybe that was because she was expecting him to try to tap dance around his real feelings, if what Sandra Mayotte-Jefferson had told them was true.

"What kind of employee was he?"

"Excellent," he said with an alacrity born of having answered the question dozens of times at the time of the murder. "Always willing to do whatever was asked of him and then some. In fact, that ambition was no doubt at the root of the actions that cost him his life."

"Had you assigned him to be out in the field on the day he was killed?"

"No, ma'am. He'd gotten a tip, I suppose. Happens all the time around here. Procedure was, he should have passed it along. We've got agents up the wazoo all over the state whose job it is to handle things like that, but Frank had something to prove. He wanted a promotion. I suppose he thought that taking the initiative, making that bust on his own would prove he had what it takes to move up."

"Would he have been promoted, if he'd succeeded?"

Haines adjusted the cuffs on his fancy suit before answering. "No, in all honesty, I have to say it would probably have gotten him fired."

"Even if he'd taken out a still and shut down a bootlegger?" Jenny Lee said. "Wasn't that everyone's goal around here?"

"Well, of course it was," he said hurriedly, obviously reacting to her hint of disapproval.

To Amanda it sounded as if he wanted to placate the little woman he'd unintentionally riled. Maybe he saw his hopes for a date disappearing. She could have told him he couldn't tap dance fast enough to have a crack at Jenny Lee. Not as long as Larry Carter was in her life. Even ignoring the age factor, Haines and the photographer were light years apart in style and personality.

"Did you have it in for Frank Jefferson for some reason?" Amanda asked, hoping he was once again distracted enough by his ill-concealed fascination with Jenny Lee to blurt out an honest answer.

"Hmm?" he murmured.

Then, as the implication apparently sank in, his head snapped around for the second time during the meeting. At this rate, he'd suffer a whiplash.

"Of course not," he said. "Why would you even ask such a thing?"

"How many African-American employees do you have?"

"You'd have to check with personnel for a count," he said stiffly. "I really don't see . . . "

"What's their average tenure?" Amanda interrupted. Perhaps she could goad him into making a slip.

"That's a personnel matter."

"Are they promoted at the same pace as whites?"

His jaw set and his eyes began to glitter. "Honey, are you trying to turn this into some sort of racist thing? Because if you are, you are way off base and you might as well walk out of here right now."

Jenny Lee blanched, her gaze suddenly anxious as she awaited Amanda's reply. Amanda fought for calm.

"First of all, I am not your *honey*," she said quietly. "And second, I'm not trying to turn this into anything. I'm just looking for answers. Facts will do nicely. If the facts happen to add up to racial bias, then I'll report it. If they don't, then it will never become an issue. Are we clear?"

"Perfectly," he said tightly. He seemed to be grinding

his teeth. "Perhaps you would like to assemble your *facts* through our public relations person. I'll make him available." He reached for a business card, scrawled a name on the back, then picked up the phone.

"In a minute," Amanda said. She was not about to allow him to foist her off on some minion, who would spout the Department line. "First, I would like a straightforward answer from you about what you think happened on the Ashford property."

"I think that Frank Jefferson went sticking his nose in where it didn't belong, without knowing proper procedure, without notifying his superiors of his intentions, and got a shotgun blast in the stomach for his trouble," he said heatedly.

He sucked in a breath as if forcing himself to calm down. "Do I regret the man's death? Of course. Do I think he was a hero, killed in the line of duty? I'll admit flat out that I have some trouble with that concept." He glowered at her. "Anything else, Ms. Roberts?"

Amanda smiled at him. "Not a thing. You can make that call for a Department spokesman now." She handed him a business card. "Have him call me at the magazine with the personnel information I requested. If I'm not there, he can give it to Jenny Lee."

Haines cast one last lustful look at Jenny Lee. "Perhaps I should have your card as well."

"No need," Jenny Lee said cheerfully. "It's the same number."

"And your home number, in case it's after hours when the information is assembled?"

"There's an answering machine on at the office."

He seemed to accept defeat gracefully enough. He didn't walk them to the door, but within seconds after they'd exited, Amanda heard it click quietly shut behind them. And, if she wasn't mistaken, the lock turned as well.

She lingered in the vicinity of the secretary's desk for as long as she could, her gaze locked on the phone. Sure enough, a line lit up almost at once. Amanda doubted he was that anxious to call for his media person.

"You know," Jenny Lee said thoughtfully as she and Amanda walked back to the car. "Do you recall that phrase *a wolf in sheep's clothing*?"

"Yes."

"I think whoever came up with it must have met Cutter Haines."

Amanda was almost sure of it. It might be possible to dress a *gen-u-ine* good ole boy up in an expensive, sophisticated suit, but there didn't seem to be a darn thing that could be done about the stereotypical functioning of his brain.

Given the way her energy level was suddenly flagging, Amanda figured she had about one more interview left in her. She opted for Randy Blaine Alcott Jr., son of the first murdered Revenue agent.

She handed her car keys to Jenny Lee. "You drive."

"Me? You want me to drive your car? Why?"

The suspicion was natural enough. Amanda rarely let

anyone touch her precious convertible. "Because I'm liable to fall asleep halfway there. It'll be better if I'm not behind the wheel when that happens."

Jenny Lee looked doubtful. "Maybe you ought to go home instead."

"Not until I've talked to Alcott. I have to get the big picture and I have to do it now."

"Why the hurry?"

Amanda thought of Miss Martha waiting impatiently for answers, waiting for a release from what she viewed as a long-overdue obligation so that she could die in peace. She couldn't very well tell Jenny Lee that. "Because I want to get this story in before Oscar changes his mind and before Carol runs to tattle to Joel. I don't need the additional flak."

"Okay," Jenny Lee said, accepting the keys with obvious reluctance. "But if you start telling me how to drive before we leave the parking lot, I'm pulling over."

"Jenny Lee, I do not tell you how to drive."

"Amanda, you tell everyone how to drive." She huffed. "Like you're some kind of expert. How many tickets did you have at last count?"

"Just drive, okay?" Given her urge to remind Jenny Lee to watch for oncoming cars as she was backing out of the parking space, Amanda decided it was just as well she was exhausted. She closed her eyes and promptly fell asleep.

When she awoke an hour later, they were pulling into the parking lot of a big old barn of a building that looked more like an auction warehouse than a church. Beige siding was topped off by a sloping tin roof. Small, standard sash windows dotted the sides. Double doors opened onto the gravel parking lot. There was no steeple. Nor was there a speck of stained glass. In fact, the only thing identifying the structure as a church was the hand-lettered, fading sign on the front lawn: CHURCH OF OUR LORD'S BRETHREN. RANDALL BLAINE ALCOTT, PASTOR.

"Exactly what religion is Pastor Alcott?" Amanda asked.

Jenny Lee shrugged. "My guess is he made it up."

"Is that legal?"

"I don't know why not. Nobody ever said faith was restricted to Baptists, Presbyterians, etcetera." She glanced at Amanda worriedly. "Did they?"

"I'm a little lax on my understanding of such things. The last time I was in a church I was waiting for Donelli to show up for our wedding. He didn't and his best friend was killed by a bomb blast. It rattled my beliefs."

"Maybe Pastor Alcott can change that," Jenny suggested.

Amanda looked over the setting and shook her head. "I don't think I'll be holding my breath for that." Then again, she was fairly sure miracles had taken place in far less impressive locales.

They found the pastor in a cramped, cluttered office at the side of the church. For some reason, probably that Junior tacked onto his name, Amanda had been fooled into thinking that Alcott would be a young man. In fact, he was past seventy. If she'd done the proper calculations back to the date of his daddy's murder, she would have realized that he had to be well past his prime.

Still there was something very charismatic about his

lively, vivid blue eyes. They burned in a narrow face that had been weathered by sun and time. The instant he spotted them, he rose and came forward, hands held out to encompass theirs in a gesture that was less a polite greeting than a blessing. Despite the heat in that tiny office, he was dressed in a black suit and white shirt with a tie knotted at his throat.

"Praise be, sisters. What can I do for you?" He had a gravelly, powerful voice that could probably reach the rafters when he chose.

"We'd like to talk, if you have the time," Amanda said.

"There is always time for the Lord's work. Would you like to go into the church and pray?"

"No, this will be just fine," Amanda said and practically bolted to a vacant chair beside his littered desk. Jenny Lee took up watch from the sofa on the opposite wall.

"Can I offer you something, then?" He gestured toward a cabinet on which an electric coffeepot was perking away. He reached for a plate, peeled away the foil covering and held it out. The aroma of chocolate filled the air.

"A brownie, perhaps? Fresh from the oven. Mildred Ives brings 'em over every few days about this time, bless her soul."

Amanda didn't have to be asked twice. She reached for the still-warm brownie, took one bite, and practically swooned. If Pastor Alcott had wanted to bribe her, he'd picked exactly the right offering. Mildred Ives deserved all the blessings he could heap on her.

"I'll wrap another one for you to take along home," he said.

"Really, I couldn't," Amanda said.

"Of course you can," he contradicted, folding one tidily into a paper napkin and handing it to her before offering the plate to Jenny Lee. "Nothing makes Mildred happier than having someone appreciate her baking. It's wasted on me. I'm allergic to chocolate."

"You've never told her that?" Amanda asked.

"Absolutely not," he said, a twinkle in his eyes. "I find I have an increase in visitors on the days Mildred bakes. Much as I'd like to believe people worry more about their souls on those days, I suspect it's Mildred's brownies they come for. Now, tell me why you're here."

"Actually it's a subject you might find rather painful," Amanda admitted.

Pastor Alcott stopped where he was, plate in hand, and regarded her expectantly.

"I wanted to ask about your father's death," she said quietly.

The benevolent, jovial expression on his face washed away. With that the plate of brownies fell from his hand and clattered to the floor. His mouth began to work, but no words came out. He looked as if he were having some sort of a spell.

Jenny Lee jumped to her feet and rushed to his side. "Are you okay?"

Still silent, he nodded and made his way to his chair, ignoring the mess on the floor. Since he didn't seem to mind its being there, Amanda ignored it as well.

"I'm sorry," she said. "I should have prepared you. I shouldn't have asked out of the blue like that."

He waved off the apology. "You could not have prepared me for a question like that," he said. Those penetrating eyes of his burned into her. "You see, since 1942, I have had no father."

"Because that was the year he died," Amanda said, faintly puzzled by something in his voice, an odd note she couldn't identify.

"No," he told her tersely. "Because that was the year I discovered that my father was a son of Satan."

CHAPTER

Nineteen

Jenny Lee looked as if the devil himself had joined them in the room. She turned positively pale following Pastor Alcott's quiet declaration labeling his father a "son of Satan." Amanda felt a little unnerved herself. She fully expected the old man to hold up a cross to ward off evil spirits if his father's name or existence were mentioned again. Unfortunately, she was just getting started.

"Would you tell me what happened back then? I'd like to know everything you remember about his murder," she said.

The fierce, burning light in the old man's eyes grew even more intense. There was a bit of a fanatical cast to it. "I vowed I would never speak of that time again."

"Please," Amanda cajoled. "I really need to understand what led up to your father's death."

"Evil, plain and simple," he said succinctly. "I really

don't care to discuss this any further. I have no idea who you are or why you're here."

"I'm trying to save a young man who may spend the rest of his life in prison for a crime he didn't commit. Surely you would want to see justice done," Amanda said.

His gaze narrowed. "And digging around in my past will accomplish that? I can't see how dredging up so much evil from half a century ago can help anything."

Pastor Alcott seemed to be stuck on a single track, one so upsetting to him that it didn't seem likely to lead to productive answers. Amanda tried to steer him off on a less controversial course, hoping he wouldn't just decide to toss them out the door. "Your father was an agent for the Department of Revenue, is that right?"

"He was paid to rid the community of sin. That much is true," he conceded eventually. He looked as if every word he spoke, every memory, pained him.

"Everything I've read indicated he did his job exceedingly well," she said, wondering if he would contradict her, wondering if he would lay out her own theory that his father had been taking bribes from William Ashford. "You worked with him. Surely you know how effective he was."

"He was . . . " Alcott's voice faltered. He looked even more deeply troubled by the old wounds that were being ripped open again.

Or was he hiding something? Was he searching for words that would answer her questions, but keep his secrets? Judging from the agony in his eyes and his tight jaw, she feared he might clam up at any second. Maybe she'd better direct him away from Department of Revenue business and onto more personal ground, after all. Or maybe there was no safe line of questioning when it came to this particular father–son relationship. She'd just have to keep switching gears, hoping to keep him off balance enough that he'd answer at least one out of every two or three questions. Sooner or later the revelations would have to mount up.

"Let's go about this another way. Was he a good father?" she inquired, lowering her voice to a soft coaxing note.

Alcott's face twisted into an angry mask. "He made a mockery of the word *father*. He was rigid, harsh. There was no comfort, no compassion in him." He shuddered. "I can't talk about this, I told you. I won't talk about it."

Amanda spoke as if he hadn't warned her off again. "Yet you followed in his footsteps," she pointed out, unrelenting. "You went to work for the Department of Revenue, just as he had. On some level, you must have admired him a great deal, perhaps because he was so good at his job."

He sighed heavily, apparently giving in to her pressure. "I was seeking his approval. Always, all my life, I tried in vain for his approval." He sounded weary and far away, as if he were back in those terrible, lonely days he was describing.

He glanced at Amanda, back in the present. "Withholding love, that is not the Lord's way," he said with fervor. "Suffer the little children to come unto me. That was the Lord's command."

"At some point, though, your desire for your father's approval apparently died."

"I hated him," he said categorically.

"Why? What happened? Can you recall when things changed for you?" As powerful as it was, she resisted the urge to mention betrayal. She didn't want to put words in his mouth. She wanted his emotions, his exact memories, in the article, not her own.

He gazed at some far-off point, as if on some level he'd left the room and gone back to that earlier time. "Two weeks before he died, I made a discovery."

Even now, his hands shook as he recalled it, Amanda noticed. She was trembling herself, but with anticipation. He was on the verge of making a critical revelation. She could feel it. She waited, silent.

"He was planning to betray me," he said in a whisper.

His voice was so low and filled with anguish she could barely hear him. "How?" she asked.

Suddenly he blinked, as if coming out of a trance. He stared at her and visibly withdrew. "No more."

"Please, tell me how he planned to betray you," she pleaded.

"This is private, a matter between me and my father, between my father and the Lord. It is not for mortals to dissect and judge. And it surely can have no bearing whatsoever on the fate of this young man you are trying to help. I wish him godspeed and I will pray for his soul, but that is all I can offer you or him."

Amanda knew from the forbidding expression on his face that she had lost. There would be no more answers, not today. At least, not about Randy Blaine Alcott Senior. It was time to try another tack.

"Did you know Franklin Jefferson?" she asked. It was a longshot, but perhaps he had stayed in touch with the Department even after he'd left. Perhaps he had even continued to pass along tips about hidden stills that should be closed down. No doubt he would have viewed such tips as part of his Christian duty.

"The Revenue agent who was shot? I read about it," he admitted.

"Did you know him?"

"No, we never met."

Amanda wondered at the cautious wording. A simple denial would have been a straightforward *no*. Adding that he and Jefferson had never met hinted that they had been acquainted in some way—on the phone, perhaps. Or was she looking for clues that simply weren't there? She couldn't be sure. The entire interview had spooked her.

He rose. "If there's nothing else, sisters, I should get back to preparing my sermon."

Jenny Lee looked more than willing to bolt, but Amanda didn't budge." I just have one or two more questions," she said. "A few names, actually. Did you know Henry Boggins?"

"He attended church here on occasion."

Startled, Amanda lost her train of thought for a second. If Boggins had attended Alcott's church, would the pastor have been duty-bound to visit him in the hospital? "Did you see him before he passed away at Grady Memorial?"

"Several times."

"Today?"

He shook his head. "No, the last time was several days ago. To be frank, I was expecting to see him back in church this Sunday. Praise the Lord, he had made a miraculous recovery. I was stunned to learn of his death when the hospital called earlier today."

His reaction seemed genuine, Amanda decided. She tried out a few more names. "Do you know the Babcocks?"

He hesitated, his expression thoughtful, then shook his head. "I don't believe so."

"Kenny Loftis?"

Another considering pause, then, "No."

"Cutter Haines."

"No," he said at once.

The last seemed too rushed, especially when Amanda thought she caught a flicker of panic in his eyes before he looked away. "You're sure about Haines? He's the head of the Department of Revenue Alcohol–Tobacco Tax unit now. Maybe you've seen him around out here."

He shook his head, still avoiding her gaze. "No, I'm sure I would have recalled."

"Any idea who's running stills in this area?"

"I would be the last person to whom anyone would mention a thing like that," he said with a faint hint of amusement in his voice.

"Don't you keep your eyes and ears open, though? I would think such old habits would die hard."

"Not in my case."

Amanda had to fight to keep a note of exasperation

out of her voice. "One last thing," she said. "What made you decide to become a preacher?"

He assumed a pious posture, hands folded as if in prayer. "It was my calling."

"But before that your calling was to be a Revenue agent," Amanda reminded him. "Did the change have anything to do with your father's death?"

Vivid blue eyes seared her. "I believe I said there would be no more on this topic."

Defeated, Amanda stood up and held out her hand. "Thank you for your time," she said as he folded her hand in his own. His was icy. An indication of nervousness, perhaps?

Outside, she drew in a deep breath of fresh air, realizing for the first time that she had begun to feel choked in Alcott's office, as if all the oxygen had been used up in that claustrophobic little room once Satan had been introduced as a topic of conversation. Jenny Lee shivered beside her.

"That man gave me the creeps," Jenny Lee said.

"He didn't exactly warm my heart, either," Amanda conceded. "I wonder what he's hiding."

"Maybe he's not hiding anything. Maybe he's just a twisted old man, who's using religion to salve his own conscience."

"Why would he need to do that, if he weren't hiding some guilty sin?" Amanda persisted.

"Such as?"

"Who knows? Maybe he used to sell moonshine himself. Maybe he fornicated with a woman other than his wife. I can't begin to imagine what makes a man like that tick. Talk about dysfunctional families, though. The Alcotts—father and son, anyway—strike me as being about as dysfunctional as anyone I've ever met, if Randy's recollections are to be believed."

"Do you think Randy Junior was involved with the murders in some way?"

Amanda shrugged. "I don't know. But I would bet my last dime that he knows a hell of a lot more about moonshining in these parts than he told us."

"How do you intend to get him to talk?"

"Gather enough evidence so that he can't deny it." She sighed. "Whatever *it* is."

"Where to now?"

"Home," Amanda said at once. "I'll drop you off downtown, then head out to the farm. I suddenly have an urgent need to see my husband and my son. Maybe we can spend the evening eating popcorn and playing Monopoly."

Jenny Lee looked as if Amanda had suggested she planned to take up knitting. "Monopoly?"

"Why not?"

"I just can't see it."

"Okay, maybe we'll get on the computer and break into somebody's files together."

Jenny Lee grinned. "Now that I can imagine."

It was already dusk by the time Amanda reached the farm. She found Donelli at the stove stirring a pot of homemade spaghetti sauce. The room was heady with garlic and oregano and tomatoes. She drew in a deep breath and savored it before going over to slip her arms around her husband's waist from behind so she could savor his clean, masculine scent and the solid, reassuring comfort of just touching him.

"You feel so good," she whispered against his back. She felt grounded again, centered. It was amazing, the effect the man had on her.

"Rough day?" he asked.

"Weird day."

He picked up a bowl of cleaned mushrooms and an onion and handed them to her over his shoulder. "Sit over there and chop these and tell me about it."

Reluctantly, she released him, took the mushrooms and onion, and set them on the table. She washed her hands to rid herself of the day's grime, if not its accumulation of troubling thoughts.

"Boggins is dead," she said, as she pulled a knife out of the drawer and returned to the table.

"You're kidding. How?"

"I'm waiting to find out. I had to get Jim Harrison to talk to the medical examiner. More than likely he had to talk to Willie, too, to try to stop the burial, so an autopsy could be performed."

"That reminds me. Willie called a little while ago. He wants to see us as soon as possible."

Amanda started up. "Why didn't you say so?"

He shot her a quelling look that had her sitting down again. "Because we are not going back through that door tonight," he said emphatically. "You need to get some rest. I told him we'd be by in the morning."

Amanda was too tired to argue. "Did he say what he wanted?"

"He said something about an unexpected visitor, but he wouldn't say who."

"Did he sound upset? Worried? Angry?"

Donelli laughed at the barrage of options. "Amanda, I don't know him well enough to do an instant analysis of his mood, but offhand I'd say he sounded more surprised than anything."

"Hmm," she said, thoughtful. "Wonder who it could have been? Maybe it was just Jim Harrison to ask him about stopping the burial."

"He'll tell us in the morning." He glanced back at her. "How are those mushrooms coming?"

She glanced at the untouched bowlful in front of her. "Hang on. They'll be ready in a minute. Where's Pete?"

"Upstairs."

"Doing his homework?" Amanda asked doubtfully.

"Are you kidding? I think he's in the nursery measuring."

"Measuring for what?"

"He wants to do wallpaper this weekend. He says you mentioned wanting wallpaper, rather than paint. He seems to be torn between football helmets and ducks."

"He's already looked at paper?"

"I believe he was able to talk his friend Michael's mother into taking them by one of those hardware superstores this afternoon after school." Donelli grinned. "Don't panic. He brought home samples. I understand you and I are to be given some say in the decision."

"How thoughtful," Amanda said, but she was grinning. "Obviously we're not going to have to worry about sibling rivalry."

"Actually we may have to worry more about getting to spend any time with this kid ourselves. Pete has plans."

"Oh?"

"I am under the impression that his baby brother . . . "

"What if it's a girl?"

"I don't think he's accepted that possibility."

"Uh-huh."

"Anyway, he and his baby brother are going to do stuff together every day after school. He seems to feel that baby Joe—his choice, not mine—will be capable of playing most sports by the age of two."

Amanda regarded Joe worriedly. "Do you think maybe we ought to get Pete a puppy to take some of the pressure off the baby? The kid will have performance anxiety or something."

"No, my guess is that the first time Pete has to change a diaper, he'll have second thoughts about wanting to be pals with his brother or sister before he or she reaches kindergarten at the earliest."

Pete sauntered into the kitchen just in time to overhear that. "Hey, don't be worrying about no diapers. I can handle that." He plucked a wad of wallpaper samples out of his back pocket and tossed them on the table in front of Amanda. "What do you think?"

He kept his gaze on her expectantly as she smoothed the samples out and spread them over the table. There seemed to be a preponderance of designs for little boys. The duck pattern was about as neutral as they got.

"I like the ducks," she said, but without much enthusiasm. "Of course, you don't have anything here for a little girl."

"A girl?" He said it cautiously, as if testing out a foreign concept.

"It could be, you know."

"I suppose," he conceded with apparent reluctance. "When are you gonna know?"

"There's a test, amniocentesis, I'll probably have done in another couple of months. That would tell us, if we want to know. Or the doctor might be able to pick it up on a sonogram." She glanced at Joe. "Do we want to know the baby's sex?"

Pete didn't wait for Joe's answer. "Sure we do," he said at once. "How else will I be able to pick out wallpaper and stuff? I can't make the room all pink and frilly and have it turn out to be a boy. It could mess the kid up for life."

Amanda grinned. "I see the problem. Joe, what do you think?"

"I think if we're ever going to eat, I'm going to have to chop those damned mushrooms myself." He sat down, dumped the mushrooms on the cutting board, and chopped them in less than a minute with the kind of deft skill that came from practice. The onion was diced almost as quickly. "See, Amanda, it's not so difficult."

"Especially when I have you around to do it," she agreed.

"You are hopeless," he said, but he dropped a kiss

on her forehead as he returned to the stove. "Pete, set the table, okay?"

Pete obeyed without a word of complaint. He had fallen into the evening routine almost at once after coming to live with them. In fact, he seemed to savor every tiny act that hinted of the kind of normal family life he had missed during his first thirteen years.

During dinner Amanda shared more of the information she had gathered during the day. Though Donelli had several observations, Pete remained abnormally silent.

"Pete, are you okay?" Amanda asked eventually.

"I was just thinking," he said, regarding her worriedly. "Maybe you should stop with this stuff till after the baby's born."

"An interesting idea," Donelli chimed in quietly.

Amanda scowled at her new son. "Traitor."

"Well, geez, Amanda, you get into an awful lot of trouble sometimes," Pete reminded her. "And it won't be long before you'll be too big to run very fast. Michael's mom can barely squeeze behind the steering wheel."

"Thanks for the vote of confidence."

"Face it," he persisted. "You weren't all that fast to begin with."

"Okay, here's the deal. I am not going to stop asking questions. I am not going to quit my job. I'm not going to take an early maternity leave." She shoved her chair back from the table, stood up, and glared at the pair of them, even though Joe had remained mostly silent. "That's final."

Donelli and Pete exchanged looks of resignation.

"Well, geez," Pete complained. "You don't have to get your drawers in a knot."

Amanda choked back a laugh. "Sorry." She started from the room.

"Where are you going?" Pete demanded. "I didn't mean nothing."

She paused and ruffled his hair, a gesture he would never have permitted a few weeks earlier. "I know you didn't mean *anything*. I'm going in to work on the computer for a while. I need to check out some legal stuff."

Joe's gaze homed in on hers. "About?"

"Assisted suicide."

He sighed. "Then it's true?"

Amanda nodded. "She's made up her mind. And she finally admitted to me that she does have cancer and that she's refused chemotherapy."

"Who's made up their mind?" Pete asked, glancing back and forth between them. "Assisted suicide? Is that like killing yourself with somebody's help?"

"Exactly."

"Oh, wow," Pete said softly. "Cancer? That stuff's bad news. My grandmother had that. She screamed all night long sometimes." He paused and shook his head. "I guess you have to be in a lot of pain to think dying's better, huh? I wish my grandma had known about this assisted suicide thing."

Tears sprang into Amanda's eyes at the compassionate note in his voice. Pete might be only thirteen, but he sometimes shocked her with his intelligence. More important, he had a heart the size of the whole damned state.

"Maybe you'd like to meet Miss Martha one of these days," she said, giving his hand a squeeze. "She's a wonderful woman and I think she would like you very much."

CHAPTER

Twenty

Amanda's declaration that she was going to see Willie Ashford with or without her husband apparently persuaded Donelli to take the morning off. She wasn't kidding herself, though. It probably helped that it was raining cats and dogs. The fields were awash with deep puddles by dawn and there was no sign of a letup in the leaden sky.

Before he'd get in the car, though, he insisted she eat a real breakfast: cereal, toast, and half a grapefruit. Amanda knew within three bites that it was a very bad idea, but under Donelli's watchful gaze, she finished it, then ran for the downstairs bathroom and promptly threw it all back up. Joe wiped her face with a cool washcloth, apologizing the whole time.

"Stop," she said when he'd practically rubbed all the skin off. "Next time, just serve me Saltines."

"After the way I've seen you eat later in the day,

I had no idea your stomach was such a mess," he said.

"Hormones," she said. "The doctor says they'll even out eventually and the morning queasiness will pass. Meantime, I just make up for it at lunch and dinner. You can buy me a burger after we've seen Willie."

"We'll see."

He said it with a gleam in his eyes that suggested she was going to wind up with some pseudo turkey-burger for the second day in a row. She wondered if she could ditch him before noon.

At the jail, the guards produced Willie within minutes. Whoever had been to see him the day before had apparently improved his mood. He was practically bouncing with excitement.

"What happened?" Amanda asked at once.

"I'm gonna skate on the charge," he said with complete confidence.

Donelli regarded him doubtfully. "Where would you get an idea like that?"

"Remember I told you I'd had a visitor yesterday? Well, this guy said he was here to help me. He said if I'd cooperate and cop a plea, he'd get me out on time served."

"On a murder charge?" Amanda said with blatant skepticism. "Willie, it doesn't work that way."

Willie's jaw set stubbornly. "He said he'd work a deal."

"Nobody can work that big a deal with the system," Donelli told him. "Who was this guy? An attorney?"

"I guess. He didn't give me a card or nothing."

"Did he actually say he was here to represent you? Did he tell you his name?"

"It was Johnson or Johnston. Something like that."

"And he didn't show you any ID," Amanda persisted.

"Look, I don't get it," Willie snapped. He was looking more sullen by the minute over having his story picked apart. "I thought you two were supposed to be on my side."

Amanda looked straight at him. "Willie, are you innocent?"

Clearly outraged by the suggestion he might not be, he glared right back at her. "I told you I was, didn't I? Damn, with guys like you in my corner, I'll probably end up with life imprisonment."

Amanda held up a hand to stop the tirade. "If you're innocent, why would you want to plea bargain?"

"I don't want to sit around here waiting for a trial. I want to get out now."

"With a record?"

"Shit, what difference does that make, as long as I'm free?"

Donelli hitched up a chair and sat down facing him. "Let me explain the facts of life to you, son. First of all, you're talking murder. I doubt there's a charge that could be reduced to that would get you out of here with a slap on the wrist. Second, I don't think anybody can promise you're gonna walk out of here, if you cop to a plea. Maybe the judge gets contrary and decides to make an example of you. Maybe he's got sentencing guidelines you don't know about. Now maybe before you rush into this, you'd better think long and hard about why some man you don't even know would be so anxious to convince you to plead guilty to anything."

Willie blinked rapidly as Donelli laid it all out in front of him. His optimism fizzled out like a cola left too long in the sun. "He said he'd help," he repeated plaintively.

"And maybe he will," Amanda consoled him. "Just don't be too eager to give up on proving your innocence. Give us time to check this guy out, find out what his angle is."

"Describe him for me," Donelli suggested.

Looking resigned, Willie closed his eyes as if he were trying to picture the man. "Clean-cut, I suppose you'd say. Brown hair. Very establishment. Kinda old. At least forty. He looked like a lawyer. You know, successful. Fancy clothes. He wasn't wearing a jacket or tie, but I could tell he'd paid a bundle for the threads. Had one of them fancy monograms stitched on his cuff."

Amanda's pulse immediately began to hum. She had seen just such a monogram the day before, only the man wearing the expensive, personalized shirt hadn't been a lawyer. He'd been head of the Alcohol–Tobacco Tax unit at the Department of Revenue. Coincidence? She wasn't a big believer in that much coincidence. But why would Cutter Haines, if that's who it was, have an interest in saving Willie's hide? And why would he have lied about his identity?

She reached for Willie's hands and clasped them tightly. "Willie, if this man comes back do not agree to anything, not without talking to us," she said urgently. "Promise me. And if he has one of those monograms on his shirt again, try to get a real close look at it. I want to know exactly what initial it is. Ask him for a business card."

Donelli listened to this without changing expression. "You think you know who it was, don't you?"

"I have an idea. And if I'm right, his name isn't Johnson or anything even close. What I'm not so sure about is his angle."

"In that case, Willie, you'd better listen to Amanda. The advice she just gave you could save your neck."

Willie looked thoroughly defeated, but he nodded. "I'll sit tight until I hear from you. Could you hurry, though? I've got a business to run."

Amanda suddenly thought of those fading lilacs she'd found in his house. "And a girl to get back to?"

He blushed a fiery shade of red. "Maybe, if she hasn't run off with someone else, while I'm locked up in here." There was a trace of unmistakable anxiety in his voice.

"Has she been to visit?"

"Nah. It's too tough for her to get here. She works real hard and her hours are crazy. Her dad's real strict, too. She's practically never out of his sight."

Bells went off in Amanda's head. "You're not talking about Suzi Babcock, are you?"

Willie's eyes widened. "How'd you know?"

Amanda exchanged a look with Donelli. "Wild guess."

"Did you meet her? Is she okay? Did you talk to her about me?"

His eagerness was touching. Amanda wished she had more news to impart. "She waited on us the other night, but we didn't talk about you. I didn't even realize the two of you were close. I thought you were tight with her brother. That was the name you gave us."

"Yeah, well, I didn't want to get Suzi involved. Her old man would have a cow. Suzi's the best, but that old man of hers . . ." He shrugged. "I'll just be glad when I can get out of here and marry her, like we planned. She's got to get away from him."

"What's his problem?"

"He's nuts. He'll be acting all normal and then, *bam*, out of nowhere he goes whacko. Between him and his loony wife, it's a wonder Suzi and Steven haven't flipped out themselves."

Amanda wasn't all that sure that Steven hadn't. "You said the two of you planned to get married. How does her father feel about that?"

A fleeting expression of guilt passed over Willie's face. "We haven't told him." He regarded Amanda hopefully. "If you see her, will you tell her I'm thinking about her day and night? Tell her I love her, okay?"

"If I see her, I will," Amanda promised.

"One other thing, though," Donelli said. "Tell me about this big real estate deal you've got cooking."

Willie's eyes practically popped out of his head. "You know about that? Where the hell have you been snooping?"

"We took a look around out at your place," Donelli admitted. "After all, that is where the murder took place."

"Not inside," Willie bellowed. "Man, you two are something else! Ain't anything private anymore?"

"Willie, a man on trial for murder has absolutely no

secrets from the police," Donelli said sternly. "He'd better not be keeping any from the people trying to help him either. Now tell me what's going down with the real estate deal."

"It's a pipe dream, man. I told you Daddy and Granddaddy bought up a lot of property. I filled in some of the spaces. Then I read about that big theme park that was planned for up in Virginia till the local environmentalists and historians and all got crazy and the Disney people killed it. I decided maybe I ought to go for the deal down here. I put out a few feelers to some of the big amusement park companies. That's all there was to it."

"You weren't using those feelers to pull in some investors, were you?" Amanda asked. "Maybe by suggesting that they'd be getting in on the ground floor of something big?"

Willie stared at her blankly. "Why would I cut anybody else in on the deal? I already own enough land to build the park and more hotels and motels than they got in all of Orlando."

"You're sure about that?" Donelli persisted.

"I told you, man. I got this deal covered. What does my real estate stuff have to do with anything anyway?"

"Maybe somebody thought you'd duped them into a bad real estate venture, or maybe they got greedy and decided they could have it all, if they got rid of you," Donelli suggested. "Either way, it could provide a powerful motive for framing you."

"It makes a great story," Willie said. "But I'm telling you it's not possible. I was going solo on this."

"Okay," Donelli said. "We'll get back to you. Remember what Amanda said if that guy comes back."

Willie faced Amanda. "Some cop was here yesterday, too. He wanted me to sign a paper so that they could autopsy Henry Boggins. I thought he died a long time ago."

Amanda shook her head. "No, just yesterday. The timing seemed suspicious to me, so I had Jim Harrison do some checking."

"You think somebody killed him?"

"It's possible."

Donelli, his expression skeptical, warned, "It could also be that he died of natural causes."

"Man, this thing just gets crazier and crazier," Willie said just as the guard indicated their time was up.

When Willie had been taken back to his cell, Amanda turned to Joe. "What do you think?"

"If what Willie says about his relationship with Suzi is true, it might give old Tommy a motive to frame him. Add to that any moonshining disputes they may be having and he'd be a real tidy suspect."

"Do you think he was telling the truth about the theme park deal?"

"He sounded sincere," Donelli conceded in a way that said he thought there was room for doubt. He regarded Amanda intently. "Now, tell me who you think Willie's visitor might have been."

"In a minute. We can't hang out here forever and there's something I need to do. Can we get a look at the list of visitors?"

"We can, if you can distract the guard outside long enough. What name are we looking for?"

"I'd better do the looking," she said at once. "It will probably say exactly what Willie said, something close to Johnson. I want to compare the handwriting to a sample I picked up yesterday." She dug in her purse for the card Cutter Haines had given her with his media contact's name and number scrawled on the back.

The visitor's log wasn't all that difficult to check, after all. The guard, bless him, insisted they sign out, something the guard on their last visit hadn't required. While Donelli chatted with the young, by-the-book man on duty, Amanda flipped back a page and scanned the previous day's entries.

She found one Orville Johnson at 4:13 in the afternoon. Though she was no expert, she thought she detected distinct similarities between his handwriting and Cutter Haines's. Both had open, looping strokes. She turned the page back to where it belonged and moved to Donelli's side. He slipped his arm around her waist and finished discussing the prospects for this year's Braves team, a subject guaranteed to stir passions and keep attention diverted.

Five minutes later, they were out the door.

"Well?" he asked at once.

"I'd swear that Willie's visitor was the head of the Alcohol–Tobacco Tax unit, Cutter Haines. Joe, I think he's in this thing up to his neck and I'm certain he's counting on getting Willie to take the fall."

"Now, wait a minute, you can't go around accusing a state official of murder or conspiracy without proof.

You don't have clues. You don't have a motive. You don't have diddly."

"Except his signature on a visitor log using a false name," she reminded him. "And Willie's description, right down to the monogrammed cuff on his shirt. Plus his attempt to convince Willie to plea bargain. Clearly, he was trying to impersonate a defense attorney. That's not legal, is it?"

"He never said he was an attorney," Donelli pointed out. "Willie said that himself. For starters, I think you'd better get a picture of Haines and show it to Willie to make sure it's the same person. His description sounded pretty vague to me."

"You didn't meet Cutter Haines. I did. Willie had him nailed." Amanda regarded him curiously. "Why do you sound so doubtful?"

"Don't you think a man whose family has been moonshining as long as Willie's has would make it a point to know what the head of the Alcohol–Tobacco Tax unit looks like? Bootleggers probably put Haines's face on posters and use it for target practice."

It was an angle she hadn't considered. "Damn, instead of being so blasted discreet, I should have asked him that point-blank," she lamented.

"Not necessarily. For once, you were exercising a little caution. Suggesting that Cutter Haines might be running a scam on Willie might very well get you embroiled in a slander suit."

"I still think it was him," she said stubbornly. "Maybe Willie just doesn't have a thing for remembering faces."

"And maybe you'd better get some proof."

"Have I mentioned lately that you are an irritatingly by-the-book kind of guy?"

"Not recently," he said, grinning at her. "Maybe that's just because I've stayed out of your investigative path."

Amanda nodded. "I am beginning to see the benefits of your being a full-time farmer." She regarded him hopefully. "Don't you want to rush home and get all those cute little seedlings you've been nursing along all over the dining room into the ground this afternoon?"

He glanced up at the dark, cloudy sky. "Nah, they'll just drown." He beamed. "I guess I'm all yours for the rest of the day."

"Swell."

Just then her cellular phone rang. She dug in her purse, amazed as always that something the size of a phone could manage to disappear in a pocketbook. She was convinced that if she carried only two things in her purse, one of them inevitably would be lost when she went to grab for it. She finally latched onto the phone on the fifth ring.

"Yes?"

"I was about to give up on you," Detective Jim Harrison said. He sounded as if the prospect had pleased him.

"Sorry. No such luck. I'm here. What did you find out? Were you able to get an autopsy done on Henry Boggins?"

"Do you know how thrilled the medical examiner was to be asked to autopsy a man a hundred years old who died in a hospital, a man on whom a signed death certificate already existed?"

"I can only imagine," Amanda conceded. "Did he agree to do it?"

"With that kid's okay and after I used up my chits into the next century, he did it as a favor to me."

"And?"

"And, as he predicted going in, it was a waste of time."

"Boggins died of natural causes," she said, filled with disappointment.

"I didn't say that. He didn't say that. The results were inconclusive. It looked like natural causes. He was an old man. His heart stopped."

Amanda's adrenaline began to pump at the tiny opening she thought she detected in his voice. "But?"

"But nothing. He was willing to do a little speculation for me. He said eighty millequivalents of potassium in an IV push could have caused his heart to stop and it would never turn up on an autopsy. A couple hundred units of insulin could have knocked him out, too. Neither would be traceable. The body has potassium and insulin in it all the time."

Amanda uttered a sigh of resignation. "No traces. No proof. That's the bottom line, isn't it?"

"Unless you happen to have a suspect who's a nurse or someone who's diabetic and has a ready supply of insulin on hand. But you'd need more than that to make a case. A lot more. Do you have anything at all, Amanda? A motive? A strong suspect? Opportunity?"

Though she claimed otherwise, Sandra Mayotte-Jefferson had motive and opportunity. Randy Alcott had opportunity, but as far as Amanda knew for certain he didn't have a motive, nor did he have ready access to the likely substances.

Suddenly she thought back to the previous afternoon in Pastor Alcott's office and his claim that he was allergic to chocolate. What if it wasn't an allergy at all, but a diabetic condition that kept him away from those brownies? She would have to find out for certain before she could start hurling accusations in his direction.

"I don't have anything solid," she admitted finally. "Just suspicions."

"Keep me posted if anything more turns up. Otherwise, I have no grounds for investigating this any further."

"Okay. Thanks for trying, Detective."

"Amanda?"

"Yes?"

"You know those favors I now owe to the medical examiner?"

"Yes."

"You owe me double. You will never get out of the debt you owe me. And there is only one payback I want. Am I making myself clear?"

"Stay off your turf?" she guessed.

"Staying off my turf would be a start. Stop plaguing me for inside information. Perhaps it's time for you to start writing gardening tips."

"In your dreams, Detective," she said succinctly. "Besides, you know you'd miss me."

"In *your* dreams, Amanda."

CHAPTER Twenty-one

"Where to now?" Donelli asked as he and Amanda got back into their car. "Or do I need to ask?"

"I was thinking of lunch at Babcock's Cafe," she admitted.

"Somehow I knew that. Let's go." He held out his hand. "I'll drive."

"I want to get there in time for lunch, not afternoon tea," she retorted, climbing behind the wheel herself.

"If you get stopped by the Georgia Highway Patrol, I will tell them the exact reading on your speedometer," he warned as he climbed into the passenger side. "And I will not pay the fine. In fact, I may even encourage the officer to recommend driving school."

Amanda scowled at him. "I am not a dangerous driver, Donelli. It's people like you who poke along who make the rest of us take unnecessary risks."

"Yeah, right."

Still, she dutifully stayed within the speed limit until they reached the outskirts of the city. Then, with traffic light and most cops probably inside someplace warm and dry drinking coffee and eating doughnuts, she could no longer restrain herself. All that open road called to her. She hit the accelerator, ignoring her husband's pained expression.

They reached Babcock's unticketed and in one piece. Donelli seemed amazed. Amanda was exhilarated.

Inside the small cafe, they found another crowd of truckers diving into the day's special of rabbit stew. Amanda swallowed hard against a tide of nausea just reading about it on the chalkboard menu.

They slid into a vacant booth in the back. Two minutes later Suzi rushed over, her order pad out, her hair falling into her eyes, a streak of mustard down the front of her T-shirt. There were also deep, dark circles under her eyes that Amanda found worrisome.

"Suzi, are you okay?" she asked.

The waitress seemed startled by the concerned inquiry. "Just tired," she said at once. "This place hasn't slowed down since dawn and Daddy's home sick. Stevie worked for a while, then he took off for who knows where. I'm the only one waiting tables. What can I get you?"

"I'll have a grilled cheese sandwich and fries," Amanda said, shooting a defiant look at her husband.

"I'll try the rabbit stew."

"Not while I'm at the table," Amanda declared.

Apparently he'd learned his lesson about her stomach

at breakfast, because he readily changed his order to a hamburger.

"And a cup of coffee, when you get a minute," he added.

Suzi gestured over her shoulder. "If you're in a rush, the pot's behind the counter. Go on and grab a cup. If you can wait, I'll be back with it in a few minutes," she promised as a customer yelled at her from the register. "Hold your britches on, T.C. I'm hurrying as fast as I can. You think that big ole rig's gonna drive away without you?"

Amanda grinned. "I can see her with Willie, can't you? She'll give that boy fits."

"You're assuming he can overcome his current difficulties and they can get past daddy," Donelli pointed out.

"He'll overcome his difficulties," Amanda said grimly, extracting her notebook from her purse. "I'll see to that."

"I admire your confidence. What do you have so far?"

Making a big circle on a piece of paper, Amanda listed all of the people they'd interviewed: Willie, Kenny Loftis, the Babcocks, Henry Boggins, Sandra Mayotte-Jefferson, Randy Alcott, and Cutter Haines. Then she tried linking them with lines to indicate any connections. In no time at all she had an indecipherable mess. She crumpled the paper up in disgust.

Donelli reached over, grabbed it, and smoothed it out. "Okay, let's see what you have here."

"I have absolutely nothing conclusive," she muttered in despair. "How can I tell that to Miss Martha? She's counting on me."

"Hey," he protested, "where's that famous Amanda Roberts spunk?"

"It's running on empty."

"Then let's go back to basics," he suggested with the equally famous, if often irritating, Donelli patience. "Who are your suspects in the murder of Randy Blaine Alcott Senior back in 1942?"

"Practically none of the people I've talked to were even alive back then."

"Boggins was. Kenny Loftis was. Randy Junior was. Salty Tufts was. Any candidates for suspect of the year among them?"

"I suppose Henry Boggins," she conceded eventually. "We know he hated William Ashford, either because of what Ashford did to his daughter or because he was ticked that his blackmail attempt hadn't worked."

"Okay. How about Loftis?"

She shook her head. "Nothing he said indicated any emotion whatsoever about that murder."

"But someone either on his property or darned close to it took a shot at you, while we were at Willie's," Donelli reminded her.

"Not him, though. He didn't have time to scramble through the underbrush in the woods and get back home afterwards. You said so yourself."

He beamed as if she'd just passed a course in police investigative procedure and evidence analysis. "What about Randy Junior?" he prodded.

Amanda hadn't much liked him, but murder? She couldn't reconcile that with his current profession. "Besides, would he have killed his own father?" she asked doubtfully.

"You told me he hated him, that he felt his father had betrayed him."

Unable to ignore the possibility of motive, Amanda nodded. "Okay, he stays on the list."

"Who was the last one? Salty Tufts? What about him?"

"Nope. Miss Martha said he and William were best friends. Besides, if we're looking for a link between the two murders, he can't be involved. He's dead."

"But his descendants aren't. Suzette's alive, if slightly out of touch with reality. Suzi and Steven are around and Tommy may only be an in-law, but who knows how tied into the old family vendettas he might be."

One by one Donelli led her through the convoluted maze of potential suspects, nudging her toward conclusions, pulling her back from guesswork. In the end, she was left with Boggins, Alcott, and Haines, possibly in some sort of triangular connection between past and present. She liked those three as suspects, but she didn't have a clue about their motives or how they fit together. Or even if they did fit together.

"Damn, this is making me crazy," she muttered finally, as she dipped her last fry in ketchup, then ate it slowly. "How am I supposed to tie the three of them together, especially since Boggins is dead?"

"The same way a cop makes a case or you investigate any other story: patience. You keep digging for clues.

Just be careful about focusing so intently on those three that you miss other people who might crop up."

"Aren't you on Miss Martha's payroll? Shouldn't you be doing some of this investigation?"

"Actually, I have a few things in mind, but I need to get back on the computer to check 'em out."

"Well, I hope you're not in any hurry, because I do not intend to go home until I've talked to Suzi again and maybe gone by to chat with Pastor Alcott one more time."

Donelli sat back with his cup of coffee, clearly settling in for the long haul. "Go for it," he said.

Unfortunately, going for it was slowed considerably by the size of the lunch crowd. Suzi could have used roller skates to keep up. Amanda dawdled over a piece of homemade banana cream pie and a cup of decaf until the cafe finally cleared out.

Suzi, looking considerably more bedraggled than she had earlier, stopped by with the coffeepot. "More?"

"No thanks," Donelli said.

"Can you sit a minute?" Amanda asked.

Suzi cast a longing look at the booth bench. "I should start cleaning up. Believe it or not, the dinner crowd will start showing up in a couple of hours. Some of these guys like to eat early and get in a few more hours of driving."

"Just for a minute," Amanda said. "We've just been to visit Willie Ashford."

The transformation of Suzi's expression was something to behold. Her entire face lit up. "Is he okay? Is he furious because I haven't been by to see him? I've wanted to go, but I think Daddy's deliberately giving me more to do around here to make sure I don't have time to go visit." She dropped readily onto the seat beside Donelli, facing Amanda.

"Willie understands. He wants you to know he's thinking about you, though. He's determined to get out so you two can get married."

Suzi sighed. "Daddy'll kill me before he lets me marry an Ashford. He's barely tolerated me seeing Willie at all and that's just because he thinks Willie's hanging around with Stevie, not me. He'd stop Stevie from going around with him, too, if he could, but Stevie just ignores him."

"Why does he dislike the Ashfords so much?"

"Beats me. It's almost like one of those stupid Hatfield and McCoy feuds that goes back for generations with no one even understanding anymore what started it. I've asked and asked, but Daddy just tells me to leave it be, that I might as well accept that he knows best."

Amanda figured her next question was going to take her into treacherous waters. She approached it cautiously. "Does he disapprove of what Willie does for a living?"

"You mean developing shopping malls and housing tracts?"

Amanda bit back her surprise. "That's what Willie's doing?" He'd left that particular tidbit out when they'd spent all that time talking about the theme park. Apparently he had a backup plan for all that land of his.

"Well, sure. His family bought up acres and acres of land over the years. Now he's selling off some and developing other pieces."

Suzi seemed so certain that real estate was Willie's primary business. Amanda couldn't help wondering if she honestly believed that's all he did or if she'd just become accustomed to covering up for the moonshine trade he was really in. Perhaps hiding moonshine and bootlegging were simply second nature to her. Amanda had to find out which, but the only way she could think of to do it was to discuss generalities first. Maybe that would tell her how much Suzi knew or whether she was genuinely as naive as she sounded.

"Suzi, do you know anything about moonshining around this area?"

"Well, sure," she said at once. "It goes on all the time. I don't see what the big deal is. Most of the people are just making stuff to drink themselves. Some folks sell it, but it's not like it's some terrible sin or something, not the way Pastor Alcott carries on about it."

"You've heard Pastor Alcott preach?"

Suzi rolled her eyes heavenward. "I wouldn't go near the place, but Daddy insists we go every single Sunday and sit right up front. Seems downright hypocritical to me considering Daddy's making moonshine himself. If he believes all that stuff Pastor Alcott says, he must be scared half to death of dying." She shrugged. "Or maybe he just figures he can build up enough points to sneak past Saint Peter. You know, like cozying up to the man in charge to get some sort of heavenly hall pass."

Amanda laughed. Donelli choked on a sip of coffee.

Suzi seemed surprised by their amusement. "You two are okay, you know. How come you know about Pastor Alcott?"

"I went to talk to him the other day," Amanda said. "I thought he might be able to help me figure out what had happened years ago when Willie's grandfather was accused of murdering a Revenue agent, just like Willie is today."

"Oh, boy," Suzi said, sounding awed. "You talked to him about the Ashfords? That must have been something to hear. Willie came to church there one Sunday, figuring it would be a good way for us to see each other. Pastor Alcott lost it. He came screaming down out of the pulpit, calling him names. He chased him out of the church. Half the congregation got into a frenzy, shouting *Amen* and carrying on. You'd have thought the devil himself had paid a visit. I felt so bad for poor Willie. Those very same people sneak over to his place every single weekend to buy a jug of moonshine and here they were acting all self-righteous. It made me sick."

It took fully a minute for Amanda to absorb that image. Anger on Willie's behalf rose inside her. "Did you ever see an old man named Henry Boggins in church?" she asked Suzi.

"Sure. He was usually sitting in the front row right beside Daddy. Sometimes we drove over to pick him up, when he didn't have a ride to services." She grinned suddenly. "He was something. All the ladies in the congregation knew not to get too close. Old as he was, he still liked to pinch fannies. It's too bad about him dying. I just heard about it. He didn't want a regular funeral, but I understand Pastor Alcott's going to do a memorial to him as part of Sunday's service."

The threads linking Alcott and Boggins grew stronger. "Suzi, have you ever seen a man named Cutter Haines around here?" Amanda asked.

"The guy from the Department of Revenue? Are you kidding? If he set foot in the county, warning sirens would probably go off, like those air raid things they test sometimes."

"Does Willie know what he looks like? Has he ever met him before?"

The young girl looked doubtful. "I don't know. I mean everybody talks about Haines, but I'm not so sure anybody's actually seen him. Even when they write about him in the paper, they never publish a picture. Sorta like some undercover cop thing, you know. Keeping his identity under wraps."

Amanda nodded. It seemed possible, then, that Haines could have been the one to visit Willie and he wouldn't have been recognized. She needed to find a picture of the man. Meantime, though, it seemed there was little more she could gain from Suzi.

"Thanks, Suzi. You've been a big help. I'll tell Willie you're doing okay."

"Tell him I miss him," she said. "I go by the house and check on it for him."

Amanda thought of the shots that had been fired at her when she and Donelli had visited the house. "Be careful over there."

Suzi apparently heard the note of alarm in her voice, because a frown suddenly creased her forehead. "Is something wrong? Is there some reason I shouldn't go there?"

"Joe and I were there the other day. Somebody fired a shotgun at me, probably just warning shots, since I was in the clear and he missed, but it might be safer if you avoid it for a while."

Suzi winced. "Oh, geez, I'm sorry."

Amanda stared at her. "You know who shot at me?"

"Stevie," she admitted. "I was on my way over and I saw two people snooping around. I didn't know who you were or anything, so I went and got my brother. He's the one who fired the shots and you're right. He just wanted to scare you off."

Amanda sighed. One mystery solved. Too bad the solution to the bigger one still seemed far too elusive.

CHAPTER

Twenty-Two

Even though she didn't have a lot of news to report, Amanda suddenly felt an almost desperate need to pay a call on Miss Martha after talking with Willie and with Suzi Babcock. She wasn't sure why she couldn't get the older woman out of her head. Intuition, maybe, that she was getting worse.

Whatever it was that had brought on her uneasiness, a visit certainly wouldn't be wasted. Maybe the older woman could even shed some light on Randy Alcott or, for that matter, on Cutter Haines. Miss Martha had contacts in all sorts of fascinating places. If she didn't know Haines personally, she was bound to know someone in the Georgia state government who did.

"I'd like to see Miss Martha," she told Donelli. "Do you want me to drop you off at home and then drive back?"

"That's absurd. Her place is right on the way. Stop on the way home. I'd like to see her myself."

Surprised, Amanda grinned at him. "You're a brave man, Joe Donelli."

"Meaning?"

"For one thing, whether you admit it or not, she's always intimidated the daylights out of you."

"She has not."

Amanda laughed. "Has too. And on top of that, she's paying you and you don't have a halfway decent suspect for her."

He winked and waved her own messy diagram in her face. "Sure I do, thanks to you."

She stared at him with disbelief. "That's not investigating," she accused. "That's stealing."

"I've got names. That's all that matters," he taunted. "Don't fret, Amanda. I won't charge her for the time you spent chasing all over hell and gone to come up with three halfway decent suspects. So far, this one's on the house." He paused. "Or on *Inside Atlanta*."

"Thanks for the token credit."

"Amanda, I'm always willing to share with you. You're my wife."

She scowled at him. "Don't you try to sound noble, you sneaky, conniving information thief."

"Just be glad I don't work for the competition."

"If you did, we wouldn't be running around the countryside working the same story, much less sleeping in the same bed."

He laughed at her indignation. "Have I mentioned lately how much I love you?"

"It's your only saving grace," she shot back, finally allowing herself a grin. She glanced over at him. "I love you, too."

"How much? Desperately? Passionately?"

"Don't press your luck, Donelli."

"I was just trying to figure out if there was sufficient incentive for cutting this visit short," he said, dropping his voice a seductive notch.

"I'm mad at you," she reminded him.

"Passionately furious or just a little mad?"

"Mad is mad."

"Not when it comes to making up," he pointed out.

Amanda laughed at his hopeful expression. "I was thinking of staying for tea."

"You hate that insipid tea Miss Martha serves."

She shrugged. "Maybe I've finally developed a taste for it."

"What you've developed, Amanda, is a knack for tormenting me."

"I know. Don't you love it," she said, grinning with satisfaction.

She was still tormenting him when they reached Miss Martha's. Della admitted them with a scowl and a cursory warning not to get Miss Martha all stirred up.

"Not that I expect you'll pay a bit of mind to me," she added.

Amanda led the way upstairs, pausing to tap on Miss Martha's door before entering.

"Yes, who is it?" Miss Martha called out irritably.

"Amanda and Joe."

"Well, what are you lurking around in the hall for?

Get in here," she commanded. She waved them toward chairs with a weak flutter of her hand.

The room was filled with shadows. The drapes had been drawn against the afternoon sun, which had finally broken through the dark, rolling clouds.

"I can't see you," Miss Martha said. "Amanda, open the curtains. Della can't get it through her head that I don't like it all closed up in here. I'll be shut away in a dark box soon enough."

Amanda hurried to comply with her instructions. Sunlight streamed through the sheer curtains and spilled over the bed. Amanda turned around and reacted with shock at her first glimpse of Miss Martha. It was the first time she'd stopped by unexpectedly and the old woman had had no time to prepare for the visit. Her white hair was mussed. Her skin was ashen. And her eyes seemed dulled by pain. Amanda had to bite her lip to keep from crying. For the first time, she could no longer deny that Miss Martha really was dying.

Forcing herself to act as if nothing were out of the ordinary, she went back to her seat beside Donelli. Fortunately, he'd covered her stunned silence by quietly outlining some of the things he and Amanda had picked up on. Despite his teasing in the car, he gave Amanda credit for the few scant clues they had picked up.

"It's not enough," Miss Martha said wearily. Her head shook from side to side, almost as if she had no control over the motion. "Not nearly enough. What will you do now?"

"I thought perhaps you could make some calls to your friends in the State House and see what you could find out about Cutter Haines," Amanda suggested, wondering if Miss Martha had the energy left for even that much activity.

"Hand me the phone," she ordered without hesitating.

Her voice instantly seemed stronger, putting Amanda's worries to rest, at least for the moment. It was as if having something to do gave her an immediate burst of energy. Even though her fingers trembled visibly as she punched in the number, her manner was as imperious as ever as she demanded to speak to the governor. Obviously, she saw no point in wasting time with lesser mortals.

"Clayton, how are you?" she said within seconds. "Yes, it has been a long time, too long. How is Adelaide?"

Apparently Georgia's first lady was just fine, because Miss Martha spent precious little time listening to the governor's answer. "That's lovely," she said before he could have said much more than *fine*. "Clayton, I was wondering what you could tell me about Cutter Haines over at the Department of Revenue."

She nodded, as she listened. "Highly respected, yes? Ambitious? Of course. Isn't that what it takes to survive in government these days? Any clouds at all over his administration? Yes, yes, of course I'm asking off the record. Did you think I'd gotten a job reporting on the eleven o'clock news?"

The dry comment was followed by a lot of *uh-huhs* and *I sees*. "Well, of course, I had read about the murder. Tragic. Mr. Jefferson seemed such a nice young man.

That would be a blight on Haines's record. Other than that, he has a fine reputation? Good. I'm glad to hear it."

"Ask about any hints of bias?" Amanda coached her.

Miss Martha nodded to acknowledge that she'd heard. "You know, Clayton, there have been rumors about Mr. Haines. Of course, I'm not one to put much stock in idle gossip, but it has come back to me on several occasions that he might be less than fair when dealing with employees of color. As you know, that is not the sort of thing that's considered politically correct these days. I would hate to see your administration tainted by such charges."

She held the phone away from her ear while the governor ranted loudly about the dirty tactics of his political opponents in even suggesting such a thing.

"Clayton, for goodness sake, I didn't accuse *you* of anything. I was just asking about the head of a department. I wouldn't want his ill-advised actions to rub off on you. Of course, I'm absolutely sure that you'll nip anything like that in the bud. Never doubted it. Yes, Clayton, lovely to speak to you, too."

She hung up and scowled at the phone. "Prissy old fool."

"Well," Amanda said. "Did he have anything on Haines?"

"The man's an absolute paragon, according to Clayton." A faint gleam of anticipation sparked in her eyes. "I suppose we'll know if he really believes that when we see whether Mr. Haines still has his job in another few days. If there's any smoke at all that Clayton has been ignoring, he'll figure he'd better put it out now before there's a full-fledged fire."

Amanda couldn't hide her disappointment at not getting a more concrete response. "So we have to wait."

"That's right, dear. We wait." Miss Martha turned to Donelli. "And while we do, young man, suppose you get on that fancy computer of yours and poke around in this Mr. Haines's financial affairs."

"Good idea," Donelli agreed, as if he hadn't had that very thing in mind all along.

Miss Martha still looked pale, but she was sounding much livelier by the minute as they compared notes on Haines, Alcott, and Henry Boggins. She didn't have a lot to add on Alcott, but the sheer act of being involved was clearly good for her.

Unfortunately, Donald Wellington, Miss Martha's nephew, chose that precise moment to turn up. The former senator, who had returned to his law practice full-time following his defeat in the last election, stood in the doorway, took in the scene before him, and immediately puffed up with anger.

"What do you all think you're doing?" he demanded. "Aunt Martha, you are supposed to be resting."

Miss Martha didn't bat an eye. In fact, she managed a welcoming smile. "Donald, dear, I had no idea you were planning to drop by this afternoon."

"You're supposed to be resting," he said again, shooting an accusatory scowl at Joe and Amanda.

"There'll be time enough for that, all of eternity, in

fact," Miss Martha shot right back. "I feel better right now than I have all day."

"I don't like it. The doctor says . . ."

"That I'll die if I don't take it easy," she retorted. "Don't you think I know that? Heavens, Donald, I'm going to die one of these days anyway. I'm not immortal, much as I might like to think I am."

"You would have plenty of time left, if you wouldn't allow yourself to get agitated." He turned to Joe and Amanda. "I think it would be better if you left now."

Amanda was more than willing. She had never liked Donald Wellington. He'd always struck her as an insufferable bore. She supposed, though, that he did have his aunt's best interests at heart. Before she could make a move to stand up, however, Miss Martha ordered her to sit right where she was.

"We have not finished," she insisted. "Donald, why don't you go down and have Della fix you a cocktail? Perhaps it will improve your mood and your manners. We can visit shortly."

With obvious reluctance, Donald did as he'd been ordered. Few people dared to argue with Miss Martha. Donald certainly wasn't one of them.

Miss Martha sank back against the pillows when he'd gone. "He has no idea that he's the one whose visits wear me down. I have to watch every word around him. If he finds out . . ." She glanced worriedly at Joe.

"It's okay," he said gently. "I know."

Miss Martha reached for his hand and squeezed it.

"Thank you for not jumping to judgment. I know there are people who would disapprove of my decision."

Joe kissed her hand in a gallant gesture that brought color to her cheeks. "I think you are a remarkable woman."

Miss Martha beamed at him. "You know there was a time when I thought Mack Roberts was the right man for Amanda. I regret that now. I am so very glad she has you in her life. She needs someone solid and dependable."

Donelli grinned at her. "Would you mind reminding her of that from time to time?"

"It will be my pleasure." She glanced at Amanda. "Dear, dry your eyes. I will not have you sitting around here weeping on me." She sighed. "As I was saying, if Donald finds out what I intend to do, I'll wind up in a nursing home under twenty-four-hour guards. I do so wish I could talk to him," she said wistfully. "As it is, I won't be able to say a proper good-bye. Too bad I don't live in Oregon, where people had the good sense to vote to treat human beings with as much dignity and compassion as they would a dying pet. I just hope that judge out there has the good sense to let the law stand eventually, instead of keeping it tied up in the courts forever."

Before either Joe or Amanda could respond, she drew herself up. "That's enough of that for today," she said briskly. "I promised myself that I would not grow morbid. Amanda, dear, would you bring me my makeup? I feel the need for a little armor before I have to deal with

Donald again. Then, before you go, tell me about that young man you adopted. Pete, is it?"

Because Amanda's throat was too choked to say a single word, Donelli told Miss Martha all about their teenage son, including the fact that Pete would like very much to meet her.

"Then bring him by. It will be good to hear the sound of a boy in this house again. It's been all too silent since Donald and his brother visited as children. I've grown weary of the often inconsequential chatter of grown-ups with inflated egos."

"Pete may not be exactly like the sort of polite, prep school boy your nephews were," Amanda warned.

Miss Martha chuckled delightedly. "All the better. Perhaps you'll come for tea on Sunday. I'll have Della bake. She'll be ecstatic to have someone around who has an appetite."

"Pete can definitely qualify on that count," Amanda said. "We'll see you on Sunday, then."

They left her putting the finishing touches on her powder and blush. On the way downstairs, Amanda slipped her hand into Joe's and clung to it. Every time she walked away from Miss Martha's room, she was terrified it might be the last time she saw her.

Unfortunately, before she and Joe could escape, Donald Wellington stepped into their path. "I'd like a word with you, if you don't mind," he said in a tight voice.

Apparently assuming their compliance, he led the way into a parlor that Miss Martha herself rarely used because she'd always found it too stuffy and formal. Naturally

Donald appeared perfectly at home in such a setting. He gravitated to it as if it had been designed for him. Amanda found his subtle claiming of Miss Martha's home as his own to be in extremely bad taste.

Donelli must have observed the souring of her mood, because his grip on her hand tightened perceptibly. Under other circumstances, he might very well have clamped his hand firmly over her mouth. At any rate, the effect was the same. Amanda bit her tongue and prepared to hear Donald Wellington out.

"Can I offer you something?" he inquired wearily. "A glass of sherry, perhaps?"

"Nothing for me," Amanda said.

"Nor me," Joe added.

Donald poured himself a drink from the heavy crystal decanter sitting on a silver tray on an antique table. He seemed to be building up courage, or perhaps a head of steam. Amanda couldn't be sure which, but the delay was irritating her.

"I'm sorry about what happened upstairs," he said at last.

The apology surprised Amanda. "I'm sure seeing your aunt so ill is very distressing," she said, willing to meet him part way.

Donald rubbed a hand over his eyes, then downed the remainder of his drink in one gulp. His eyes seemed faintly unfocussed when he finally turned his gaze on Amanda. "Look, I know you are aware of . . . certain things," he began.

His attempt at circumspection left Amanda in a quandary. How much did Donald Wellington actually know?

Was he hinting that he knew about his aunt's intentions? If he didn't know, if he was merely on a fishing expedition, Amanda had no intention of enlightening him.

"Certain things?" she repeated cautiously. "What might those be?"

He shook his head, as if to clear it. "I'm not making any sense, am I? It's just that I am in this incredibly awkward position. As a lawyer, as an officer of the court, I cannot knowingly or willfully permit my aunt to do anything that might hasten her death. Nor can anyone else, for that matter," he said, looking pointedly at Amanda. "The Georgia legislature made such acts a felony, punishable by one to ten years in prison for those assisting. Had I been there I would have voted with the majority. I believe no one other than God has a right to make such decisions about life and death."

He knew! Amanda fought to hide her shock. Somehow he had guessed what Miss Martha was planning and now he was caught in a terrible moral dilemma. For the first time she studied him closely and realized how haggard he was, how much anguish there was in his eyes.

"I'm sorry," she said softly.

He waved off the expression of sympathy. "I just wanted you to understand that I'm not the cold-hearted beast I might appear sometimes. If I were, I suppose I could prevent what she intends. I know that legally and morally that's what I should do. Somehow, though, I can't bring myself to do that to her."

"How long have you known?"

"I guessed weeks ago when I saw that storehouse of

sleeping pills in her bedside stand. She's been hoarding them for who knows how long. I am dealing with it the only way I know how, by pretending not to know, by allowing her her dying wish."

"You're also cutting yourself off from the chance to share this time with her," Amanda said.

"No," he said. "If we speak of it, I would have to tell her how I feel, that I believe she is committing a mortal sin, as well as a crime. It would only cause a rift between us. As it is, I see her every day. I will be here at the end. Della has promised to see to that." A single tear tracked down his cheek. "A final secret in a house that was once filled with them."

His gazed honed in on Amanda. "You're keeping that secret for her, I assume," he said with an unmistakable note of doubt. "I wonder if you'll do the same for me?"

The question, with its hint of cynicism and self-interest, changed everything. Amanda was dumbstruck that he would think she was capable of capitalizing on Miss Martha's tragic decision by writing about it. Or that she would betray a friend.

Donelli replied for both of them, an edge of anger in his voice. "Actually, Wellington, there is no choice. Not for any of us. You saw to that by citing the law, didn't you? We're all coconspirators now."

Donald shrugged, admitting that his words had been deliberately planned to lock them all into silence. "It seemed the wise thing to do."

Donelli gave him a look of disgust. "I pity you, man. To live without trust, to live without understanding anything at all about friendship must make your life hell. I'm in just as much of a dilemma here as you are. I was raised Catholic. I'm an ex-cop. Everything in me wants to protest what your aunt is doing. I think it's wrong. But after seeing her just now, I also see that she is in pain that will only get worse. She has been diagnosed with a terminal illness. And she knows exactly what she's doing. Her decision to die with dignity is a very private matter. It's not my business, nor the state of Georgia's."

A crimson tide climbed slowly up Donald Wellington's neck. He had the grace to look ashamed.

"Amanda and I will keep your aunt's secret because we care about her, not because we fear reprisals for ourselves," Donelli continued. He glanced at Amanda. "Anything you'd like to add?"

Amanda shook her head. "No, I think you summed it up pretty well." She looked at Donald, who refused to return the direct gaze. "If you can't bring yourself to admit what you know and to tell her that you understand and forgive her, then at least tell her that you love her. She needs desperately to know that."

He sighed and started for the stairs. He was partway up, when he looked back. "I'm truly sorry if I misjudged you. I just had to be sure, for all our sakes."

CHAPTER

Twenty-three

The confrontation with Donald Wellington had left Amanda thoroughly drained. Donelli had zeroed in on her weakened state and extracted a promise that she would take Saturday off. He made it worth her while by promising that he would spend the afternoon digging around in computer files to see what he could learn about their three primary suspects—Henry Boggins, Pastor Randy Alcott, and Cutter Haines.

"And Tommy Babcock," she added when he was finally sitting in front of his computer.

"You don't honestly suspect him," Donelli accused. "You just want to get something on him to use as leverage if he tries to stand in the way of Willie and Suzi's marriage."

"That, too," she admitted. "But something about him has bugged me from the beginning. Half of what he told us turned out to be lies. And the whole family seems to be trigger happy."

"You have a point there." He glanced over his shoulder at her. "I can't do this if you're going to be hovering. Go take a nap."

"I don't need a nap. I slept for ten hours as it was. I wasted most of a perfectly good morning sleeping."

"Then go look at that new batch of wallpaper samples Pete brought home yesterday. If you like something, you two can go and buy it."

Amanda finally sighed and relented. The search for clues in the various computer data bases to which Donelli had access wouldn't go any faster if she were pacing the room. She also had a hunch that Donelli was as worried about interference from Pete as he was from her. Their son had an almost scary knack for breaking into files that were supposed to be confidential. It was a trait they were trying to discourage.

She found Pete at the kitchen table leafing through a magazine. "New comic?" she inquired, opening the refrigerator door in search of a snack that contained more calories than an orange. Chocolate—whatever the form—would be a start.

Pete's face caught her attention. He had blushed the fiery shade of red reserved for teenage males caught in the act of reading forbidden material. Somehow, though, Amanda got the feeling it wasn't *Playboy* he was perusing, since he didn't make any move to hide it. She gave up on her search for food and leaned over his shoulder to see what he was so embarrassed about.

"Baby furniture?" she said incredulously.

Pete scowled at her. "Well, somebody's gotta figure out what the kid's gonna sleep in. You guys don't have time."

Amanda grinned and pulled a chair over beside him. "What did you find?"

Pete had turned down the corners on an amazing array of pages. Some of the rooms he'd chosen, however, were clearly meant for someone a decade or more older than a new baby. She had the feeling he'd been doing a little wishful thinking of his own. Ever since he'd moved in with them he had been careful to ask for absolutely nothing. It was as if he feared they might reject him if he became too demanding. As a result, his room still looked as if it were the impersonal guest room it had once been. Other than his clothes and a few pieces of sports equipment, the only personal touch he'd added was the snapshot of her and Joe he'd tucked in his mirror.

"You know," she began casually, "we could think about redecorating your room, too."

He shrugged off the idea, but there was no mistaking the tiny flare of interest in his eyes. "Nah, the baby needs stuff now."

"Not for another seven months. In the meantime, we could buy some wallpaper for your room, maybe a new bed and a wall unit for your books and stuff. Pretty soon you're probably going to need a computer setup of your own for your schoolwork."

His eyes lit up with unabashed excitement. "Really? There was one room in here that was totally awesome."

He flipped through pages and pointed to a room designed with a Southwestern motif. "What do you think?"

"I think finding all this will keep us out of Donelli's hair for the rest of the day," she said. "Let's do it."

Pete suddenly looked worried. "He won't be mad 'cause we're spending all this money on me, instead of the baby, will he?"

Amanda winked at him. "We have to practice, don't we?"

Pete grinned. "Yeah, practice is good. Joe says that all the time. I wouldn't want to mess up the wallpaper in the baby's room."

"So, let's do it."

The shopping expedition took most of the afternoon. It was after six when they finally staggered in the back door, laden with packages. Pete's new furniture was being delivered the following week. Given free rein to choose, he had gone from prudent caution to exuberent shopper in no time at all. Amanda prayed he never discovered the Home Shopping Network.

It was good to be home again. The expedition had worn her out. It was even better to discover that Donelli had lasagne in the oven and a salad on the table.

"Successful shopping spree?" he asked. Given the number of packages, it was a massive understatement.

"The best," Pete said. "Wait till you see." He began extracting wallpaper and sheets and a bedspread from the bags until the entire kitchen was littered with their finds. Frowning, he glanced at Donelli. "It's not too much, is it?"

Donelli turned to Amanda, his expression amused. "I was expecting cute little duckies. Maybe some cuddly little teddy bears. Did the agenda for this shopping trip change just a little?"

"A little," she conceded. "Since neither Pete nor I has ever hung wallpaper, we thought we'd practice our decorating skills on Pete's room first."

Grinning at Pete, Donelli held up his hand for a high-five. "All right, my man. I see you like the Southwestern theme. Ever been out west? Ever had a hankering to be a cowboy?"

"Not really," Pete said, flushing. "I kinda liked all those old John Wayne movies, though. Besides, it's just little kids who think they can really grow up to be cowboys, isn't it?"

"Not necessarily," Donelli said. "It's always been my conviction that you can be absolutely anything you want to be when you grow up, as long as you work hard for it. Have you ever ridden a horse?"

Pete shook his head.

"How would you feel about riding lessons? There are some horses over at Cahill's. Their farm's not far. I think I could arrange for someone over there to teach you."

"Wow! That would be radical!" Pete gave Donelli another high-five.

Amanda watched the pair of them and thought about how far they'd come since Pete had first come into their lives. He'd missed out on so much in his young life. Thank God, they were able to give some of those things to him now. Most of all, though, Pete just wanted their love and approval. He'd long since earned that, but given his insecurities, it never hurt to reinforce the message.

"Okay," she said eventually, "that's enough of this male bonding stuff." She stared pointedly at her husband. "Let's get down to what you did with your afternoon."

Donelli and Pete exchanged a tolerant look.

"She's been a pain ever since we walked out the door," Pete revealed. "I had to stop her from calling here every five minutes and bugging you."

"You weren't supposed to tell him that," Amanda accused. "The bottom line is, Donelli, I left you in peace. Now what did you find out?"

"I was awfully tired," he said, his expression all innocence. He yawned for effect. "With the house so quiet, I caught a few winks."

She glared at him, not entirely certain if he was teasing. "Don't you dare tell me you slept while we were gone."

"Hey, when the opportunity comes along, take it. That's what I always say." He grinned at Pete. "Isn't that what you say?"

"Absolutely, man."

Amanda stood up and reached for the nearest weapon, a rolling pin Donelli hadn't put away yet. She advanced on him.

"Uh-oh," Pete said, laughing as he backed out of the way, clearing the path to Donelli. He never took sides, possibly because he considered their feigned arguments as entertaining as they did. On the few occasions when voices rose in genuine anger, however, he visibly blanched.

"Okay, Joe Donelli, tell me again about that nap," Amanda suggested in an ominous tone.

Donelli laughed. "Yes, indeed, pulled that old quilt up under my chin and dozed right off the minute you walked out the door. Slept like a baby."

"I'm going to kill you," she warned, lofting the rolling pin until a perfect downward arc would bring it neatly onto her husband's head. He never even flinched.

"Before you hear my news?" he queried.

Her gaze narrowed. "What news?"

He used her faint distraction to snatch the rolling pin away.

"What news?" she demanded.

"It seems your fine Pastor Alcott is in one heap of debt."

Amanda stopped where she was and thought about that. "Which means he's been squandering his Sunday collections on something other than the Lord's work, I'd bet."

"No doubt about it," Donelli agreed. "I couldn't come up with a list of his partners, but he's formed himself a little company that invests in real estate."

"Real estate?" It didn't require a giant leap of imagination to guess that some of those purchases had been made from Willie Ashford. "He was buying property from Willie?"

"You got it. Maybe for those strip malls Suzi mentioned. Only Alcott's cash flow has been a little slow these past few months. The economy's tight. Maybe folks are spending a little too much on moonshine and not enough on protecting their souls. At any rate, he's missed a few payments. The owner of the property has threatened to foreclose."

"Which would give him serious motivation to frame Willie. At the very least, it would buy him some time. And it could get him relieved of all debt, if Willie's sent to prison for life and his property is sold off to the highest bidder for legal fees," Amanda said. "Have you talked to Willie?"

Donelli nodded. "I was able to get a message to him about fifteen minutes ago. He called back right before you came in. He had no idea that the company he'd been selling property to belonged to Randy Alcott. He'd held the notes himself, considered it a nice base income every month. When the payments stopped coming, he had his lawyer and accountant notify the company of the intent to foreclose."

Amanda grinned. "My, my, my, I can hardly wait until tomorrow."

"What's tomorrow?" Pete asked. "I thought we were going to visit that lady, Miss Martha."

"We are, right after we go to hear Pastor Randy Blaine Alcott preach what might very well be his last sermon."

CHAPTER
Twenty-four

Donelli protested Amanda's intention of snooping around in Randy Alcott's office for the entire drive to Dahlonega. She could have told him from the outset that he was wasting his breath, but it probably wouldn't have done any good. He liked to believe that Amanda was a woman of reason. And, on occasion, she was. Today, though, she was operating on gut instinct and adrenaline. She was determined that they would know the whole story of both murders—and possibly what had happened to Henry Boggins as well—before the end of the church service.

She was not, however, foolish enough to go charging into Randy Alcott's office until she was very certain that he was leading his congregation in a hearty rendition of "Rock of Ages." In fact, she sat on a pew at the back of the church until he was well into his passionate eulogy for Henry Boggins, lauding him as an outstanding member of the community, a dear friend whose years on earth had been well spent. It seemed a stretch to Amanda, but then again, Alcott had known Boggins better than she had.

The Babcocks, seated together in the front row, nodded their agreement with Alcott's every word. Amanda scanned the congregation in search of some sign of Cutter Haines, but couldn't spot him. Too bad. She'd really hoped to find some way to tie him to this entire mess, if only by guilt through association.

As soon as Alcott seemed totally caught up in his topic, Amanda slid out of the pew and headed for the closest door. Out of the corner of her eye, she saw Pete shift positions to follow her, but Donelli held him back, whispering something that caused him to stay right where he was. She had a feeling Donelli wanted two pairs of eyes keeping watch in case anyone else in the church decided to make an early exit. Either that or he was more concerned about Pete being charged with burglary than he was about her.

Outside, the spring air was unseasonably warm and still. Amanda slipped around the side of the building and cautiously approached Alcott's office. She paused for a moment to listen. She could still hear the pastor's voice rising and falling eloquently. Time to get busy.

Without her lock-picks, which had been confiscated by the police over in Myrtle Beach a few months earlier, she was armed with bobby pins and credit cards. She doubted that the lock on Alcott's door was too sophisticated for such improvised tools.

Keeping her ears attuned for the slightest sound, she

went to work on the lock, fiddling with a pair of bobby pins until she heard the tumblers click. The door swung open. She dutifully murmured a prayer of thanks, wondering if a bolt of lightning would be the reply.

Inside the claustrophobic little room, she began a methodical search through the papers on the top of Alcott's desk. Nothing there but sermon notes and pink message slips, she realized fairly quickly. She moved on to the drawers. Not much there, either. The big surprise was the jug of moonshine tucked away in the back of the bottom drawer. Perhaps he simply used it for a show-and-tell sermon on the evils of demon rum, but she doubted it.

Disappointed with what she'd found so far, she weighed whether to check out the bathroom off to her left, the closet, or a set of file cabinets. It depended on what she hoped to find. Papers linking Alcott to real estate deals with Willie Ashford would be nice. So would a packet of syringes and insulin, which could conceivably tie him to Henry Boggins' death, even if it wouldn't be sufficient proof of guilt for a court of law.

A scuffling noise outside sent her heart leaping straight into her throat. She made a dash for the bathroom and closed the door, then waited to be discovered after contemplating the room's tiny window and realizing she could never in a million years squeeze through it.

Eventually, her pulse rate returned to normal. She climbed onto the sink and glanced out the window just in time to catch sight of a dog chasing a squirrel. That, no doubt, had been the cause of the noise she'd heard.

Chiding herself for her jumpiness, she conducted a

thorough survey of the bathroom. To her everlasting regret, she found no evidence that Alcott might be diabetic. There wasn't so much as a tissue in the trash can, much less a used needle. A medicine cabinet contained nothing more than a razor and Old Spice aftershave.

Back in the office, a glance at the clock revealed that she'd already been searching for more than fifteen minutes. Alcott might be a windbag who loved to hear the sound of his own resonant voice, but she couldn't risk staying too much longer, just in case he decided to send Henry Boggins off to heaven in a hurry.

She tackled the file cabinet next, where she struck a modest amount of pay dirt: the church budget and a folder filled with property deeds. She flipped on the small copy machine, made herself a set of the appropriate pages, then replaced the originals in the files and turned off the machine.

Another glance at the clock warned her to get out. She tucked her copies in her purse and started for the door. She'd almost made it when she realized she hadn't taken a look in the small cabinet on which the coffeepot sat.

Opening the door, she realized at once that it wasn't a cabinet at all, but a small refrigerator. And inside, big as life, sat a box of insulin.

Bingo!

Pulling a pocket-sized camera from her purse, she snapped a picture, careful to get the prescription label in the shot. She'd have the photo blown up nice and big, when she turned it over to the police as evidence.

All in all, a very satisfying morning, she decided as

she whirled around . . . and walked right straight into the waiting arms of Cutter Haines.

"Ms. Roberts," he drawled as he held her upright. "Fancy meeting you back here. I thought all the excitement was going on inside the church." He waited just a tad too long before releasing her.

"I guess that depends on how you like to get your kicks," she said.

He glanced around the office with evident fascination, as if he'd never seen it before. "Find anything interesting?"

"Not really. Actually, I just came back here to use Pastor Alcott's restroom. Too much coffee this morning. You know how it goes."

He nodded agreeably, though she had the feeling he no more believed her tale than she believed this was his first visit to Alcott's office.

"What brings you back here?" she inquired.

"Just stretching my legs," he said, gazing directly into her eyes as if daring her to contradict him. "I saw the door ajar and decided I'd check it out."

"You must be a loyal member of Crime Watch."

"I try to do my part."

"So, tell me, how acquainted are you with Pastor Alcott?"

"Never met the man."

"And with Henry Boggins?"

His mouth turned up a bit. "Now Henry and I went way back. I made it a point to make his acquaintance as soon as I got this job."

"Why is that?"

"Old Henry was a very observant man. Very little went on in these parts that Henry didn't know about."

"And share with you?" Amanda speculated.

"When it suited his purposes."

"Or when you paid him enough."

He laughed. "Oh, yes, Henry did love to bargain with his information."

"What had he shared with you lately?"

Haines shook his head. "Now, Ms. Roberts, you know that's confidential."

"Is it really? I would have thought it to be a matter of public record. I'll have to call and check on that first thing tomorrow."

"You do that and if you happen to speak to the governor, give him my regards," he said cheerfully, then turned and walked away.

A chill shot down Amanda's spine as she closed the office door and watched him stroll off toward the parking lot, whistling something that sounded suspiciously like "Onward Christian Soldiers." That man was too damned confident for her taste. And that little jibe about the governor had certainly been meant to let her know that he wasn't the least bit afraid of her or her friends in high places.

Either that meant that Cutter Haines had nothing to hide or it meant that he had powerful allies—more powerful than hers—who could bail him out of any trouble. Before she could decide which it might be, the back doors of the church opened and the congregation poured out. Pete and Donelli were in front of the pack.

"You okay?" Donelli asked at once. "You look as if you've just seen a ghost."

"Just engaging in a little banter with the head of the Alcohol–Tobacco Tax unit."

Pete frowned at Donelli. "That must have been the guy who slipped out the side door. I told you I saw somebody leave. You shoulda let me go check."

Donelli nodded. "Yes, I should have. I'm sorry." He studied Amanda intently. "Any harm done?"

"No, he was just making idle threats, if you want to call them that. Actually, I think he just wanted me to know that he was on to me."

Donelli's gaze shot to the parking lot, where Haines was just ducking into his car. "Want me to go bash his face in?" he inquired, only partially jesting.

Amanda shook her head, less because the idea didn't appeal to her than because Pete seemed a little too anxious to participate. It appeared she and Donelli were going to have to curb any tendencies for retaliation as long as they had an impressionable teenager living with them.

"Let's just get out of here," she suggested. "I'd like to find someplace to stop for a nice Southern Sunday dinner."

"Babcock's Cafe, I suppose," Donelli said.

"No, actually I think I'd rather go someplace else, someplace where we can look through the papers I found and see if anything adds up."

Donelli groaned. "Amanda, tell me you didn't steal papers from Pastor Alcott's office."

"Of course not," she said with what she considered just the right touch of indignation. "I made copies."

CHAPTER Twenty-five

The real estate papers Amanda had retrieved from Randy Alcott's office merely confirmed that Good Deeds, Inc., a name she found to be just too cute for words, had been buying up vacant land around town for decades. Small parcels, big parcels, it didn't seem to matter. Nor did the locations, which she charted on a local map she had insisted on stopping to buy at a gas station on their way to lunch. Unlike Willie, Alcott wasn't looking for a single big development score, apparently.

Munching idly on a Southern fried chicken leg, she studied the map. "I don't get it," she admitted finally. "What's he up to?"

Donelli conceded he was at a loss as well. "Not all the properties belonged to Willie Ashford, either. Did you notice that? In fact, only a handful did."

Since none of the papers revealed the sale prices,

Amanda resigned herself to paying a visit to the county records department on Monday. She needed to know how much money Alcott had forked out for all this land before she could tell if he'd been stealing it from the church budget. Maybe Jenny Lee could spend the morning going through the records.

Amanda reached for her cellular phone, which for once was on top of most of the debris in her purse.

"Who are you calling now?" Donelli asked.

"Jenny Lee. I want her to get over to county records first thing in the morning."

"Isn't she in Washington with Larry this weekend?"

Amanda stared at him. "Is she?"

"That's where she told me she was heading when I talked to her Friday. She's your assistant, Amanda. Haven't you talked to her lately?"

Amanda winced. "Obviously not recently enough. A lot can change in twenty-four hours apparently. She didn't say a thing about a trip when I saw her. Did she share any other news with you?"

"Nope."

"How about Larry? Have you heard from him?"

"Oscar talked to him last week."

"You've talked to Oscar?"

Joe shook his head. "When this is over, perhaps we should talk about your priorities. When you get caught up in a story, you ignore everyone around, including your boss. Oscar's resigned himself to getting updates from me. And I only know what you're up to, because you do still come home at night. Is this the way you're going to treat the baby?"

Pete listened to the exchange, his expression growing more worried by the minute. He clearly hated it when they fought for real. "You guys," he protested.

"It's okay," Donelli reassured him. "We're just having a discussion."

"It sounds like the beginning of an argument to me," Pete said flatly. "You don't have to worry about the baby. I told you I'd help."

Amanda forced a smile. "Pete, this isn't really about the baby. Joe just likes to remind me every now and then that I tend to get carried away and lose perspective on what's really important in my life. What he doesn't seem to realize is that this particular story is important because solving these two murders matters a great deal not just for the sake of a story, but because it means a lot to someone I care about."

Donelli had the good grace to look duly chastised. "I'm sorry. I know you're doing this for Miss Martha."

"And right now she is more important to me than Oscar or Jenny Lee. Does that mean my priorities are screwed up?"

"No. I stand corrected," he said. "This time."

"You like this old dame more than Jenny Lee?" Pete asked, clearly struggling with the subtleties of adult relationships. "I thought Jenny Lee was your best friend."

"She is. That doesn't mean I can't care about other people and occasionally put their needs first," Amanda explained. "Loving people means giving them the freedom to do what they need to do, not demanding exclusive rights to their time."

"I guess I get it," Pete said, but he still looked troubled.

Amanda patted his hand. "You'll understand once you fall in love and still want to play ball or go out for a beer with your pals."

Donelli grinned. "Are you kidding? In this day and age, the woman Pete falls for will probably play third base."

Pete squirmed in his chair. "Geez, you guys, stop talking about girls and stuff. I'm not going to fall in love until I'm really old, maybe as old as you guys."

Amanda exchanged a look with her husband. "Do we kill him now or later?"

"Later. After he's met Miss Martha. Maybe she can put a civil tongue in his head."

An hour later, they were all seated in Miss Martha's bedroom. Della had helped Miss Martha into a dress, but had abandoned any attempt to get her down the stairs. Instead, she was already seated in a velvet-covered wingback chair waiting for them. An elaborate tea service had been set up beside her. The strain of the arrangements had clearly cost her, though. She also seemed slightly more vague than usual, as if she'd given in and taken a powerful painkiller to get her through their visit. There was a pinched expression around her mouth, and her eyes seemed tired.

Until she spotted Pete, that is. Then they sparkled with interest. "Come right over here and sit beside me, young man. I want to get to know you."

Pete, to Amanda's relief, didn't even hesitate. He hitched a chair a little closer to Miss Martha and accepted the delicate china cup she offered as if he'd been going to tea parties his entire life.

"How about some of these little sandwiches?" Miss Martha asked.

"I've never seen sandwiches that little before," Pete said candidly. "What are they?"

"I believe Della has made cucumber, watercress, and egg salad. Here, you must try them all."

She put one of each on a plate and handed it to the skeptical-looking Pete. He balanced it awkwardly on his knee, then glanced toward Joe for approval.

"Amanda? Joseph? What can I get for you?" Miss Martha asked.

"One of each would be lovely," Amanda said.

"I'll have the same," Joe said.

He looked pained. Amanda knew he was taking them only to set an example for Pete. He hated the wimpy little things. So did she, for that matter.

While they ate, Miss Martha drew Pete out as if he were the most celebrated guest she'd ever entertained. In no time at all, he was regaling her with stories about school and his attempt to turn Donelli's roadside produce stand into a costly natural foods franchise. He'd had tourists lined up to pay his exorbitant rates for vegetables he'd claimed would make them healthy.

"Joe made me stop. Then he made me put the money into one of them CD things," he concluded, shooting a look of disgust at Donelli. "I won't get it forever."

"A wise, safe investment," Miss Martha declared, winking at Amanda. "I myself, however, prefer to take an occasional gamble with stocks. There is some risk, of course, but the rewards can be so much more interesting when one guesses correctly."

Amanda winced as Pete's eyes lit up. "What kind of stocks?" he asked. "How do you know about this stuff? Can anybody buy them?"

Miss Martha spent several minutes educating him about the *Wall Street Journal*, biotec companies, pharmaceuticals, and consumer products. It was clear, though, that her energy was flagging. And despite the struggle she was putting up and any painkiller she might have taken, she was clearly hurting. Every now and then, she winced and made a soft gasp that she quickly tried to cover with a clever remark.

"Perhaps we'd better be going," Amanda said. "We don't want to tire you out."

For once, Miss Martha didn't argue. She smiled graciously at Pete. "You must come again, young man. We can discuss your financial affairs further."

"Yes, ma'am," Pete said. He started toward the door with Amanda and Joe, then turned and ran back. He leaned down and kissed Miss Martha's cheek. "I hope you feel better real soon."

Miss Martha's hand shook as she touched his cheek. "I expect I will, as soon as Amanda finds me the answers I've been looking for."

"Tomorrow," Amanda promised with a confidence that was probably unjustified. "I think I'm getting close."

"I'll be waiting."

When they were outside again, Joe scowled at her.

"Do you think you should have told her you'd have this wrapped up tomorrow?"

"She needs something to keep her going," Amanda declared.

Pete's expression turned sad. "Why do people have to get sick and die?"

Donelli put an arm around his shoulders. "Now that is one of those deep, philosophical questions that people have been asking all through eternity."

"So, what's the answer?"

"It's the natural cycle of things," Amanda said.

Pete frowned. "Well, the cycle sucks."

Looking back toward Miss Martha's room, Amanda sighed. "Amen to that."

Amanda's sense of urgency tripled after the visit to Miss Martha. She was on the phone to Jenny Lee again at the crack of dawn, after failing to reach her all Sunday evening.

"Amanda, are you sick or something? Why are you calling me this early?" She groaned. "It's not even six o'clock, for heaven's sake."

"I'm calling at this ungodly hour because I couldn't get you yesterday."

"I told Joe I was going to Washington."

"So he said. Obviously you don't check your messages."

"It was after midnight by the time I got home. Who was I going to call back at that hour?" She allowed her point to sink in, then added, "Aren't you going to ask how my visit with Larry went?"

Amanda had learned that asking about their volatile relationship lately was something to be approached with caution. "Did you have a good time?"

"It was okay," Jenny Lee said noncommittally.

"Did you like Washington?" she asked, realizing that whatever Jenny Lee had to say, she was going to have to pull it out of her.

"It wasn't bad."

"And Larry's apartment? Was that okay?"

"It will be, when I get it fixed up."

Uh-oh! Amanda thought. "How often are you planning to visit?"

"No more visits," Jenny Lee announced. "We're getting married!"

Amanda started laughing. "Congratulations! I am so happy for the two of you."

"Won't you miss me?"

The plaintively asked question hinted of Jenny Lee's conflicted feelings. Amanda could understand them only too well. Balancing career choices and a personal life often took skills she wasn't sure she possessed. "Of course I will miss you, but I know this is what you've wanted. So, when's the wedding?"

"Next weekend. We decided not to wait. Larry will be going off to do an assignment in Alaska at the end of April and he wants me to go too. It's for a whole month."

"Oh, Jenny Lee, that's wonderful. What a terrific honeymoon."

"I know. I can't wait. So, why did you call? Was there something you wanted me to do?"

"It doesn't matter. I can handle it."

"No. I haven't given Oscar notice yet. Tell me," Jenny Lee insisted.

Amanda described what she needed from the county records department.

"No problem. I'll have it for you by noon. Should I meet you at the office?"

"No, I think we should meet at Babcock's Cafe." She told Jenny Lee how to get there. "Depending on what turns up, we may want to pay another visit to Randy Alcott."

"Yuck!" Jenny Lee groaned. "I'm almost sorry I agreed to do this."

"Come on, don't get fainthearted on me now. Think of this as the last test of your intrepid spirit."

"My intrepid spirit will get a very nice workout from Larry, thank you very much. Where are you going this morning?"

"I want to stop by the hospital. Something's nagging at me and I'm hoping I can catch Sandra Mayotte-Jefferson before she goes off duty. If I miss her, maybe Henry's doctor will be able to clear it up."

"Okay, I'll see you at that cafe at noon."

Amanda headed for Grady Memorial the minute she got off the phone. She missed Sandra Mayotte-Jefferson by minutes, but Ryan Paltrow was on the unit.

"Do you have some time?" she asked the doctor. "I keep going over and over Henry Boggins' death and I can't come up with any answers."

"I have rounds in twenty minutes, but we can talk until then," he said. "Let's go in the lounge."

The staff lounge wasn't especially quiet. Doctors and nurses were coming and going, pausing to grab a cup of coffee. Amanda had to lower her voice to assure that no one overheard when she told the young resident what she suspected about Henry's death, as well as a couple of scenarios spelled out by the medical examiner.

"And neither potassium nor insulin would be detectable in an autopsy," he concluded, one step ahead of her explanation.

"Exactly. The only way to build a case, then, is to show that someone had motive and opportunity. I figure I have to start with opportunity. Was there anyone at all on the unit that night who didn't belong here?"

He thought for several minutes before responding. "Nobody. The patients on this floor don't get a lot of visitors even in the daytime. They almost never have anyone staying with them overnight. We would have noticed a stranger."

"Damn." She tried to come up with another angle that made sense. "Was there an employee on the unit who ever expressed any particular dislike for Boggins? Maybe blatantly steered clear of his room? Or was in there when they shouldn't have been there?"

Paltrow looked apologetic. "Sorry. Not that I noticed. We're so short-staffed that most people don't even have time for their own patients, much less spending time in other rooms. And the others would complain bitterly if anybody tried to pass off a patient for personal reasons."

"Sandra Mayotte-Jefferson said she sometimes spent extra time overnight talking with Henry."

Paltrow smiled. "Sandy? She's terrific. And she was really distraught about the old man's death."

That confirmed exactly what the nurse had already told her. Amanda sighed. It just wasn't falling into place the way she had hoped it would. Maybe there had been nothing suspicious about Boggins' death, after all. Or, if there was, she might never be able to prove it.

"Thanks for your time," she said eventually.

"No problem. I wish I could have been more help."

He walked her to the elevator and punched the button for her. Back at the nurses' station, Amanda heard the phone ring. Then the clerk called out, "Hey, anybody seen the chaplain around this morning?"

The chaplain! "That's it," she said, turning and racing over to the desk. Paltrow followed, his expression puzzled.

The same young girl was on duty. Amanda glanced at her nametag to refresh her memory. "Debbie, remember me? We spoke the other day."

Debbie looked her over blankly, then caught sight of Ryan Paltrow behind her. Apparently that triggered her memory. "Oh, sure. You were asking about Mr. Boggins right after he died. I hooked you up with the doc, here."

"Right. And right before we talked, you had a call looking for the chaplain. Somebody said he'd been on the unit earlier."

Debbie gave her another vague look. "I guess. It happens all the time."

"Who's the chaplain?"

"Let me think a minute. You're sure it was the chaplain, not the priest?"

"I'm sure."

"Last week? Okay, it wasn't the regular chaplain, because Reverend Lewis has been on vacation. I guess it was that guy who usually fills in for him."

"Do you know his name?"

"I do," Ryan Paltrow said. "It's Pastor Alcott."

Something in Amanda's expression must have indicated her glee, because the young doctor immediately looked alarmed. "What?" he demanded. "Surely, you don't think . . ." He glanced at Debbie and allowed his voice to trail off, until he had drawn Amanda back away from the desk. "You can't possibly think . . ."

"I don't have conclusive proof of anything," she admitted. "But I do know that Pastor Randy Blaine Alcott is diabetic. I took a photo just yesterday of the insulin supply in his office."

Ryan Paltrow turned ghostly pale. "Oh, shit."

"That would be my sentiment exactly," Amanda said.

CHAPTER
Twenty-six

"The evidence is circumstantial, Amanda," Detective Jim Harrison repeated for the umpteenth time when she reached him as she was driving to her meeting with Jenny Lee. "But just in case he's the serial killer you want him to turn out to be, stay away from him."

"Can't you at least bring him in for questioning?"

"We don't even know that a crime was committed. What am I supposed to question him about? Whether he was praying for the soul of one of his parishioners or jabbing him with a jolt of his own personal supply of insulin?"

"You don't have to be sarcastic."

"Maybe not, but I do feel a need to bring you in and put you in protective custody. You're heading straight out to see Pastor Alcott now, aren't you?"

"Of course not," she said and hung up before he

could get her to reveal that that was the second stop on her itinerary.

Jenny Lee was waiting for her at Babcock's Cafe, nursing a large soda and ogling a cute trucker sitting two tables away.

"Better get that out of your system now," Amanda teased, sneaking up on her. "After next weekend, Larry's liable to object."

"That's his problem. I'm getting married, not going blind," she retorted.

Suzi came out of the kitchen just then, spotted Amanda, and came straight over. "You're getting to be a regular in here. What can I get you today?"

Amanda introduced her to Jenny Lee. When they'd placed their orders, Suzi headed back to the kitchen. On her way she paused to flirt with Jenny Lee's trucker.

"See what I mean," Jenny Lee said. "Flirting and looking are perfectly normal. Isn't she the girl you told me was crazy about Willie?"

"So she claims. He's certainly counting on it." She eyed the bulging folder of papers that Jenny Lee had on the table in front of her. "What did you find?"

"Nothing that makes much sense to me. Maybe it will to you."

Amanda reached for the folder, but Jenny Lee stopped her. "Don't waste your time. I made a summary." She pulled a sheet of numbers from the front of the folder and handed it to Amanda.

"What are these?"

"The name of the seller, size of the property, and the

selling price. I numbered each property. The paperwork's in here."

Amanda studied the list, wishing she knew a whole lot more about property appraisals in the area. The price Randy Alcott had paid for the land seemed awfully low to her. In one or two instances, the five or ten thousand dollars seemed no more than a token amount. Was she mistaken about the land's value or had Alcott practically stolen it? If so, why had the owners sold so cheap? Were they desperate? Or did the pastor have some hold over them? One thing for certain, she wasn't going to get the answers to those questions sitting here.

"Let's go," she said.

Jenny Lee stared at her. "We don't even have our lunch yet."

"I'll get Suzi to pack it to go." She was already on her feet, heading for the cash register. Jenny Lee trailed along behind.

"Why the big rush?" Jenny Lee demanded as they reached the parking lot.

"Because figuring out what really happened out here more than fifty years ago and again a couple of weeks back is more important than sitting in there eating a sandwich. I think Randy Alcott can clear it all up."

"Amanda, you can't go in there and accuse the man of murder," Jenny Lee protested. "That is what you have in mind, isn't it?"

"Not exactly," she said as she pulled onto the highway. "I'm going to get him to confess."

Jenny Lee rolled her eyes. "Yeah, right, like he's

going to be so consumed by guilt that he'll pour out his soul to a reporter. If he did have anything to do with the murder of his daddy, he's managed to keep it secret for more than half a century. How come he hasn't cracked before now?"

Amanda scowled at her. "Perhaps because nobody has ever asked him straight out if he did it."

Jenny Lee didn't look convinced, but she fell silent, leaving Amanda to plot exactly how she was going to get Randy Alcott to spill his guts. Though nothing could have persuaded her to admit it aloud, she harbored some of the same doubts as Jenny Lee did about his ability to keep a secret under stress. He'd been doing just fine for years now. Then again, maybe he'd never come up against anyone who could bluff as well as she could.

She drove into the deserted church parking lot and parked out of sight of Alcott's office. She glanced over at Jenny Lee, who was nervously ripping apart her tuna sandwich. "Ready?"

"Oh, sure, let's go confront a man you're convinced is a three-time killer without telling anyone we're here."

Amanda stared at her. "Jenny Lee, are you really worried about this?"

"Aren't you? You're going to have a baby, for goodness sake. Shouldn't you be thinking about the danger?"

Amanda sighed. "Okay, maybe you're right, but who am I supposed to call? It would take Joe too long to get here. It's not in Jim Harrison's jurisdiction. There's nobody else we can trust. We're both young and strong. Alcott's an old man. We can handle him."

"He doesn't exactly have to be Arnold Schwarzenegger to be able to fire a shotgun," Jenny Lee reminded her.

Amanda thought for a minute. "How about this? I'll go in. You stay outside the door and listen. At the first hint of trouble, you use the cellular phone and dial nine-one-one."

"I don't like it, but I suppose if you've made up your mind, then I don't have a choice. Give me the phone."

Amanda handed it over, then flipped on the tape recorder in her purse while she was at it. "Let's do it."

Outside the door, she cast one last look at Jenny Lee. "Ready?"

"As ready as I'll ever be," Jenny Lee said with an air of resignation. "So help me, Amanda, if you get yourself hurt and ruin my wedding next weekend, I'll never forgive you."

Amanda grinned at her. "I wouldn't dream of it." She drew in a deep breath and opened the door.

Randy Alcott was seated behind his desk, scribbling notes. Next week's sermon, perhaps? He glanced up, recognized Amanda, and gave her a weary smile. "Back again, Ms. Roberts. What can I do for you this time?"

"I thought maybe we could have another chat."

"I can't imagine what we have to talk about. We covered some very painful incidents the last time. There's nothing more I can add."

"I suspect that's not quite true," she corrected, dropping into the chair opposite him. She put her purse on a corner of his desk, hoping the recorder would be better able to pick up anything he said.

A flash of anger flared in his eyes, but died just as quickly. "Okay, get on with it. I have work to do."

"You told me you weren't at Grady Memorial on the day that Henry Boggins died."

"Did I say that? Then it must be true."

"Not according to the staff there. They indicated that you were substituting for the regular chaplain last week. A nurse saw you on the unit not more than an hour or so after Henry died."

"So?"

"The doctors are very suspicious about his death," she said, stretching things a little. Okay, quite a bit. "Frankly, so am I. I keep thinking about an old man recovering from pneumonia suddenly dying of something totally unrelated. Perhaps from an overdose of insulin."

Alcott's hands shook visibly, but his expression never changed. "Can you prove that?" he inquired, a smug note in his voice.

"No, but I can place a diabetic with his own supply of insulin in the vicinity of that room around the time of the murder. You, Pastor Alcott." When he opened his mouth, no doubt to protest, she cut him off and continued, unrelenting. "I began to suspect you might be diabetic after you talked about your allergy to chocolate. I confirmed it when I found the insulin right here in your office."

He rose up and leaned across his desk, a thunderous expression on his face. "How dare you! Who gave you the right to come snooping around in my office? I will have you charged with breaking and entering."

Amanda shrugged. It was time to go for broke, to lay out every theory she'd been able to come up with and see which, if any, hit its mark.

"And while the police are questioning me about that, I'll tell them about the rest of your shady little business deals," she said quietly. "I'll also mention that I suspect you, not William Ashford, were the one who killed your father years ago. Why, Pastor Alcott? Were you greedy even then? Did he find out you were accepting payoffs to protect moonshiners in the area? Did he threaten to turn you in?"

She saw from his horrified reaction that she was cutting close to the truth. "That must have hurt you deeply, knowing that your own father would betray you that way. How did you do it? Did you lure him to the Ashford property on some pretext? Were you in it with Henry Boggins? He hated Ashford. You were furious with your father. It was a good way to kill two birds with one stone. Who pulled the trigger, you or Henry?"

She allowed the question to hang in the air, using the time to study his face. There was a sheen of perspiration on his upper lip. His eyes were darting here and there, avoiding her. "I think it was you. I think you pointed that shotgun at your father and killed him, but Henry knew about it. He'd been blackmailing you for years now, hadn't he? He had a history of it. He'd tried to blackmail Ashford, too."

Again she fell silent and let her words sink in. "What happened, Randy?" she asked eventually, deliberately using his first name to strip him of the protective power of his religious title. "Did you get tired of paying? Had he threatened to talk? Or had you started up your little game again, forcing people to sell you property dirt cheap in return for keeping silent about their moonshining activities? Maybe Henry found out about that, too, and wanted in on the action."

He held his hands over his ears, his face mottled red. "Stop! Stop it! My father was a son of Satan. He had to die. Can't you see that? I had no choice."

Amanda lowered her voice to a coaxing tone. "And Henry? Did he have to die, too?"

"Yes, but he was an old man. What did it matter if he lost a few months? He could have cost me everything. No one should ever have guessed about that. No one."

That was two admissions, but she still didn't know how Franklin Jefferson fit in. Or Cutter Haines. Had Jefferson gotten wind of the payoffs? Had his boss been in on the take?

"So, tell me about these land deals," she prodded. "Who's been in on them with you?"

Before he could answer, she heard a startled yelp, then a scuffle outside. Randy Alcott's gaze shot to the door, as did Amanda's. Obviously someone had come upon Jenny Lee. The question was whether it was someone who would be on their side or on Alcott's.

The door swung open and a struggling Jenny Lee was ushered in by a shotgun-toting Tommy Babcock. "Lookee what I found hiding in the bushes, Pastor. I see you've got company, too."

He dropped Jenny Lee onto a chair as if he were releasing a sack of potatoes. He propped his filthy boot right next to her thigh.

The last piece of the puzzle fell into place for Amanda. Babcock, desperate to keep his daughter and Willie separated, had stolen a page out of history. He'd probably been guided through the tactic by his good friend, Pastor Alcott. Amanda wondered if they were such good friends that they were in on the land deals together.

"Who exactly are the partners in Good Deeds, Inc.?" she asked Alcott with what she hoped was nothing more than friendly curiosity. She wanted answers, but she wasn't sure she wanted to antagonize a man with a gun. Unfortunately, after a silencing scowl in the direction of Alcott, Babcock was the one who answered.

"Now what would you be knowing about that?"

"Not much. Just that the company seems to own an awful lot of land around here. Pastor Alcott's name is on some of the title transfers, but I'm assuming there are partners. Are you one of them?"

"So what if I am? There's nothing wrong with buying land, is there?"

"I suppose that depends on how the price was negotiated."

"Fair and square," he asserted.

"I don't know. Some of those prices struck me as below market value. Then again, maybe the sellers were getting something other than money in return."

Babcock's gaze narrowed. "Such as?"

"Protection from the Department of Revenue."

He laughed. "Honey, how do you suppose the pastor and me could protect them from the state government?"

"Perhaps by paying off Cutter Haines, who, in turn, steered his agents in other directions. Until Frank Jefferson got a tip, that is, and decided to do some investigating on his own."

She had expected angry denials, perhaps even threats. What she hadn't expected was the expression of weary amusement that appeared on Babcock's face.

"Well, now, ain't that a shame?" he said to Alcott.

"What?" Amanda asked cautiously, since Alcott couldn't seem to get a word out.

"I do so hate the thought of ruining two pretty faces by filling 'em full of buckshot."

Amanda swallowed hard. She wasn't exactly wild about the notion herself. "What would be the point? The cops will be all over you like ants on roadkill."

"Maybe. Maybe not. Depends on what the pastor here has to say, don't it? I'm pretty sure they'd believe a man of the Lord if he said the killings were self-defense. And that's what it would be, right, Pastor Alcott?"

Randy Alcott's complexion had turned ashen. He rose to his feet unsteadily and came around the desk. Then, to Amanda's astonishment and tremendous relief, he latched onto Babcock's gun and twisted it away. His movements were so unexpected that the other man barely had time to react. He started to fight for the weapon, but Jenny Lee and Amanda leapt up in unison and jumped him from either side.

When they had wrestled him to the floor, Amanda shouted for Alcott to call the police. There was no movement, not so much as a whisper of sound. She glanced up, scanning the office for some sign of the man who'd just saved their lives. He was gone.

''Jenny Lee, I'll stay on Babcock,'' she said, hoping she could manage it. He was bucking like a bronc. ''You call the police.''

''What about Pastor Alcott?'' Jenny Lee asked, just as a shotgun blast shattered the air.

Babcock's body convulsed involuntarily at the sound. Even Amanda jumped. ''I don't think we have to worry about him,'' she said softly. ''I think he's just resolved his own fate.''

Babcock must have thought so, too, because he stopped struggling. Fifteen minutes later the police showed up and took him into custody.

They found Pastor Alcott's body on the front steps of the church. Amanda couldn't help thinking that at the end, he hadn't been able to bring himself to take his life inside the building where he'd spent so many years preaching against sin.

CHAPTER
Twenty-seven

"How is she today?" Amanda asked Della when the housekeeper opened the door.

"She's not having one of her good days, I'm afraid. The pain's getting mighty fierce and she refuses to take those pills Doc Flanders gave her to ease it."

"Do you think she's up to visitors? I have someone with me who would very much like to meet her."

With that Willie Ashford, dressed up in a suit and tie, his hair slicked back, stepped out from behind Amanda. Della's hand rose to her bosom and her eyes widened.

"Saints protect us, if you ain't the spitting image of your granddaddy. You get right on up those stairs. I think seeing you may be the best medicine she could have."

Willie glanced nervously at Amanda. "You're coming, aren't you?"

"For a minute, just long enough to introduce you."

"Won't need no introduction," Della said. "Ain't no mistaking who that boy is."

Still, Amanda climbed the stairs with Willie and rapped on Miss Martha's door.

"Come," she commanded. Her tone was as imperious as ever, but the volume had faded.

Amanda squeezed Willie's hand, then preceded him into the room. "Miss Martha, I've brought someone to see you."

"Well, get on over here. I can't see you if you hang around out there in the hall." Her gaze sought out Amanda, then shifted behind her to fix avidly on the young man accompanying her. "Oh, sweet heaven," she whispered. Tears tracked down her cheeks as she held out her hand. "You must be Willie. How very glad I am to meet you."

"I wanted to thank you," he said, moving to her side and taking her hand, while Amanda hung back.

"There's no need for thanks. What I did for you is what I should have done for your grandfather all those years ago." Still clinging to his hand, with her other hand she patted a space on the bed. "Sit right here beside me so I can see you. We have your whole lifetime to catch up on."

Amanda listened for another minute as Willie hesitantly began to talk. Then, encouraged by Miss Martha's obvious thirst for his memories of his grandfather, for every tiny tidbit of insight into his own life, Willie spoke more readily. Miss Martha's rapt gaze never left his face.

At last, clearly a third wheel, Amanda stole away. The story had come full circle.

* * *

When Amanda opened the *Atlanta Constitution* to the local section the next morning, the headline leapt out at her:

> LOCAL SOCIETY LEADER DIES
>
> Miss Martha Wellington, long the reigning queen of Georgia society and the driving force behind local preservation efforts, died at her home yesterday after a long illness. She was 86.
>
> Her nephew, former Georgia senator Donald Wellington, said that his aunt died as she had lived, "with incomparable grace and dignity. The entire state has lost perhaps its last true Southern belle, a woman of strength, courage and compassion. She will be sorely missed by all of us who knew and loved her and by thousands more who will benefit from her commitment to preserving our great past."
>
> Wellington and *Inside Atlanta* publisher Joel Crenshaw, a longtime admirer of Miss Wellington's good works, announced the formation of the Martha Wellington Foundation, which will be committed to historical preservation.

Amanda found herself smiling through her tears. Della had called to tell her of the death, but seeing it in print made it real.

She reread the final paragraph about the foundation to be named in her honor. She thought she detected Carol Fields's hand in that. She had found a way to turn her defeat over the publication of Miss Martha's story into a public relations coup for the magazine and she had convinced Joel to go along with it. Carol might be a lousy assignment editor, but there seemed to be some hope that the woman had a knack for marketing. If some good could come out of Miss Martha's death, as it certainly had out of her living, Amanda was all for it.

She touched the crisp color photo accompanying the story. In it Miss Martha's blue eyes sparkled with wit and intelligence. That was the image Amanda would always hold dear, not the sad, pain-wracked woman she had seen so often recently.

"Good-bye, old friend," she whispered, her tears splashing on the page. "For once Donald got it right; you will be sorely missed."

Epilogue

Amanda chose the Christmas holidays for the baptism of Martha Elisa Donelli and for the official welcoming of Pete Roberts-Donelli into their family. Her parents came from New York. Joe's father's recurring health problems kept his family at home in Brooklyn, but a happily married Jenny Lee and Larry made the trip from Washington.

Mattie, as they'd decided to call her, cried through the entire service at the church.

"Just like her mother," Donelli commented at the celebration back home as he held the dark-haired, dark-eyed beauty he clearly adored. "She can't stand not being in control."

"She already has you wrapped around her fingers," Amanda commented. "You're pitiful."

"Hey, Pete, come take your baby sister," Donelli called. "Her mama's getting jealous. I need to pay her a little attention before she pouts all through the party."

Pete claimed Mattie at once, cooing over her. Mattie watched him, wide-eyed. Her tiny mouth formed a brilliant smile. Amanda tucked her hand in Joe's and sighed contentedly.

"Happy?" he asked.

"Astonishingly so."

He folded his arms around her waist and held her. "You're not restless yet?"

Oscar apparently overheard the question, because he immediately joined them. "Isn't this maternity leave of yours due to end soon?"

"Who knows," she said. "Maybe I'll take an extension."

"Yeah, right. I'm surprised you're not climbing the walls already."

She shook her head. "Not yet."

"Damn, Amanda, don't go soft on me."

"There's not much chance of that," Donelli said. "I caught her muttering at the local news last night. It's only a short hop from that to chasing down political corruption."

"Very funny," she said, just as she spotted one of Miss Martha's cars turning into the lane leading to the house. For a moment the sight of it brought a lump to her throat. Della had decided to come, after all. Miss Martha had left the car and driver at her disposal, but Della rarely took advantage of it. She seemed content enough to stay at home in the house Miss Martha had declared hers for the rest of her days. Only after Della was gone would Donald Wellington get his hands on it. Amanda thought that was as it should be, though Donald had made noises for a while about fighting it. Amanda's quiet reminder of his complicity in Miss Martha's suicide had silenced him quickly enough.

In the months since Miss Martha's death, Della had aged noticeably. Now she struggled across the lawn, using one of Miss Martha's old canes. Amanda went outside to meet her.

"Let me help you inside."

"I won't be staying," Della said stiffly. She apparently still hadn't entirely forgiven Amanda for what she believed had been the hastening of Miss Martha's death. Though whether she blamed her for chasing down the story of William Ashford or for not preventing Miss Martha's suicide was unclear.

"Miss Martha asked me to do something for her when this day came," Della said. "I'm just carrying out her wishes." She opened her black leather purse and extracted two envelopes, one much thicker than the other. "She wanted your children to have these."

That said, she turned to go.

"Won't you please come in and see the baby?" Amanda said.

Della hesitated, clearly torn between the stance she'd taken months ago and a desire to see the baby. Finally a faint, wistful smile tugged at her mouth. "I suppose I can stay a few minutes. It's been a long time since I held a newborn."

Amanda led her inside, settled her in a rocker, and

called to Pete. He brought the baby over. Della held out her arms.

Her expression softened. "Oh, my, but she's a pretty one. Looks just like her daddy," she said.

"She's much prettier," Donelli said.

"First time you've admitted that," Amanda teased.

"Go on and open those," Della said, gesturing toward the envelopes Amanda still held. All the while her gaze remained avidly fixed on Mattie's face.

Amanda handed Pete's envelope to him, then opened the second one meant for the baby. It was a savings bond. A very large savings bond. A note was attached.

Dear Amanda and Joseph, Here's a safe investment for the little one. If the baby grows up to be anything like its parents, I'm sure there will be risks aplenty. This should provide a nice cushion to fall back on. With my love and gratitude. Martha Wellington

Amanda was still absorbing Miss Martha's generosity when she heard Pete's gasp.

"Oh, wow. Look at this. Did she really mean this for me?" He was holding a bundle tied with a ribbon.

"What is it?" Joe asked.

"Stock certificates in all those companies she told me about. And there's a note, too." He handed it to Amanda.

"Dearest Pete," she read aloud. "You have Amanda and Joseph to bring all the love you'll ever need into your life. Use these to make sure your future is everything you want it to be. Fondly, Martha Wellington."

Amanda turned to Joe. "She'll always live on for us, won't she?"

"She admired you, you know," Della said. "She said if she'd been born a generation or two later, maybe she would have had your courage."

Thinking of the final choice Miss Martha had made, Amanda shook her head. "She was far braver than I."

"You didn't tell me," Della said. "What did you name your daughter?"

"Her middle name's Elisa," Amanda said.

Della nodded. "For your mama."

"And her first name is Martha."

A tear welled up and slid down Della's weathered cheek. "Oh, my, but she would have liked that," she whispered. "She would have liked that something fierce."